By Max Hardy

Novels

Angels Bleed

Her Moons Denouement

Poetry Collections

Soul Whispers

My Dark Disease

HER MOONS DENOUEMENT

For Yasmin

I hope you enjoy the book,

Cheers,

Max xx

MAX HARDY

Copyright © 2014 Max Hardy

The moral right of Max Hardy to be identified as the author of this work has been asserted in accordance with the Copyright, Designs and Patents Act, 1988.

All rights reserved. No part of this publication may be reproduced or transmitted in any form or by any means, electronic or mechanical, including photocopying, recording, or any information storage and retrieval system without permission in writing from the author or publisher.

ISBN-10: 1503033937

ISBN-13: 978-1503033931

For Mum & Dad

Her Moons Denouement

Ah, her succinct instinct haemorrhages denial

elementally raw, she, Carpathian hewn

pale beauty shaded scarlet in alacritous

humorous allegory of her wanton moon

Ah, her bridled burden a sullen mood constrained

midst the tacit verve, she, in sated succour strewn

ignominy the riddle of illicit names

naked edged the carrion of her hollow tune

Ah, her frozen glow carves tears upon virgin lips

an echo bereft, she, breathless of amour's swoon

soul scarred and sewn, beating with their eternity

no warmth of life tonight to light her aching womb

Chapter 1

The rusting, squeaky rubber wheels bounced erratically over the uneven shoe-shined cobbles on the narrow, steeply inclined side street leading up towards the Royal Mile in Edinburgh. The wheels supported a twelve-foot high distressed mahogany cabinet that was agitatedly shaking and rocking while being pushed up the incline. A hunched back man, dressed in Jester's motley, dull and threadbare, all vivacity faded from the colours, was pushing from behind it. Tarnished silver bells jingled on the end of the Fools Hat framing his ruddy, sweating face, which was grimacing under the strain of his labour.

Up ahead, streams of people passed the entrance to the alleyway and the vociferous hubbub of the main street in the middle of a Fringe Festival began to pervade the alley, drowning out the jangling bells as with one last huge effort, the Jester rolled the cabinet off the cobbles and onto the flag stoned pavement of the Royal Mile.

The din was infectious, swirling through the open air under a cloudless midday sun streamed blue sky, intoxicating the milling throngs who were devouring the street entertainment. A slow meandering wave of people navigated their way around crowds surrounding the jugglers, magicians, living statues, fire-eaters and sword swallowers, bobbing heads trying to catch sight of the wares. Up and down the pavements, sandwich boards and posters proclaimed the evening gigs, touts standing next to them shouting out the same message and forcing flyers into the hands of every person that passed by.

Her Moons Denouement   **Max Hardy**

The Jester slowly negotiated the cabinet along the pavement, patiently going with the flow, until he came to a small square by St Giles Cathedral, where there was a relatively open space in front of the imposing building. He manoeuvred the cabinet into place in front of steps to the entrance of the Cathedral, the front doors of it facing out onto the street. He opened a drawer in the bottom of the cabinet and proceeded to remove half a dozen buckets filled with stones from within and placed them in a semi-circle about five metres in front of it.

A few passers-by stopped to watch as the Jester skipped back to the cabinet and started to unfasten the doors. Swinging one of the doors open, he turned to the small crowd, smiling broadly.

'Good morrow to you kind Lords and Ladies. Today, I have for you revelations of the like you will have never encountered. They will truly blow your mind. Please, please, avail yourselves of a stone or two from the buckets in front of you while I finish setting up the show.' he encouraged animatedly, his hunched body prancing to open the other door, revealing a large white sheet, fully ten foot tall by ten foot wide covering something within the cabinet. At the top of the cabinet three metal rods with clasps on the end held the sheet in place. Emblazoned on the sheet in blood red letters, each a foot tall were the words 'Even Fallen Angels Have Wings'. Words that were also written on the inside of the open doors.

The jester turned back towards the growing, inquisitive crowd with a broad, almost manic grin on his face and skipped towards the throng building behind the buckets. He had picked up what looked like a metal tube with a bladder on the end from the bottom of the cabinet, which he proceeded to tap off the heads of the crowd as he jauntily skipped the line.

'Fear and Faith. Faith and Fear. Fear and Faith.' he started to sing while bopping the bladder off people, who smiled in nervous expectancy. He suddenly stopped in front of a young, tall skinny man in the middle of the line and stared into his eyes intently.

'In whose faith is your fear founded?' the Jester started to sing, rattling the bladder and shaking the tarnished bells on his hat in rhythmic accompaniment. 'Which God's atonement do you seek?' he continued, turning to the young woman who was with the man and tapping the bladder off her forehead, chest and shoulders in the sign of a crucifix. 'Whose penance keeps your soul grounded, when spirits avarice is preached?' he finished, stooping down and grabbing a few stones from the bucket in front of him. He skipped back a few steps and took in his ever-growing audience.

'Ladies and Lords. Would you help me uncover the truth? Would you help me tear down the veil of deception? I am not without sin, but I am prepared to cast the first stone.' the Jester preached, raising one of the stones above his head in his free hand. He smiled broadly as he watched the crowd look down at the stones they held, then turned and threw his towards the clasps holding the sheet in place, tapping from foot to foot as he took a second stone and threw that. He turned back to the crowd, grinning and skipping. 'Help me derail the veil, help me expose the truth.' he encouraged, throwing another stone which pinged off one of the clasps, slightly dislodging the sheet.

A stone shot out from the crowd and smacked into the sheet well below the clasps with a dull thud, causing the blood red words to billow and dance. More followed, from the hands of people whose faces were still perplexed, but also enlivened with the temptation of the revelation, joining in the crowd reflex. Stones pinged off the woodwork, splatted into the sheet, the odd few making contact with the clasps, shaking them and loosening the cover.

Suddenly, the sheet came away from the clasp on the right side of the cabinet and fell down, partly revealing what lay behind. There were panicked gasps and screams from the crowd and as one, the group shuffled back, dropping whatever stones they still had in their hands to the ground. A few started to push their way out and away from the scene. Many more, the majority, stood transfixed in morbid curiosity, staring intently at an outstretched, blood-stained arm, the hand of which being nailed through the palm to a wooden plank.

The Jester stopped skipping and walked slowly over to the cabinet, his stride imperceptibly lengthening, his shoulders widening as his gait started to un-hunch, even though the lump was still on his back. He grabbed the flapping corner of the sheet and yanked it forcefully off the remaining two clasps to further screams and gasps of astonishment.

In the cabinet was a crucifix, ten foot tall. Nailed to it palm and foot was a scrawny silver haired man, naked apart from a dirt stained loincloth. He was unconscious, head lolling to one side, blood meandering down his brow from the barbed wire crown that was gouging into it. Behind the crucifix, on the back of the cabinet there were pictures. Smiling faces. Smiling faces of young, vibrant women, their carefree snapshots resonating with the beautiful bright day, but at odds with the macabre scene in front of them.

'Is your fear founded in his faith!' shouted the Jester, turning back to the remaining crowd and pointing his bladder towards the man on the crucifix. 'Do you want to know the truth of his faith! What he does in the name of his faith!' His voice was rising in volume, simmering with vitriol as he stood up fully from his feigned stoop and pointed the bladder towards one of the pictures.

'Demi Simpson, twenty three, a prostitute, went missing in 2008.' he pointed to the next picture. 'Josie Richards, nineteen, a lap dancer, went missing in 2010.' And the next. 'Shelley Crabtree, seventeen, seven-fuckin-teen,' he spat, 'still in sixth form, went missing three weeks ago.'

Her Moons Denouement   **Max Hardy**

The crowd were in stunned silence, but through the Jesters rant could be heard the raised tones of someone pushing through them, the bobbing peaked cap of a police officer visible above their heads.

'Come on people, let me through, what's all the screaming about.' PC Simpson started just as he got to the front of the crowd and saw the vista in front of him. 'Bloody hell mate, what's going on here!' he said as he walked into the open area in front of the cabinet, his incredulous gaze moving between the crucifix and the Jester.

Instantly, the Jester pulled the bladder from the end of the tube he was holding and pointed it towards the PC. The tube was the barrel of a gun. 'Please stop there PC?' he asked calmly, holding the gun steadily at the police officer's chest.

Pandemonium broke out behind them as those in the front of the crowd saw that it was a gun the Jester was holding, panic pulsing in waves as people turned to flee, screaming, while some stood fast in their curiosity and still more on the periphery sought to see.

'Simpson. Bill Simpson. Now I don't know what your beef is Sir, but could I ask you to just keep calm and put the gun down please.' Simpson asked as he stopped suddenly, putting both hands out in front of him in placation.

'You have nothing to fear from me Bill. Quite the contrary. Today I am here to help you. Today I am here to expose the crimes of this man to the world.' the Jester answered, smiling radiantly, the gun not wavering at all.

'What do you think this man has done?' asked Simpson, his eyes darting from the crucifix, to the Jester, to the frantic crowd and the other peaked caps he saw pushing through it.

'It's not what we think Bill, it's what we can prove. In the bottom drawer of the cabinet are folders, each one of which contains conclusive evidence of that man's, no, that *monsters* involvement in the murder of those seven poor women.'

'Okay Sir, so perhaps you could put down the gun and we can talk about that. Talk about who this man is and what he has done.' Simpson suggested, seeing other police officers emerging from the pulsing crowd and gesturing for them to hold back.

'His name is Liam O'Driscoll. Archbishop Liam O'Driscoll.' he shouted, so that the curious still in the crowd behind the ever expanding line of police officers could hear. 'The highest authority of the Catholic Church in Scotland. You may have unburdened your sins to him in confessional. He may have asked you to do three Hail Mary's. That wasn't enough of a penance for these women. No. Their penance was to be bound face down on the altar in the Cathedral behind you as he sodomised them while strangling them to death. All in the name of his God.'

'Jesus.' stuttered Simpson, losing his composure for a moment at the revelation. 'Please don't think about shooting him. If you have evidence that can prove he has done those things...' he continued before the Jester interrupted, laughing.

'Bill, Bill, I'm not going to kill him. I am giving him to you so that justice can be exacted, so that the lies and deceit that are spread in the name of his God can be exposed. For far too long his seed have committed debauchery under the fear of his faith and we say NO MORE!' he finished the sentence shouting, flexing his shoulders, his eyes alive with fervour.

'We will no longer sit in the shadows of your Gods and let their impotence prevail. Even Fallen Angels Have Wings!' he sang, stretching his arms out as he did, still keeping the gun levelled at Simpson. There was a rip of Velcro from the hump on his back and out of the Jesters Motley, two giant feathered wings sprouted, fully the

Her Moons Denouement Max Hardy

length of his arms, shimmering and fluttering in the brilliant sunlight. Simpson stepped back in surprise, an astonished shriek escaping his gaping mouth, in tandem with gasps from the rest of the crowd.

'We want justice. Justice for Demi, justice for Josie, justice for Shelley. We want justice for every Angel that has died. Justice for every Angel left to bleed in the fear founded by the disease of their seed. We want the world to see the truth.'

The Jester quickly turned the gun in his outstretched hand from pointing at Simpson and forced it into the temple of his own head.

'We are the Fallen Angels!' he shouted, smiling wildly at the crowd, and pulled the trigger.

Chapter 2

I am in a padded cell, my hands and feet nailed to a chair in the middle of it, naked. My mind is swirling, trying to comprehend where I am, what is happening. The walls are pulsing, the stained and ripped individual pads ululating as the material starts to morph, starts to coalesce into faces. Faces of Sarah, my wife. Faces of Jacob, my son. Hundreds of faces staring at me imploringly, their lips screaming in silence. I cannot hear the words, but they echo in my mind, condemnatory.

'Why John, why did you choose her?'

'Why Daddy, why did you forsake me?'

An explosion flashes, startling my gaze from the walls to a point in front of me where the very air itself is torn apart. In the rip I can see a building engulfed by an inferno and I can feel the searing heat emanating from the explosion blistering my naked skin. Behind the aberration, the faces of Sarah and Jacob still silently scream at me.

Then through the flames a shadow appears: the dark, charred, stuttering outline of a person, the nauseous stench of their still burning flesh invading my nostrils on the breath of the searing heat. The outline moves closer, away from the burning house, towards the rip in the air in front of me. Pieces of darkness start to fall away from

Her Moons Denouement   Max Hardy

the shadow, evaporating into nothingness, revealing the pristine suited form of a man beneath, Dr Ennis. He sneers toward me as he walks closer to the rip in the air, taking a glove out of his pocket, a Vampire glove, impressed with sharp metal pins. As he pulls it onto his hand, he speaks in silence, but the words echo around my mind, along with the other words in there.

'In my world Saul, this type of pain is a precursor to pleasure.'

'Why John, why did you choose her?'

'Why Daddy, why did you forsake me?'

The words swirl around in my head, biting, scratching, clawing and gouging at my understanding, awakening my pain. And I suddenly remember what he does next. What that malicious gloved hand does to my penis and I start shaking furiously in my bindings, strapped to the seat, screaming 'No!' silently at the top of my voice, catching the maniacal image of him climbing through the rip in the air as I try and turn my head away. I can't. It is strapped tight to the chair around my forehead. I try to close my eyes, but they won't close. I am forced to watch him approach, forced to watch that hand get closer and closer to me, forced to watch his rictus grin salivate over what he is about to do.

I see his face. I see Sarah's faces. I see Jacob's faces. I see the gloved hand getting closer, and I start to understand my hell.

Then I see the glove start to disintegrate, breaking up into pieces that float away into nothingness. His clothes, his skin, his hair, his face all do the same. Slowly revealing the naked form of a woman, her body emaciated, hair ripped from her head, her skin pock marked, scarred and ravaged. It is Rebecca. Her gaunt, sunken ghostly countenance smiles beseechingly at me, revealing the withered stump of a tongue as she pleads with me silently, words bursting into my mind, joining the crescendo.

Her Moons Denouement   Max Hardy

'You have to believe me John, I am not Madame Evangeline.'

'In my world Saul, this type of pain is a precursor to pleasure.'

'Why John, why did you choose her?'

'Why Daddy, why did you forsake me?'

Her hand, which is still reaching out as she stops in front of me, hovers over the nail rammed through my right hand into the chair. She gently strokes her fingers over it. I wince with the pain, eyes angled down to watch what she does. Skin starts to peel from her fingers as she strokes the head of the nail, then from her hand and from her arm. I watch as the battlefield of harm seems to evaporate from the left side of her body, leaving smooth, lithe skin. Long red hair sprouts from the riven scalp, framing the left side of a face starting to flush with colour, forming the familiar countenance of my lover, Jessica. Her eye is a deep emerald, as is the eye on the right, on Rebecca's side of the face. They both implore me, half wizened, half voluptuous lips silently pleading, screaming in my mind.

'I am not Madame Evangeline. I thought you believed that, I really thought you believed that.'

'You have to believe me John, I am not Madame Evangeline.'

'In my world Saul, this type of pain is a precursor to pleasure.'

'Why John, why did you choose her?'

'Why Daddy, why did you forsake me?'

The walls breathe, the faces seethe in front of me, while inside my mind their voices scream a tornado to my ignominy. My eyes fall from their faces in shame; to the last vestiges of ravaged flesh flaking away from Jessica's half of their stomach. To the forked tongue of the snake tattoo inveigling its way from their vagina.

Her Moons Denouement   Max Hardy

To the forked tongue that flicks.

To the snake head that pulses, then bloats and becomes real.

Its head turns to me, beady eyes entrancing me in a stare as it starts to meander up the stomach, over Jessica's arm and onto the chair where my right hand is nailed, more and more of its body coming out of their vagina. I hear a sibilant hiss in my head, followed by words augmenting my torment.

'You had a choice John. It was all down to you. Jacob or Jessica. Only you knew the truth. Only you had the facts.'

'I am not Madame Evangeline. I thought you believed that, I really thought you believed that.'

'You have to believe me John, I am not Madame Evangeline.'

'In my world Saul, this type of pain is a precursor to pleasure.'

'Why John, why did you choose her?'

'Why Daddy, why did you forsake me?'

The snake crawls up my arm and its body circles my neck, coiling around it, the head slowly angling in front of me again as the coils start to constrict. It hisses silently, eyes piercing me, as do the eyes of Rebecca/Jessica, as do the hundreds of eyes of Sarah and Jacob. Screaming words start to change in my mind as all of the lips in front of me start to sync.

'You had a choice John. It was all down to you...'

The coils start to constrict further, tightening around my throat, crushing my windpipe, slowly choking me. All of their lips now whisper sibilantly, accusing me.

'Only you knew the truth, only you had the facts...'

Her Moons Denouement   Max Hardy

I try to scream, but my throat is too constricted, my tongue fattening and filling my mouth, my eyes bulging in my skull as I am starved of oxygen. I begin to palpitate and shake in my bindings, unable to move, unable to stop the descent into my hell as with the last whisper of breath in me, gutturally I plead 'Forgive me!'

My eyes start to roll in my head, the room around me swirling, the images spiralling into a vortex of faces blurring into each other, all mouthing the same damning incantations. Consciousness starts to leave, everything turning dark, sinking into the distance, my body slumping as the last vestige of my human being escapes. The voices fade. Darkness. Silence. The emptiness of forever.

Then, crystal clear, a voice, coming through the darkness, through the silence, through the emptiness of forever.

'John, think on one thing: Even Fallen Angels Have Wings.'

I wake with a start, sitting bolt upright in the leather chair I fell asleep in. The nightmare is still resonating through my mind so the very first thing I do is raise my hands, just to make sure they aren't nailed to the chair, just to make sure I am not back in that cell. The bandages are weeping slightly and are soaked in sweat, as is the rest of my body, and as I lift my left hand, I see the Nagant M1895 revolver still tightly clasped in its palm.

Statistically, you would think the odds of blowing your brains out with a Nagant playing Russian Roulette would be seven to one. After all, there are seven chambers in the cylinder and only one bullet, right? Wrong. What people don't generally take into account is gravity. When you spin the cylinder, the chamber with the bullet in is heavier than the ones that are empty, so nearly every time, that chamber will end up near the bottom. So statistically, the odds of blowing your brains out are very long. That's how magicians get away with it.

Her Moons Denouement   Max Hardy

Slivers of light are seeping in through tiny gaps in the closed blinds, suggesting daylight outside. They are strobing talons through the semi-darkness, revealing the contents of my studio, revealing the collage of evidence I have pinned to every spare surface in the room. I put the revolver down on the writing desk in front of me, stand up gingerly, slouch my way to the far wall through the discarded takeaway containers, empty vodka bottles, ripped up notes and photos festooning the floor. It still hurts to walk. I take in glimpses of the evidence, of images, of loved ones gone on the wall in front of me.

Two weeks ago, my wife and son were killed in an explosion at a country house called Fetherstone Hall. My son had been kidnapped, incarcerated inside a crate in the Hall and was being used as bait. Bait to try and ensure that I investigated the murder of a dead body, Michael Angus, which was also in the Hall. A murder where his mother, Rebecca Angus, had already been committed to a mental institute for the crime. An 'Unknown Caller' set a challenge. He wanted me to find the real killer of Michael and return to the Hall with that killer, within twenty four hours, before midnight, or the crate would explode. All the evidence pointed to a woman called Jessica Seymour, my lover, being the real killer of the dead body. But I knew she couldn't be. I knew that at the time Michael was killed she was with me.

I thought the 'Unknown Caller' was a man called Gordon Ennis. He ran a mental facility called the Fielding Institute, where Rebecca Angus was committed. I had investigated him in the past for suspicious deaths caused by 'Face Down Restraint' and thought that he was out to exact some kind of warped revenge against me. He wasn't directly involved, but he was a killer and during the course of the investigation, he nailed me to a chair, sexually molested me and would have ripped my heart out if the real 'Unknown Caller' hadn't intervened and saved my life.

I say real 'Unknown Caller', but I still don't know who he was. He was a trinity. Father, Son and Holy Ghost. One in the same. An older man

Her Moons Denouement

called 'Ben Hanlon' who had spirited Rebecca Angus away from under the nose of Gordon Ennis. A young paediatric physician called 'Rob Adams' who was looking after my son, Jacob. A nebulous voice of the 'Unknown Caller' who no one ever saw. They were all the same person and he wanted me to choose.

He wanted me to choose between Jessica and Jacob. He wanted me to believe that Jessica had an alter ego. An alter ego called Madame Evangeline who had seduced Rebecca Angus and somehow been involved in Michael's murder. But I knew Jessica could not have been Madame Evangeline. Even though Jessica was in Edinburgh when Michael was killed. Even though Rebecca and Michael had been seen in a Limousine owned by Jessica. Even though Jessica owned Featherstone Hall, where Michael was killed. Even though Jessica had the exact same Snake tattoo on her abdomen, I knew she couldn't have been Madame Evangeline.

So I chose Jessica: and Sarah and Jacob died at midnight on that fateful evening when the Hall exploded. Shortly after that, while I was being taken to hospital to have my injuries seen to, Jessica died too, in a car crash. In the space of an hour, everyone I had ever loved was gone.

And I still don't have a clue why. There was a serpent, there was temptation, there was forbidden fruit and someone wanted me to make a choice. I chose wrong. All I do know is that it wasn't chance.

But I will find out. If chance lets me, today I will go and see Allie, Sarah's friend and see if she knows which Private Investigator Sarah used to have Jess and I followed. I chose wrong, which means Jessica could have been Madame Evangeline. Nothing in the evidence I have can corroborate that. This Investigator may have seen something while following us, which could help.

If chance lets me.

Her Moons Denouement   **Max Hardy**

I turn from the wall of frustrated hope and stagger to the other side of the room, picking up the revolver from the desk as I pass. There is a six foot tall blank canvas leaning against the wall, my signature, John Saul, in the bottom right corner. It will be called 'My Last Lament' when it is finished. I'm not sure exactly when that will be. It could be in the next few seconds, it could be in a day, or a week. Only chance knows that.

While statistically there is very little chance of blowing your brains out during Russian Roulette if you let the barrel come to a natural stop, that's not true if you stop the barrel mid spin. I flick the barrel on the revolver out, slip the single bullet into my palm and then quickly slide it back into a different chamber. When you stop it mid spin, the odds are seven to one. When you have tried it seven times, statistically, the odds are even. Every time you try it after that, statistically, you will blow your brains out.

I turn, standing with my back to the canvas and spin the barrel of the revolver, stop it mid spin, put it to my forehead, and for the fifteenth time, pull the trigger.

Chapter 3

The squeal of seagulls swirled around in the thermals the birds were riding. They glided in circles, occasionally swooping down towards the white plastic barrier that had been erected around the Crime Scene in front of St Giles Cathedral. The noise was sharp and biting, cutting through the jovial buzz that had returned to the Festival activities taking place on the Royal Mile. One particular Great Black-backed gull swooped low inside the barrier, its dark wings shimmering in descent as it skimmed the heads of four people, excited by the odour of blood, and defecated onto the drab, dirty raincoat of one of the four stooping over the outstretched wings of the dead body lying on the ground.

The guano splatted onto DI Bentley's shoulder, spattering onto the side of his face on impact. He stood up animatedly, raising a balled fist and shaking it furiously at the ascending bird as he shouted, 'Fucking flying rat!', while using the other arm to wipe the white deposits from his cheek, dislodging dog hair from the sleeve of his raincoat which gently floated down onto the body below.

'Ne pas contaminer mon Crime Scene vas te faire encule sale!' screamed Marcel Laurent, a svelte, tall angular faced man dressed in white Personal Protection Equipment. The Forensic Examiner straightened up as he shouted the insult and faced up to DI Bentley, shoving him backward, away from the body.

Her Moons Denouement   Max Hardy

'What the hell do you think you are doing?' Bentley responded in surprise as he stumbled before gaining his footing and standing his ground. He tried to push back against Laurent, but the Frenchman was strong and determined and held him in place.

'I said, don't contaminate my Crime Scene you filthy fuck!' Laurent repeated, in English this time, his features taut with fury.

Bentley tried again to push his portly, broad frame against the palm of the hand in his chest but still couldn't move it. Anger flowed over his paunchy ruddy cheeks, coursed through his body, diverting the balled fist that he had shaken at the receding bird and angling it towards Laurent's head.

A hand shot out and stopped it just before it made contact with Laurent's skull. 'Gentlemen, please, we have enough blood shed to investigate here today without the two of you adding to it.' intervened Dr Le Fenwick, the Medical Examiner, as he positioned himself between the two men. 'There are a also a good number of Junior officers and investigators here today, not least the lovely DC Tait, and I don't think you are showing them a particularly good example of how senior professionals are meant to behave. Calm down, the pair of you, or I will report you both for gross misconduct. Do I make myself clear.' finished Le Fenwick, his bulbous blue eyes radiating disapproval as his bald head moved back and forth, glaring at them.

'Il est une telle chatte ecossias inconsidérée!' mumbled Laurent under his breath, still simmering.

'And you are a stinking oily four legged amphibian.' Bentley growled, gutturally.

'Great, you are an inconsiderate Scottish Twat, and you are a slimy French frog. You don't like each other. I get it. But we have a dead body behind us. We have a potential Serial Killer to investigate, so could you please put your bigotry to one side and let's get back to work please gentlemen.' asked DC Tait, a tall, pallid young woman with blonde hair tied tightly in a ponytail. Le Fenwick looked at her in admiration and winked.

The two men grumbled an acknowledgement, begrudgingly nodding their heads. All four of them turned back to the dead body that was lying on the ground dressed in Jesters Motley, wings spread out from either side of its back.

'Cause of death is due to a single gunshot fired directly at the left temple. The bullet passed straight through the brain and exited via the right temple. Death was instantaneous.' Informed Le Fenwick as he crouched down beside the right side of the head, next to the blood pooling from the exploded exit point. The Jester's eyes were wide open, glazed and empty, a rictus grin still singing from his lips.

'And the wings?' asked Tait, standing back from the body.

Laurent bent over the body and rolled it onto its right side, the left wing rising as he did. Their gaze followed the arc of the wing, all the way to where it met the Jesters back. Through the torn Motley they saw a metal bracket with hinges, the end of the wings attached to the hinges. The bracket was strapped around the Jesters chest. Laurent reached inside the Motley near the bracket, seeing a cable heading off up towards the shoulder and traced it all the way down the left arm, to a metal band circling the Jesters wrist.

'The wings were contained in a metal harness, strapped around his body, with control wires on each wrist to activate them. So, not a real Angel then.' Laurent finished, smirking towards Le Fenwick.

'And you thought it was.' sneered Bentley. 'Do you have any idea who he is? Any ID? Anything?' he added.

'No, nothing to identify him yet.' Laurent answered curtly.

'What about the Archbishop, Dick. How are his injuries?' Bentley asked Le Fenwick as he turned and took in the rest of the area. Other Forensic Investigators in White PPE were examining the cabinet and various Manila files and boxes were being taken out of the drawer at the bottom of it. A number of police officers congregated at the side of the cabinet talking to PC Simpson.

Bentley walked towards them, Tait and Le Fenwick following. 'Nails hammered through his hands and feet, proper crucifixion, but nothing life threatening. He has a few cuts and bruises from the stones that were thrown but otherwise is in reasonable shape. He had been sedated and the effects of that are starting to wear off. An ambulance has just taken him to hospital to have the wounds treated and he will be taken to the station after that.' Le Fenwick answered.

'Catholic bastard.' grumbled Bentley under his breath as he approached PC Simpson.

'Simpson, you okay?' Bentley asked without concern, quickly adding, 'Good, now tell me what happened?' before Simpson had a chance to answer.

'Gents.' Bentley added, addressing the other Police Officers, 'Go and make sure the perimeter is secure. I don't want the press getting any more pictures than they already have.' he finished, his tone admonishing.

The other officers left, each patting Simpson on the shoulder as they did, mouthing words of encouragement. Bentley looked on in irritation.

'So Simpson, what happened?' Bentley reiterated.

'He blew his brains out. He blew his fucking brains out. Right in front of me.' Simpson said, looking up at Bentley with imploring eyes.

Her Moons Denouement

Max Hardy

'Yes, he blew his brains out. Get over it. Who was he and why did he have the Archbishop?'

'Jesus Bentley, show a bit of compassion, the man has just seen someone die.' interrupted Le Fenwick, kneeling down alongside Simpson while wrapping a consoling arm around his shoulders.

'Comes with the territory. Simpson, you are still on shift and we need to know what happened here.' Bentley continued, unabashed.

Simpson looked up into the stern uncompromising face of Bentley, then down towards Le Fenwick's considerate countenance. He spoke to Le Fenwick.

'He said they were the Fallen Angels. He didn't say who he was particularly. He said that they would no longer sit in the shadows of your Gods and let their impotence prevail. He said, even Fallen Angels Have Wings! And then the wings came out and he fucking shot himself!' Simpson said, his voice rising in intensity as he shook in the seat, eyes wide with shock and panic.

'And what the fuck does that mean! What about the Archbishop? What did he say about that Catholic twat?' demanded Bentley abruptly. The harsh words seared through Simpson's panic, bringing him back through his emotion, to fact.

'He said that the Archbishop had killed seven women. He sodomised and strangled them to death on the altar in the cathedral. He said there were files in the cabinet containing the relevant evidence.'

'He said a Roman Catholic Archbishop killed seven women on the altar of a Presbyterian church?' Bentley reiterated, paraphrasing.

Tait looked up at Bentley in astonishment. 'I think he told you the Archbishop killed seven women and you have been given the evidence to prove it. Is Catholic or Presbyterian really that important in the context of seven murders?'

'Isn't it. It seems to be important to the Fallen Angels. Important enough to crucify him. Important enough for one of them to commit suicide in broad daylight in front of an audience of hundreds. Important enough to make a religious statement. 'We will no longer sit in the shadows of your Gods.' What the hell do you think that is if not religious?' Bentley said with sarcasm, shaking his head as he looked at Tait in disdain. Tait turned away sheepishly and knelt down to join Le Fenwick in consoling Simpson.

'So what's in the folders?' Bentley added, marching away from them and over to the cabinet, scooping up one of the Manila folders in his stride.

'Sir!' shouted the mask covered face of one of the Forensic Examiners working the scene. 'We haven't processed that file yet.'

'Bog Off. You've got my DNA on file, and my fucking dog's, so you can easily eliminate me, right?' Bentley challenged with a forceful glare. The examiner cowered under the gaze and didn't answer, simply went back to dusting the small box in front of him for prints.

'Prick.' Bentley mumbled as he looked at the front of the folder. There was a white label in the top right corner of the cover, the name Josie Richards typed on it. He opened the cover and started to flick through the contents. The first few pages were typed notes. He read a few paragraphs, shaking his head as he did.

'It's a confession. A typed transcript of a confession detailing everything the bastard did to her.' He flicked to the end of the notes. 'And he has signed it. It looks like the bastard has signed it in blood.'

Le Fenwick came up alongside him and he scanned the notes as well, his face contorting into disbelief as he took in the graphic atrocity being described. Three words stuck in his mind. 'Vade retro satana.' he whispered.

Her Moons Denouement   **Max Hardy**

'I saw that too.' said Bentley, turning the last page of the notes over to reveal a photograph. A photograph of a naked woman laying prone on her front over an altar. A naked woman with a clear plastic bag over her head and taped around her neck with blue masking tape. A plastic bag through which her dead bulbous eyes stared beseechingly out of the picture. Beside the altar, smiling, a triumphant expression on his sweat stained face, stood Archbishop Liam O'Driscoll. He was dressed in a surplice, a loose fitting, broad sleeved white vestment which was adorned with a purple stole over the shoulders. The surplice was rucked up at the front, his still erect penis stopping it from falling down.

Le Fenwick's face lost all of its colour, his complexion becoming ashen as he gagged at the image.

'He is one sick son of a bitch.' said Bentley, flicking over to another photograph of a small, intricately carved wooden box. The same style of wooden box that was on the ground in front of the cabinet. He reached down and picked up the nearest one. He undid a small gold clasp on the front of the box and opened the lid.

Inside was a scroll, a red wax seal with the words 'Vade retro satana' embossed into it. The scroll was covered in very fine hand drawn calligraphy, the first word in bold, centred on the paper: 'Amdusias'. A clear plastic bag trimmed with a blue masking tape poked out of the scroll.

Bentley looked up at Le Fenwick.

'Vade retro satana. Go back Satan. The words used during an Exorcism. Amdusias was a demon, body of a human, head of a unicorn with claws for hands and feet. Said to control the cacophonous music of Hell. This sick bastard has been carrying out some warped kind of Exorcism, sodomising and asphyxiating those

Her Moons Denouement **Max Hardy**

girls to get at their demons. Demons he thinks he has trapped inside those plastic bags.'

Chapter 4

The last time I walked down this street I discovered my lover, Jessica, was seriously implicated in the murder I was investigating. I discovered a lot that day. I lost a lot that day. That day was only two weeks ago. I am on Grey Street in Newcastle and I stop outside Iguanas, the café where I am meeting Allie and look over the busy road toward the buildings opposite. It's a sunny day: it shouldn't be. It should be dull and oppressive, the sky should be smeared with swathes of broiling grey storm clouds rumbling overhead, threatening thunder. Every day should be like that. Instead the sun glistens off the darkened windows of what were Jessica's offices, catching reflections of people going about their business behind them. Life carries on, even as you carry the desolation of everything that has gone.

The clicking of high heels sinks into my mind, the odd click heavier than the even, Allie's signature walk. She has a raised arch on her left foot and really shouldn't wear high heels, especially not six inch high heels, but you can't tell her that. Flat shoes just wouldn't go with her image. Today the image is classically styled and still very respectful. A black shift dress with a black Bolero over the top, a deep red rose pinned to the lapel, matching the lipstick on her always heavily made up face. She reaches out her arms as she approaches me.

'John, darling!' she says, in an aching voice. If it wasn't for the Botox, her face may have creased in the brow and around the cheeks in concern. As it was, only her eyes and voice managed to convey that emotion as she hugs me tightly. It was enough.

Enough for the remorse and guilt to overwhelm me, to escape from the rickety rooms I am trying hard to contain them in so I can at least function. I feel her comforting, warm embrace, I smell the delicate sweet scent of woman and it just engulfs me in images of Sarah, images of Jessica. Loving images that scream in my mind.

'I'm sorry Allie, I truly am.' is all I can say through quivering lips.

She hugs me even tighter, gently rubbing my back for a moment before she releases the embrace, takes one step back and then slaps me hard across the face with venom, anger instantly flashing through her eyes.

'You utter bastard. How could you do that to her. How could you hurt my baby girl like that?'

The sting of the slap reverberates around my head and I clench my toes and ball my fists, straining the injuries, the nail holes in those areas to pain, adding to the intensity of the slap. I deserve it, all of it. It helps to cut through the emotion, making enough of a gap to remind me of why I wanted to meet Allie.

'I know I am. I am sorry. Let's grab a coffee and talk.'

There are tears in her eyes as she looks at me, still partly in anger, partly in sorrow. She shakes her head.

'I want to hate you John, I really do. But I can't. You are the only thing I have left of Sarah and Jacob and I know you are suffering. But don't think I forgive you for what you've done. Don't you ever think that.' she reproaches as she comes alongside, takes my arm and supports me as we walk into the café.

Her Moons Denouement   Max Hardy

A waiter shows us to a table in the window and we sit down. Allie becomes Allie, instantly flirting with the young lad, thrusting her ample fake chest out as she orders herself a skinny caramel macchiato and a double espresso for me. That irreverent glint returns to her eye for a second and to be honest, I feel it dent the glacier that is my heart. It's the contradiction that is Allie. Everything that you see of her is fake, everything she says, everything she feels is real and she can ground you and make *you* feel real in an instant.

'I was expecting you to look like a drunken bum, if I'm honest. I didn't expect you to be suited, booted and clean shaven.' Allie says, smiling as she reaches out and takes my hands, turning them palm up and staring at the clean bandages around them. 'Do they still hurt?'

'Allie, if I had come here looking like a bum, you would have slapped me twice. You should see the studio though, it looks like someone has emptied a rubbish truck into it. The wounds are starting to heal, but they still hurt.'

'Do you know how the investigation is going? I hear on the news that they are no further forward in finding out who was responsible for the explosion and that they are still sifting through all the rubble for evidence?'

I could tell there was an unasked question in her words, so I place a comforting hand over hers and answer it.

'They have what is left of their bodies but they can't release them yet. It's going to be a while before we can lay them to rest.'

Her eyes whisper disappointment as she looks down towards my hands again, running her slender manicured fingers over my bandages. 'And they really don't know who did it?'

'I check in with the team every day but there is not much more to tell other than what you have heard on the news. They are still exploring all leads but so far nothing has come up. We know there is a man who has assumed multiple identities but all investigations as to his real identity have turned up blanks so far. We still can't find Rebecca Angus. She seems to have disappeared off the face of the earth. And Jessica, well, I just don't know. That's something I want to ask you about. Sarah had a Private Investigator follow Jessica and I. Did she tell you who it was?'

The waiter arrives with our drinks and winks at Allie as he places them on the table. She smiles lewdly at him, her eyes following his tight arse as he leaves. I guess my face must have reflected the weary indignation I felt, that she could so easily be distracted from something so serious, to something so base with one wink.

'What!' she responds in playful innocence, 'I don't control my libido, it controls me! Know me, know that truth. You should know that too. After all, it was you shagging around with another woman that made Sarah hire a Private Investigator.' she finishes, the playfulness disappearing, replaced by admonishment.

'Point taken. Did she say who it was?' I reiterate.

'It was a guy from Newcastle, has an office on Dacre Street. He was called something Massah, something, something: Harry Massah. He was called Harry Massah. Why did you cheat on her John?'

Good old Allie. Keeping it real. For a second I thought about spinning her a line, something like I just didn't love her any more, anything really to drop the subject so I could get out of here and go and talk to Harry Massah. Go and talk to Harry Massah about Jessica. See if I could figure out who the hell she was. For a second I thought that. Allie is a bit like me though, she's got a bullshit sensor. But more than that, as one of my oldest friends, she deserved the truth, no matter how hard that truth was for me to tell.

Her Moons Denouement   Max Hardy

'I could tell you it was about the sex: and the sex was good. I am a bloke after all and it's our dicks that do the thinking. But it wasn't. She understood my grief. I couldn't talk to Sarah about that, I couldn't burden her with my pain when she was carrying so much of her own.'

'Your grief?' Allie asks me softly as I pause, collecting my thoughts, opening doors in rickety rooms.

'Allie, you know how hard it was for us to have Jacob. Three lots of fertility treatment in this country, then all those trips to experts in Europe: to France, to Spain, to Italy. Five years trying. You know the elation, the relief we felt when she eventually fell pregnant and the utter joy that consumed us when he was born.'

'I do. I will always feel blessed that you asked me to be there and will always be privileged that I was his Godmother.' she says as she cups both of my hands encouragingly.

'You also know how devastated we were when we found out about his condition. It broke me Allie. Seeing Jacob, day in, day out, growing up and not moving, not speaking: feeling the emptiness emanating from his eyes, it broke me. I felt like he was dead. Every single day I was grieving and it broke me. I found it harder and harder to be there with them and I know that was wrong, but I couldn't cope with the grief, I couldn't cope with the sheer guilt that Sarah bore. I know she felt it was her fault.'

I look directly at Allie as I speak, seeing anger flash into her eyes just as she squeezes my hands hard, pain searing through them. 'And Jessica, that fuckhole that you wallowed in, how did she understand your grief? How was she in a better position than your wife to help you cope?'

Allie's reaction perplexed me. I expected a little frustration when I started to talk about Jessica. After all, she was the woman who hurt

Her Moons Denouement   Max Hardy

her best friend, but there was something more in the rising anger. I continue.

'She had lost a child as well. She had an abortion. We talked about our grief, about our loss. I could talk to her about Jacob, how I felt about Jacob, the grief I felt. We talked about the stigma, the alienation of abortion, of having a child with Jacob's condition. I could talk to her and she understood, because she felt it too.'

Allie releases my hands and as she swipes her arms up in the air, she knocks her skinny caramel macchiato and the liquid spills over the table. She glares at me furiously, ignoring the drink dripping off the table edge onto her pristine dress.

'First off, your son wasn't dead. 'B', she had an abortion, the baby didn't die and thirdly, did you ever stop to give a second thought to why Sarah felt so guilty about Jacob's condition. Did you ever stop and wonder why it was so hard for you to conceive. Did you ever stop and think about talking to her. No I bet you fucking didn't! Typical bloody bloke. Much easier to find a tramp and fuck your misery away!'

Allie prods her finger into the table as she fumes at me, spatter of macchiato spraying up with every indignant poke. I was dumbfounded, the vitriol seemed way out of proportion to what I was telling her.

'Did you ever talk to Sarah, I mean, ever really talk! Did you ever talk to her about your childhood?'

Other rickety rooms started to burgeon in my mind, doors rattling in their frames. Why was she asking that? What did she know?

'No you didn't. She told me you didn't. You just clammed up. Just like you did when she tried to talk to you about Jacob. And she was just as bad because she didn't talk to you either. Perhaps if you had talked to each other, shared your sordid little secrets, you would have realised she was the one woman in the world who would have absolutely understood your grief.'

Sordid little secrets, what sordid little secrets did Sarah have? What did she know about my secrets? What was she talking about?

'The reason you couldn't conceive naturally, the reason that Sarah felt so absolutely guilt ridden about Jacob's condition is because when Sarah was thirteen, she had an abortion. She was forced to have an abortion when she was twenty seven weeks pregnant. Do you know what that meant! It meant she had to go through a full delivery. She held her dead baby girl in her arms before they took it away from her. She felt that was the cause of Jacob's condition. And do you know what happened two days after she had the abortion? The man she loved, the man whose baby it was, the man who had been locked up as a paedophile, hung himself in jail. So if you wanted to talk to someone who understood grief, who understood loss, who understood the pain of stigma and alienation: you should have talked to your wife.'

Chapter 5

Liam O'Driscoll sat calmly at an innocuous grey table, his wrists handcuffed to metal rings on the side of it. He sat in an innocuous grey chair at one side of the table, looking intermittently between the palms of his upturned hands, where the weeping, open wounded stigmata was visible, to his reflection in a large mirror that filled one wall of the police interview room. He smiled knowingly at his reflection, then looked back down at the stigmata.

The drab grey door to the interview room opened and DI Bentley, a large pile of manila folders in one hand, a steaming cup of black coffee in a chipped, stained Celtic mug in the other, entered. Following a pace or so behind him was DC Tait wearing straight grey trousers, a white blouse and an equally lifeless grey jacket. The only semblance of colour about her was the deep blue of her eyes shining from a face without any makeup, framed by blonde hair pulled tightly backward into a pony tail held in place by an elastic band.

DI Bentley stomped over the short distance to the two chairs on the opposite side of the table to Liam O'Driscoll and slouched into the one closest to the two recording decks, slurping coffee as he did. He banged the manila files with some force onto the table top, glaring at the calmly smiling Liam O'Driscoll as he pressed the record button on one of the decks.

Her Moons Denouement   Max Hardy

'DI Bentley and DC Tait interviewing Archbishop Liam O'Driscoll on suspicion of the murder of seven women. Time is 13:35. Archbishop O'Driscoll has refused legal representation.' grumbled Bentley, still glaring at O'Driscoll as DC Annie Tait sat demurely in the empty chair beside him, notebook and pen in hand.

'Good afternoon DC Tait, DI Bentley.' O'Driscoll said, his voice low and full of vibrato, with a deep powerful resonance, at odds with his slight build and bony features.

'Good? Good! You are having a fucking laugh aren't you? It's not good for these seven women. It's not good for their families. It's not good for the poor stupid bastard that blew his brains out making a point this morning! It's not good for the Catholic Church. It's not good for me having to sit here and look at your smug, sick sadistic face. So no, it's not good, not good for anyone!' fumed Bentley, one fist clenched, the other white knuckled, wrapped around the coffee cup.

O'Driscoll simply stared at him, then looked toward the mirror, the smile on his face broadening as he looked at his own reflection, then at Bentley's reflection.

Bentley followed his gaze, perplexed as he saw the smile broaden. 'Something amusing you about this it there?' he asked angrily.

O'Driscoll looked from the reflection, back to Bentley, glaring deep into the DI's eyes, O'Driscoll's gaze darting imperceptibly between the pupil, the iris, the white, from top to bottom and side to side continually, searching, his own expression becoming fixed, penetrating. Bentley shifted in his seat uncomfortably under the intense gaze, feeling the sharp, mesmerising eyes burn into the skull, methodically delving and digging into the recesses of every crack in his countenance, drinking in knowledge of him.

Her Moons Denouement   **Max Hardy**

'It's not amusing DI Bentley,' O'Driscoll began, his gaze not leaving Bentley's eyes as he gently moved his upturned palms forward toward the DI. 'It's an affirmation. An acknowledgement that what we do, is his will.' he finished, offering up the stigmata as a testament to the virtue of his suffering.

'We?' queried Bentley, the question coming out in a hoarse, dry gurgle, filled with the nervousness O'Driscoll's continued probing stare was imbuing in him. 'Was someone else involved in these atrocities?'

'You see them as atrocities, we see them as deliverance.' answered O'Driscoll, his eyes sparkling and his features glowing as he said the words.

Anger invaded the hypnotic state that Bentley was succumbing to and he quickly grabbed a manila file, thrusting it down on the table in front of O'Driscoll, breaking the gaze as he looked at the name on the front.

'Shelly Crabtree, seventeen years old, a sixth form student. Three weeks ago you put a plastic bag over her head and asphyxiated her to death while buggering her. We have the photographs. We have your confession signed in blood. How the hell is that Deliverance.' spat Bentley as he opened the folder, stabbing a finger into the photograph of O'Driscoll in front of the dead girl, glaring back up at the Archbishop.

O'Driscoll's gaze did not break from looking at Bentley as he answered. 'Shabnock. He had possessed her since she was six. He was a Mighty Marquis of Hell with fifty legions of demons under his command. We captured him. We freed hell, heaven and earth of his evil afflictions.'

'Through exorcism? What part of the rite of exorcism directs you to bugger the person possessed, to smother the person possessed and to kill the person possessed. I'm pretty sure the rite of exorcism is meant to free the individual of the demon so they can live a happy life thereafter?'

'And free the Demon into the world once more so they can spread their evil seed. We lure them, we trap them, we capture them and we imprison them.'

'So you do have an accomplice? Someone who took these sick trophy photographs?' pushed Bentley.

O'Driscoll's smile broadened as he once again looked toward the mirror, taking in his excitably grinning reflection.

'Shall we tell him?' O'Driscoll asked of his reflection, then answered in the same breath, 'We should tell him. The world should know.'

Bentley looked at O'Driscoll's grinning visage in the mirror, then turned to DC Tait with a pained expression on his face. He murmured under his breath. 'Shit, I think this fucker is a totem short of a friggin pole. He is one scary son of a bitch.'

'More a roof missing than a tile Sir.' Tait muttered in response.

'Proverbs 2:18-19 speaks of her. 'Her house sinks down to death, and her course leads to the shades. All who go to her cannot return and find again the paths of life.' She is the Night Hag, the one who came before Adam. She is my demon and she seeks atonement. She is Lilith. She knows where demons hide inside a human body. They wallow in the bowels, in the detritus of digestion, feasting on our waste. She is the incarnation of lust, and she uses me. She uses me to get to where they wallow, so she can seduce them, lead them through the writhing ecstasy of intestines, up through the churning bile of a terrified stomach, sliding and gorging on the sputum slipping down a constricting throat as she propels the demon out of the humans mouth, into the plastic bag as I orgasm, reciting the rite of exorcism, 'Vade retro satana', imprisoning the demon. She slivers back down

Her Moons Denouement   **Max Hardy**

through the dead body, back into me and their soul is delivered into Gods Kingdom. And the world is freed of another demon. For the life of one, the lives of many are saved.' he proclaimed proudly, smiling at his reflection all the while.

'What a steaming pile of horse shit. Shelley Crabtree, sodomised and asphyxiated. You killed her.' shouted Bentley in anger, hammering his finger into the picture in front of him. He reached for the next file.

'We imprisoned Shabnock. We ridded the world of the scourge of gangrene and worms.' O'Driscoll said calmly, still smiling, still holding his stigmata out.

'Demi Simpson, sodomised and asphyxiated. You killed her.' Bentley continued, veins in his temple pulsing purple, his face reddening with anger as he opened the folder and threw the picture of a dead Demi in front of O'Driscoll.

'He is Belial. No more do the Sons of Destruction roam this earth.'

'Josie Richards. Sodomised and asphyxiated. You killed her!' spat Bentley, pulling another photograph out of a folder and flinging it in front of O'Driscoll.

'He is Baalberith, he makes men blaspheme and murder. He is imprisoned.'

Bentley picked up the next folder, utter frustration and acrimony dancing on his features: which were broken by a visible uncertainty as he looked at the name on the folder, taking the photograph out as he did.

'Heather Scott. Sodomised and asphyxiated. You killed her.' Bentley said, less assured as he placed a photograph of the dead woman on an altar, the Archbishop standing in front of it with his erect penis out, onto O'Driscoll's outstretched hands.

'I do not know this woman.' O'Driscoll started, looking down at the name and at the photograph. He looked intently at Bentley, then to the DI's reflection in the mirror before continuing. 'You know this woman. Your Demon knows this woman. Your Demon knows this woman intimately. You have tasted her.'

'What the fuck are you talking about? She's there, in a picture with you and your raging hard on, dead. There's a signed confession in the folder as well.' answered Bentley, trying to imbue his voice with bravado, but there was a worry evident in it, which was even more evident in his expression, and he saw that when he took in his own reflection.

'I can see your Demon, in your reflection, he whispers to Lilith, he speaks of your transgressions.'

Bentley was obviously rattled as he pushed his chair back and stood up, leaning over the table, towering over the calm form of O'Driscoll. 'Just shut the fuck up you utter nutter. You killed seven women. And it's not just your confession and these photographs that prove it. Forensics have seven plastic bags wrapped in your stupid fucking scrolls downstairs and in less than an hour will have the necessary physical evidence that will let us lock you up and throw away the key for good you sick fuck.'

O'Driscoll's expression suddenly changed, utter terror entering his features. He started to shake his hands in their restraints, trying to loosen them as he stood up suddenly, tipping his chair as he did.

'You can't open the bags. They will escape. You can't break the seal on the bags or the demons will escape and these women's sacrifice will all have been in vain!' he screamed at Bentley, spittle flying from his mouth with the pleading words.

Her Moons Denouement Max Hardy

Bentley stood back, out of the way of O'Driscolls flailing hands. Hands which were trying to yank the dull grey table that was bolted to the floor in order to get closer to Bentley and Tait. Hands that shook it so hard, Bentley's Celtic mug toppled over, spilling the coffee. DC Tait backed out of her seat too, the two detectives slowly moving towards the door.

'You mustn't! You must not break the seal on those bags!' screamed O'Driscoll, more a forceful order than an imploring request this time, his whole person now wracked with intense broiling animosity and, with unnatural strength for such a small, frail man, he still tried to pull the table from the floor, shaking his bindings furiously.

Bentley opened the door to the interview room and shouted on one of the Officers in the corridor. 'Can you get someone to come and restrain this nutter now! You might want to get a shrink in as well. He's definitely one sail short of a yacht.'

'You will be judged and damned to suffer an eternity in hell if you release those Demons into the world! You will be judged!' screamed O'Driscoll after Bentley, banging the table furiously with his bleeding palms.

'No mate, it's you who will be judged and sent down for a long time, in with the nonces and rapists who will bugger your sick, twisted arse to damnation.' countered Bentley as he and DC Tait left the room, pulling the door closed behind them, cutting out O'Driscoll's screeching rant.

'Jesus Sir, it sounds as though he really believes there are Demons in those bags.' Tait said incredulously as they walked down the corridor of interview rooms back toward the main Incident Room.

'That's belief for you Tait. Especially fucking Catholics. He's a fag short of a packet, make no mistake.' Bentley replied, a pensive expression on his agitated, sweating features.

Her Moons Denouement   Max Hardy

Le Fenwick was approaching them from the other end of the corridor with a determined stride. 'Bentley, we need to talk, now!' he said firmly as he stopped in front of them, halting their progress.

'Oh fuck man, what the hell is it, we've got a madman and seven tossing murders to investigate, not to mention a bloody suicide, so make it quick.'

'This is particularly relevant to the investigation. It's particularly relevant to you.' Le Fenwick replied, standing firm and ignoring the disdain in Bentley's tone.

'What do you mean, relevant to me?' Bentley questioned, his whole manner suddenly becoming guarded.

'When we were examining the plastic bag that was used to asphyxiate Heather Scott we found one of your dog's hairs.' imparted Le Fenwick factually, with measured concern.

Bentley looked at him incredulously, then at Tait with the same expression, annoyance rising in the rouge that ruddied his pock marked cheeks. He looked down at his hair covered coat, then back up at Le Fenwick. 'Aye Dick, that will be from my fuckin coat. I was at the crime scene in case you'd forgotten you daft twat.' Bentley hissed, taking a step forward ready to push past Le Fenwick.

Le Fenwick stood firm, raising two conciliatory hands in front of him. 'I get that Fenny, and believe me I wish it was that simple. The problem is, we found the hair inside the sealed bag.'

Chapter 6

She had another baby. What kind of relationship did we have where she felt she couldn't talk to me about that? Especially when that was where her guilt over Jacob came from. The same kind of relationship where I couldn't tell her about the demons living behind the rickety doors in my rickety rooms. A crap relationship. And I thought I knew her. Shows how much I really knew. Nothing. God, to have gone through childbirth, to have held your dead baby in your arms. I thought looking into Jacob's vacant empty eyes was despair, but that, how the hell did she get past it. I suppose she never did get past it. What was it she said...

Mumbled words and distant shrill noises begin to invade my swirling thoughts.

'There are things that happened in my past, things I don't ever think I will come to terms with. They still haunt me now and cast a shadow over you and I.' I see her tear stained face reciting those words, standing in my studio two weeks ago, giving me my freedom, giving me her blessing to go and love another woman, to be with Jessica. I betrayed her in every conceivable way and she still loved me. Loved me enough to want me to be happy with someone else. To be happy with Jessica. Jessica's beautiful, sensuous face screams into my mind, dispersing the image of Sarah.

Her Moons Denouement   Max Hardy

Her lips are moving and I can hear mumbled words. I feel something shake my arms. I hear a car horn, coming closer. I strain to hear what she is saying and as I try to move closer to her face, in my mind, her image starts to fade as the words become clearer.

'Are you OK? Sir, are you OK? We should really get out of the road.'

Jessica dissipates and my vision snaps back into focus, back into now and there is a very concerned woman standing in front of me, gently holding my arm.

'Are you OK Sir?' she asks again. I look beyond her. Jesus. I am in the middle of the road, holding up a line of traffic. There are horns blaring, irate faces sneering at me from behind fly smeared windscreens. Crowds are gathering on either side of the street, a myriad of faces with a myriad of feelings: pity, concern, humour, anger, Jessica, empathy, derision, sympathy...

My head darts back. Jessica. I saw Jessica. I raise a hand in apology and say 'Sorry.' over and over again to the drivers and the woman as I lurch away from her, my eyes frantically scanning the faces of the crowd to the left, looking for Jessica.

I see expressions turn to worry, people stepping back from the kerb out of the way as I approach. I can't see her. People start to leave, to go about their business. I see the back of a redheaded woman walking away down a side street. She is the same height as Jessica, the same build. Jessica didn't have red hair. But Madame Evangeline did.

As I try to run, excruciating pain shoots up through my legs from the wounds on my feet, meeting the agony from my damaged scrotum as it jiggles from side to side under the exertion. I slow into a crablike hop, trying to keep a pace, but trying to keep the pressure off my injuries.

Her Moons Denouement   Max Hardy

'Jess!' I shout after the receding figure as I enter the side street, the crowd now fully dispersed. She turns into an alley halfway down the street, not acknowledging my call. My heart thumps furiously. With the exertion, with the pain, but also with the overwhelming conviction that it was her, it was Jess and she is not dead!

I reach the entrance to the alley just in time to glimpse a slender leg in a red stiletto turn left at the end of the alley onto a main street. Hobbling as fast as I can I reach the same place in about ten seconds, sweat pouring down my face with the effort. I stumble into the main street and turn left immediately, frantically looking at the melee of people walking up and down the street.

I can't see her. I shuffle on, head darting to the shop entrances, staring in, staring through their windows. On to the next, still nothing. Looking across the road, looking up the pavement, looking back into the shops. Nothing. I reach a crossroads at the top of the road and pirouette around, looking everywhere for the redhead, the red stilettos. She is nowhere to be seen amongst the constantly moving throng who are giving me a wide berth.

Was she really there? Or is my mind just playing tricks. Every time I think of Sarah, every time I think of Jacob, Jess's image just sears into my mind, opening a chasm in the fissures of grief and spawning a maelstrom of uncontrollable guilt. I should hate her. I should detest her for what happened, if it was her that instigated it. But I can't. What kind of a bastard does that make me?

I look around again, one last forlorn sweep of the static faces, and then slowly trudge off towards Dacre Street, scanning the ground for red stilettoed feet.

There is a very small, but finely filigreed bronze nameplate on the solid oak door, proclaiming 'H. Massah. Private Detective.', as I arrive in front of it. Not something I would expect. Private Detectives tend to be very practical and generally not keen on spending too much on aesthetics. I buzz the intercom and a male voice answers.

'Harry Massah, Private Detective, how can I help'

'Afternoon Mr Massah. It's DI John Saul here. I understand you worked on an assignment for my wife, Sarah Saul a little while back. I would like to talk to you about that if it's convenient?'

Pause. A long pause.

'I was wondering when you would turn up. Come on in, straight down the corridor and second door on the left.' The door clicks open into a tongue and groove panelled hallway painted a rustic lichen, with a deep walnut stain on the oak flooring. Definitely not your normal Dick. A bit more upmarket. There are some original watercolours decorating the walls as I approach the door on the left, which is slightly ajar. Some modern, with some beautiful sunset vista's over the Tyne and some more traditional.

Massah stands as I enter the office and approaches with an eager outstretched hand and an understated compassion evident in his soft, slightly paunchy features. He is tall, probably about six two, broadly built with a shock of floppy brown hair, overlong and ruffled. Mid forties. He is wearing a tailored green Harris Tweed jacket, a pink Ralph Lauren shirt and beige chinos bottomed off with scuffed brown brogues on his feet. Definitely an upper class Dick.

'Detective Inspector Saul. Please accept my condolences, I am so sorry for your loss.' he relays and he shakes my hand, cupping his second hand over the top of the shake. There is nothing but genuine warmth and compassion in his eyes. Why? He doesn't know me from Adam. But he knows I cheated on my wife. It shocks me and I look away from his gaze, mumbling a muted thanks.

Her Moons Denouement   Max Hardy

'Please, take a seat. Can I get you anything to drink? Tea, coffee, water or something stronger? A whisky perhaps? I have a very exclusive Black Bowmore 1964?'

My mind screamed single malt. My body needs it. It is aching from the earlier exertion. But I need to stay focused. 'Water will be fine, but thanks for the offer. So you were expecting me?'

'At some point, yes. I have been following the news. I see many unknowns in the reporting of the case. I know a Detective of your reputation won't let them stay unknown indefinitely.'

I scan the room while gingerly sitting as he makes drinks at a small cabinet off to the left. It has a very intimate homely charm, more like a snug or study than an office. His desk is a behemoth walnut affair topped with pictures of kids and horses and pets, with an organised chaos of papers and files off to one side. There's a pair of Hunter wellies, a brolly and a Barbour jacket in a hat stand next to the drinks cabinet. The walls, painted in country cream, are also covered in pictures of happy children. Three kids, probably fifteen, thirteen and ten. Ten year old on a horse with a friend. A familiar friend. Strange's daughter. Is that how Sarah found out about Harry, from Strange? No pictures of a mum? Divorced, separated? He's wearing a wedding ring. Widowed? Is that why so much empathy? On the wall opposite the door into the room, a large, what looks like an original Munch painting, 'Golgotha'.

'I need to talk to you about Jessica Seymour. I know that Sarah had you follow the two of us and I know that you took a great deal of pictures of our 'liaisons', shall we say.' What the fuck does that mean, 'Liaisons'. We were screwing around and he knows it.

He hands me a glass of iced water as he sits down on the opposite side of the desk and I can see his features are perplexed and ruminating on the best way to answer the question.

Her Moons Denouement   Max Hardy

'I often get irate partners banging at the door, threatening to thump me for following them, wanting someone to blame for exposing their philandering. Part of the territory. I don't judge, I just help. I don't think I've ever had someone I've been following come and ask me about their lover though.'

'Believe me, if I could ask her, I would.'

I saw his face drop and that visage of guilty ineptitude flood over it and spill into his words. 'Sorry, that was insensitive of me. How can I help?'

'Apart from when she was with me, what other things did you see Jessica doing? Did she meet up with anyone else regularly? What places did she tend to visit? Did you notice if she travelled much?'

He pulled a fairly thick manila folder from the pile of documents to his right and started rifling through notes and pictures. I noticed a few images in full that Sarah had ripped to smithereens. Of Jessica and I kissing. Guilt roared at me, but it was always shouted down by the aching emptiness of loss.

'She spent a lot of time with you, that's one thing I will say. Just about every day for the two weeks I was commissioned. Other people: she met a few ladies for coffee occasionally.' He pulled out some pictures of Jess, looking elegant and beautiful, laughing, coming out of a café with another woman I didn't recognise. Two weeks? Was I really with Jess nearly every day for two weeks? 'I saw her going out in the company limousine on a few occasions, twice she was dropped off at the train station and caught the Flying Scotsman up to Edinburgh, once meeting you at the station.'

I was never with her for two weeks solid, work and home life didn't let that happen. Did he say Edinburgh? With me?

'Did you say Edinburgh? With me?'

Her Moons Denouement   **Max Hardy**

'Yes. Here's a picture of the two of you getting on the train.'

Impossible. I have never been on a train with Jess. That's me though. What date, what time. That can't be me. I wasn't even in Newcastle on that date.

'Is everything alright, you look a tad overcome?'

'Can I see the other photographs of the two of us please?'

He passes them over and I start flicking through them, scanning the dates and times in the bottom corner. First one, yes, I remember that, we had snuck off for lunch in Corbridge. Pile on the left. Next. Yes, we were planning our weekend away in Manchester. Pile on the left. Next. No, no way. I was at the station then. In a briefing on a case. Pile on the right. Next, right. Next, right. Next, left. Next, right. Next, next, next, next, next. Jesus. Twenty 'assignations'. Ten on the left, ten on the right.

'Detective Inspector, are you alright?'

I stand up in agitation, pushing my chair back, leaning over the table as I position the two piles of pictures into rows in front of me, scanning the faces back forth from left to right.

'These pictures on the right Mr Massah, are you sure the dates and times are correct. Are you absolutely sure?'

'Absolutely. Why?'

The features are the same, the hair is the same, the build is the same, his whole demeanour is the same.

'Why. Because in these ten pictures, at those times and dates I wasn't with Jessica, I can prove without question that I was elsewhere. Which means that if your camera was set correct, somewhere out there I have a   double,   a   doppelganger.'

Chapter 7

'What the fuck are you playing at you slimey twat!' Bentley roared, a pulsing clenched fist swinging up from his side as he stormed into the Lab, approaching Laurent at a pace that belied his heavy set frame and suggested a deftness of foot akin to a boxer. It coursed up through the air, past the point at which Bentley expected impact, surprise entering his furious features. Laurent had quickly stepped to the side of the onrushing Bentley, out of the arc of the uppercut. He stuck a leg out and Bentley tripped, his forward motion causing him to flounder into the Lab bench, his splaying arms knocking over phials, tubes and samples.

'Ignorant bastard.' seethed Laurent as he raised an elbow and steadied himself, ready to ram it into Bentley's back as he squirmed trying to gain his footing.

'Marcel, stop' shouted Le Fenwick as he ran into the lab, closely followed by DC Tait. Le Fenwick thrust his arms around Laurent and pulled the falling elbow away from Bentley's back, steering the Frenchman towards the side of the room.

'It was that fat imbecile who started it!' cried Laurent in defiance as he tried to struggle ineffectually from Le Fenwick's grasp.

'I know it was, but be the bigger man and don't let petulance overwhelm you. If you do, then you are no better than him.'

Her Moons Denouement Max Hardy

'Just hold him there Dick, and I'll show him exactly who the fucking bigger man is.' rumbled Bentley as he started to rise from the floor.

'Can't let you do that Sir.' Tait said as she snapped a handcuff over Bentley's left hand, which he was using as leverage on the desk to help him stand. She quickly grabbed his right arm, which he tried to swing at her, and dragged it behind his back using the motion of the swing. She clapped the other cuff over the wrist quickly, pressing her free hand into the small of Bentley's back, forcing him onto the floor.

'You don't want to make an enemy out of me Tait, so I'd let me up right fucking now if you know what's good for you girl!' Bentley spat the word 'girl' as he writhed on the floor, trying to get any kind of footing, any kind of traction, but Tait's slight, sinewed body held him tight to the ground.

'Then I'll have to be your enemy Sir, because I can't bear to see you make a bigger fool of yourself than you already have.'

'What the hell is going on here?' squealed a high pitched, agitated woman's voice from the corridor, the sentence continuing and the tirade getting louder as the owner of the voice entered the room.

'There's so much bloody commotion going on, I've had the Super bending my ear, asking if we've got a prisoner on the loose. Then the guys tell me it's one of my Senior Detective's being an arsehole and I don't have to think two seconds about who the hell that could be, do I Bentley!'

DCI Gaynor Cruickshank came to an abrupt halt as she entered the room, throwing an admonishing glare over the vista in front of her as she banged a black patent leather pump, with a grosgrain bow on the front, hard down onto the floor, literally stamping her authority onto the room. She wore a knee length black skirt covering pronounced bandy legs, a crisp white blouse and a half length black jacket over her diminutive frame. Her beady features were as sharp as her scathing tongue and they were accentuated by her jet black hair that was pulled fiercely back from her forehead and tied in a bun.

She shook her head disconsolately, folding her arms in resigned anticipation across her flat chest. 'Well Bentley, do you want to tell me who has breathed too loudly in your direction today?'

'This French fuck is trying to fabricate evidence just because he is pissed that I contaminated his crime scene.' Bentley rumbled from the floor, his squirming diminishing under the admonishment.

'Really Bentley? You really think that is the level of professionalism in your colleagues? That they would try and involve you in a crime just because they were pissed with you? Mr Laurent, do you have anything to say on the matter?'

'Ma'am, you can watch the video of the whole procedure. Dr Le Fenwick was there too. The bag was opened in a sealed laboratory. There was nothing on the outside of the bag. There was nothing on the inside apart from a single hair, not even sputum from the alleged victim.'

'Dr Le Fenwick?' DCI Cruickshank asked, her demeanour already knowing that he would corroborate Laurent's account of events.

'The hair was inside the bag Ma'am. There is no doubt about that. But Marcel is right, this bag was different from the other six. There was no DNA at all inside relating to the alleged victim.'

'Alright. Thank you gentleman. Dr Le Fenwick, I think it's safe to let Mr Laurent loose now. Mr Laurent, I appreciate the restraint you have shown under the threat of attack.' started Cruickshank, firmly glaring at the petulant Frenchman as she continued, 'While I can fully understand that you may wish to pursue some kind of retribution towards Bentley, just think on stones, and glass houses, and how understanding management have been in other volatile encounters that you may not

Her Moons Denouement Max Hardy

have been so innocent in. None of this does our reputation any good and it stops here. Do I make myself clear?'

Laurent looked ready to burst in frustration for a second, but then Le Fenwick tightened a grip on his arm and whispered something quietly into his ear. 'I understand Ma'am.' he finished meekly.

'Good. Now Tait, help that blithering excuse for a man up and follow me to my office. Keep him cuffed. Bentley, you give her any grief and I will suspend you on the spot. And I don't want any of your colourful backchat, understand.'

'Yes Ma'am.' he grumbled as DC Tait relaxed the pressure on his back and helped him to his feet.

Cruickshank executed a clinical about face, then marched off purposefully down the corridor, inquisitive heads quickly disappearing back into offices along the way. 'Nothing to see here. If you've got time to gawp, you mustn't have enough work. If that's the case, come to my office and I'm sure I can find some menial duty to keep you busy.' she bellowed as doors clattered closed in her wake. Bentley lumbered behind her, his complexion sweaty and ruddy, his face a visage of viciousness. Tait brought up the rear, her eyes intent on Bentley, scrutinising his every movement.

Cruickshank opened the door to her office and ordered Bentley to sit. 'Take his cuffs of Tait and sit down.' she instructed while she sat down in her straight backed wooden seated chair with military efficiency, pulling in the chair and brushing down the length of her skirt in one pristine movement. There was a file open on the desk in front of her and she took a moment to read it, leaving the room in silence before speaking.

Bentley mumbled profanities under his breath as Tait uncuffed him, pushing her hands away and throwing her a dismissive nasty glare as he rubbed his wrists and shuffled agitatedly in his seat.

Her Moons Denouement   **Max Hardy**

'Right Bentley, I want you to understand that you have no choice in this and if you argue, I will suspend you. I want you to understand that if I had a choice, you would already be suspended. You are off the O'Driscoll investigation.'

'You are fu....' Bentley started before Cruickshank shot him down.

'No choice Bentley and if you swear at me once more you won't just be suspended, I'll throw your lard arse in a cell, charge you with assault and get internal affairs on to you. So shut the fuck up and listen.' she finished forcefully, her tone full and authoritative.

'You are off the O'Driscoll investigation not only because we may have found one of your dog's hairs in amongst the evidence, but because of the victim, Heather Scott. Does the name ring any bells with you?' Cruickshank asked, watching Bentley's reaction closely.

A rush of ruddy rouge ascended Bentley's complexion, married to a myriad of facial movement that made his eyes bulge and his lips tighten. For a moment he looked ready to explode into some kind of verbal tirade, but then the rouge descended and his face started to relax.

'Heather Scott. Went missing in 1990. One of my first cases as a DC. I was trying to remember why I recognised the name when I saw it on the folder. We never found her body but her husband was arrested and prosecuted for her murder. We found her blood and part of an ear in their house. Bastard would beat her to a pulp, night after night when he was pissed.'

'Glad you remember. Hopefully you can understand why I need to take you off that part of the case. It's not just the dog hair Bentley. This victim is different to the other six. Someone has already been jailed for murdering her. A case where you secured that prosecution. You would compromise the investigation straight away.'

Her Moons Denouement   **Max Hardy**

Bentley sat in measured silence for a moment as Cruickshank finished, taking in and contemplating the implications of the information. When he spoke, his demeanour was calm and reflective, all the anger and animosity evaporated from his person.

'I understand Ma'am. I apologise for my behaviour. I have no excuse other than how incensed evil bastards like O'Driscoll make me. That does not give me the right to take it out on my colleagues.'

Cruickshank shook her head as she took in his genuine words and his humbled demeanour. 'As I said Bentley, if I had a choice, you would be suspended despite your contriteness. But as I don't have the luxury of spare DI's lounging around, have seven murders, a serial killer, a suicide and a potential religious cult to investigate, and that's just today's workload on top of everything else we already have, for the moment you have a reprieve. Just for the moment. But let me make this clear. DC Tait will be working with you and she is in charge. She will be leading this part of the investigation and you will be supporting her.'

Bentley's face fell, humble replaced by humiliation. Conversely Tait's countenance wore surprise as an alien emotion. 'Ma'am, I don't think I am ready to take the lead.'

'Nonsense. You've just completed your Sergeant's exams. Barring paperwork, you will be a DS officially in a few weeks. You are the kind of progressive detective this force needs. Use Bentley for his information and his contacts. That will be invaluable to you. As for anything else, just ignore it. There is absolutely nothing he can teach you about what a good Detective should be. Isn't that right Bentley.'

Bentley's large frame visibly sagged in the chair. His head started to gently shake dejectedly. 'Aye girl, you listen to old Shankers the wanker there. She knows what she's talking about. You're a good lass and you know your stuff.' he said softly, placing a hand over Tait's on the arm of the chair and patting it gently.

'I might be a wanker, but I get things done. Good, now I want the two of you to investigate our friend who committed suicide. We've just had a DNA match back and initial details about him have come through. Here's copies of the info.' Cruickshank said, passing files over to Bentley and Tait.

'Name is Elvis Aarons. Mum must have been a fan, poor kid. Oh, he's an orphan. Even worse, poor kid. Twenty five. Got a few minor convictions for petty theft and, oh, here we go, solicitation. Looks like he's also been a rent boy for one or two of our illustrious politicians, allegedly. Got a flat on the Crombie Estate. Works at an illegal sex club down in Leith. No known religious denomination.'

'We should probably start at his flat, check that out and see if we can find anything about friends or acquaintances who might know anything about the 'Fallen Angels', whatever they are.' answered Tait eagerly, looking between Cruickshank and Bentley. Cruickshank nodded in encouragement but Bentley was still looking through the file, deep in thought.

'Sounds like the right course of action, doesn't it Bentley!' prompted Cruickshank, raising her tone.

Bentley looked up, distracted. 'Yes. Sorry, yes, that's the right thing to do. We need to go to his flat, on the Crombie Estate.' he emphasised the words 'Crombie Estate', seemingly replaying them over in his mind.

'Would you like to share your thoughts with us Bentley? What really works well as a Detective is sharing hunches, or suppositions with your colleagues.' Cruickshank reproached.

'Sorry Ma'am, it's totally unrelated, the names of places just stirred a few thoughts. Remember the case a few weeks ago down in

Northumberland, where we handed over our files on the Michael Angus murder?'

'Yes, absolutely tragic. Still no further forward in finding out who did it. Still no closer to finding Rebecca Angus either.' Cruickshank answered.

'That's just it, the thing niggling in my mind. Rebecca Angus. She lived on the Crombie Estate as well. And if it were just that you would say, so what. But she was also a part of the BDSM sex scene in Leith, and her favourite club was the same one our Elvis worked at: Sodom and Gomorrah.'

Chapter 8

Something has changed. I'm not sure what, or when, but I know it has changed.

The first thing I ever remember about my life is as vivid to me today as it was, quite literally, on the day I was born. When I say vivid, what I really mean is blurry. But the memory of those first blurred images, white wimples floating like whispered wraiths above my new born head, their near silent susurrations more pronounced in my mind than the incessant shrill of the other new born babies around me, are still so vivid. It's not that I remember everything instantly. It's just that I don't seem to forget anything. At the time I didn't know what a wimple was. I didn't know that the Nuns were speaking Italian. I had no idea that I was in an incubator. For all I knew, the myriad of tubes sticking out of me were appendages the same as the tiny, five fingered hands which fascinated me for hours. But I can take myself back there, back to that memory and relive every moment of it.

Some people might call it a gift. I often wondered if Jacob inherited it.

I am lying on the floor of his bedroom, looking up to the nightlight shining off his twirling mobile as is slowly turns above his cot to the theme tune of Pinocchio. In his short life, I did this most nights I was home, putting my hand up through the bars of the cot and either feeling his pulse, or resting it on his chest and feeling his heart beat. It was the only way I knew he was alive. I would lie and talk to him,

Her Moons Denouement   Max Hardy

about what I had seen that day. Cars, trees, animals, people. Not what I had done, but what I had seen. I would read to him from Pinocchio and then when I had finished I would just lie there and wonder how much he understood. I would try and see the world through his eyes, from his perspective.

I look straight up, not wavering my eyes at all. Jacob couldn't, so I don't. I don't know that he could hear, I have to assume he couldn't, so I mentally block out the sound of the mobile. Just see the characters gently bobbing up and down as it turns. But then I know his pupils never dilated, so I have to wonder if he could differentiate darkness and light. If he couldn't, did that mean that even though his eyes were open, it was only the darkness he saw? Only the darkness he felt? Only the emptiness he lived in.

And that's where my mind would end up. Every time I thought about my beautiful baby boy. To the emptiness of forever. The one, the only consolation I ever had was his heartbeat. In that emptiness, in that despair that always overwhelmed me, I always had the hope of his heartbeat.

His cot is empty now. Cold. But that isn't what has changed. Something is different about the room from last night, from every night I remember. What is it?

How I remember, with such vivid clarity, is to take my mind back to the moment, to find a hook in the memory and to start opening it up, an iota at a time. So last night, the mobile was turning. I had my fingers through the fourth bar in the cot, gently clasping Jacob's cold sheet. My other hand was circling a half empty bottle of vodka. The mobile was turning and the shadows were dancing. Bouncing off the glow of the nightlight, flickering from the ambient light coming in through the slightly open blinds, angled in such a way as to make the shadows dance in the chaos of the elements.

Her Moons Denouement — Max Hardy

They aren't doing that tonight. It is just the steady mechanical turning of the shadows.

I stand up quickly and shuffle over to the window. The blinds have been moved. They have been angled downwards. I didn't move them. How have they moved? Why have they moved?

I bend down and look out of the blinds, up along the angle of their decline. Dusk is settling in as I scan the tops of trees visible through the slits, my eyes coming to rest on one particular tree, with the dark, hollow holes of glassless windows staring back at me.

Jacob's tree house. It might sound strange that I had built a tree house for him. After all, he couldn't really climb and play like other boys. But we spent quite a bit of time up there, with me pointing him in a direction and explaining what it was he could see. More therapy for me I think, to at least cushion the reality of the sparseness of his life with some normality.

Now who the hell has been using that as a vantage point to look into Jacob's bedroom? More to the point, how did they get into the house to do it, and why.

I stare into the darkened windows for a moment, waiting to see if there is any movement, if anyone is still there, watching. All is still. I turn from the window and walk eagerly across the room and straight over the landing into my studio, grabbing a remote control from the pile of pictures of the other me I had been poring over earlier.

I had stuck a couple on the case wall, next to the blurred image of the Limousine driver who had taken Rebecca and Michael to Featherstone Hall on the night he died. The Limousine Driver who looked like me. Next to those was a photograph of Rob Adams and two post it's, one with the words 'Unknown Caller', one with the name 'Dr Ben Hanlon.' The only thing that makes any logical sense in the uncertainty of this case is that the other me, my double, my doppelganger was the same person as all of the other personalities.

Which means, if he was, then he knew Jess intimately. Which means that the two of them could have been colluding for years to setup the events which happened at Featherstone Hall.

Why? I don't have even a crumb of an idea.

How? Even less of an inkling.

I know she was with me all evening the night Michael died. That is fact. That is indisputable. That is what is driving me mad. That's why I had gone to lie in Jacob's room, to distract my mind, to think of something else, to think of my beautiful baby boy. That's when I noticed something had changed. Now who the hell moved the blind?

Well, I should be able to find out exactly who has been in Jacob's room. It's the one place inside the house where we installed CCTV. Sarah insisted. Her story was that she wanted to keep a record of the number of times he had fits. It wasn't. I would come home from a late shift and find her in my studio, studying the recordings from the day, looking for a stutter, a flick, a twitch. Looking for any kind of voluntary movement at all from our immobile little angel. Her anguished, empty smile as she greeted me always told me her search had been equally as empty.

There is a bank of four screens to the right of my case wall. On one of them is a frozen, slightly juddering image of the door to the hotel room where Jess and I stayed in Edinburgh. I have been playing it over and over again, willing the door to open, knowing it never will.

One of them is showing BBC One. It's coming up to ten o'clock, time to turn it up and listen to the news, see what they are saying publicly today about the case.

Her Moons Denouement   Max Hardy

I turn the volume up and then flick another button on the remote to turn on another monitor which shows a live feed from Jacob's room. I know the blinds were turned up last night, so they had to have been moved between eleven o'clock last night and me getting home tonight at seven. I press rewind on the remote.

'Even Fallen Angels Have wings.' What the hell did he mean by that? Is he suggesting she flew out of the bloody hotel room? That's just ludicrous. But how else could she get out if not through the main door. Through the window? Its three floors up onto a main thoroughfare in the centre of Edinburgh, someone would have seen her. I see images of Edinburgh start to appear on the News Headlines on the TV as the sound bites seep through my thoughts.

'Mayhem at the Fringe Festival in Edinburgh today as a lone gunmen commits suicide while exposing a senior Roman Catholic leader as a possible serial killer.'

The Fringe is on the Royal Mile, just around the corner from the hotel Jess and I stayed in. A blurry camera phone image of a screaming, running crowd is on the screen, a large cabinet with a person on a crucifix visible through the darting people.

Could Jess have climbed out of our bedroom window and walked along the ledge to the next room? Did anyone come out of the next room? Have I got CCTV footage of that? I start to rewind the image of the hotel room too, looking down the corridor. I can just see a couple of inches of the bottom of the door to the next room along.

The video of Jacob's room is rewinding, no movement visible in the room back to lunchtime.

'Our Edinburgh correspondent, Ewan Daniels is at the scene.'

Her Moons Denouement   Max Hardy

'Thanks Hew. As you can see from the amateur video, at approximately 10:30am this morning outside the Cathedral behind me, a lone gunman, dressed as a Court Jester...'

Court Jester. Why would a gunman dress up as a Court Jester? Ah, Fringe Festival, no one would think that was anything odd.

Stop! 11:28. What's that in Jacob's room? I stop the video and slowly fast forward it. About ten minutes after I left the house this morning. There. That's a woman. I put it in normal playback. A woman wearing a black coat. A slim woman with auburn hair, wearing a black coat and red high heels. The same woman I saw this afternoon! She walks with her back to the camera over to the cot, gently spinning the mobile and then picks up a small teddy from the myriad of toys. Its Ian, a cheap tatty little bear that we bought on a trip to Ikea. She puts it up to her face and I see her shoulders hunch. Is she smelling it? Taking in the scent? She puts the toy into her pocket as she starts to walk around the cot towards the window.

'The Roman Catholic Church has so far declined to comment on the allegations that Archbishop Liam O'Driscoll was involved in the murder of seven...'

Seven women, sodomised and asphyxiated. Jesus. If that's true, it's not surprising they are refusing to comment,

Turn around, for fucks sake, turn around so I can see who you are.

Stop! 12:25 am. That's a foot isn't it, stepping out of the door one down from our hotel room?

'As for the lone gunman, the police have not released any information as to his identity. Nor have they commented on the potential links with any Religious factions...'

Religious factions? Some extremist activity? Generally extremists kill other people when they commit suicide.

Her Moons Denouement
Max Hardy

Shit. That's not just a foot, that's a foot in what looks like a black boot. A high-heeled boot. A high-heeled boot like the one Madame Evangeline was wearing that evening.

'While there are many references to 'Fallen Angels' in religious texts, there are no known fundamentalist factions with that name operating today and no known references at all to the phrase emblazoned on the cabinet: Even Fallen Angels Have Wings. Back to you in the studio Hew.'

What! 'Even Fallen Angels Have Wings'. In Edinburgh? Was that the 'Unknown Caller'? Has he killed himself? What's that got to do with Jess? What's that got to do with Madame Evangeline?

Fuck. My eyes have been darting between the screens, my brain the same, but it is now completely focused on the grainy image on the CCTV from Jacob's room. The woman turns around after she alters the blinds. Her head is initially bowed, but as she walks towards the door, she lifts it, smiling directly into the camera. The bottom drops out of my stomach: It's Jess.

Chapter 9

A brilliant white, almost full moon hung in a cloudless dusky evening sky, its reflection gently shimmering off the slowly lapping waves of the Forth Estuary. The waves rebounded softly off the shoreline of a small peninsula, on top of which lived one of the large granite bases supporting the span of the Forth Railway Bridge.

A rusty old Volvo, once grey, but now almost the same colour as the bridge above it, slowly crunched up a gravel road underneath the bridge, towards a solitary property sitting on the peninsula. Brakes squealed louder than the chorus of gulls circling the nearby harbour as Bentley parked the car up. He pulled up into an overgrown, dishevelled garden, a once white picket fence marking its boundary now falling to bits, the posts rotten and mildewed green. A dirty and worn Georgian fronted house stood at the centre of the garden, looking out over the Firth of Forth, the reflection in the dirt encrusted windows making the stunning evening vista look dull and lifeless.

Bentley moaned and groaned as he forced himself up out of the car and walked around the back to open the boot.

'Come on Jackson, better have yourself a shite before you go in. You know how crotchety Dessie can get.' Bentley said affectionately to the old black Labrador that achingly stood up and jumped down from the boot, then padded dejectedly off into the overgrown grass. Bentley closed the boot and leaned up against it, looking out over the bay, the

Her Moons Denouement   Max Hardy

evening moon shining through the metal trusses of the bridge, casting dancing shadows onto the rippling waves of the estuary. Jackson trotted back towards him, tail now wagging, a gnarled bone protruding from his mouth.

'It's coming up to a full moon son, that doesn't bode well.' Bentley said as he crouched down, sighing, still looking out over the bay and stroked Jackson's head. 'You know you can't take that in.' he continued as he took the bone out of the dog's mouth and threw it back into the overgrowth. 'Come on, let's go and face the music.'

Bentley groaned again as he pushed his large frame up and walked to the front door, opening it and ushering Jackson in as he arrived.

'Fenny, Fenny, Fenny!' came the excited, almost ecstatic screech from a short, slightly rotund woman skipping down the hallway towards the front door. She wore a blue smock, a tea towel dangling from a bulging pocket in its front, over a floor length black dress. The black dress billowed as she ran, exposing her bare feet. She reached Bentley and thrust her podgy arms straight around his neck and pulled him tightly into her ample chest.

'You are Late! Did you get them, did you get them!' she admonished and questioned in one breath with a mixture of frustration and anticipation.

Bentley hugged her back with the same intensity, a look of concerned resignation on his features as he answered. 'Sorry Dessie, should have let you know but had a case to work on. Something I need to talk to you and Father about. But yes, I've got them.

'Brilliant, that's just so brilliant. Supper is ready, I've kept it warm for us. It's just normal beef stew, still waiting on the next delivery of the posh stuff. Take that grubby coat off though or Father won't be pleased.' Bentley's sister instructed, breaking their embrace and helping her brother off with his coat.

Her Moons Denouement   Max Hardy

'Jackson, in your bed son.' Bentley instructed, the Labrador doing as instructed and slinking into a small, well kept kennel by the back door.

Unlike the outside of the house, the inside was pristinely clean. The décor in the hallway was pure 1970s, with slightly faded orange starburst wallpaper on the walls and brown swirled linoleum on the floor of the hallway. There was a G-Plan lacquered teak side board on the right wall and Bentley threw his car keys into a moulded Lucite bowl which sat on top of it.

They entered the kitchen, Bentley's expression still troubled and his sister still effusive as she darted in front of him.

'Father, he has the papers!' she exclaimed as she danced around the dining booth on one side of the high gloss aubergine kitchen and sat down next to her father, shaking in excitement.

'Calm down Desiderata. Your brother needs to explain why he is so late for supper and couldn't bring himself to telephone and let us know.' said Pastor Edward Bentley. He wore a black shirt, the brilliant white clerical collar the only brightness in his dark garb and even darker expression.

Bentley eased his ebullient stomach into the narrow cushioned bench on the dining booth and addressed his Father apologetically.

'Sorry Father. I have no excuse. I apologise for my tardiness and will endeavour to be a better person. Dessie, thank you for keeping supper warm for us, I am sorry.'

'They are just words Fenny. Words I have heard too many times before. It is not good enough, do you hear me. Your sister has spent hours preparing our supper.' Pastor Edward said with a raised voice full of simmering anger. 'We have been waiting over two hours for you to come home. Now, say grace, so we can eat and then you better

Her Moons Denouement   Max Hardy

have a really good explanation or it will be the cupboard for you tonight.'

Bentley sat in diffidence, his gaze turned down to the steaming stew pot on the table top in front of him, not able to hold the ferocity of his father's glare. He reached his hands out over the table, clenching those of his father and sister who were doing the same and said grace with an obvious tremor of trepidation in his tone.

'O Lord, we thank you for the gifts of your bounty which we enjoy at this table. As you have provided for us in the past, so may you sustain us throughout our lives. While we enjoy your gifts, may we never forget the needy and those in want.'

Bentley looked back up, his eyes moving between the scolding expression of his father and the eager excitement of his sister. He let go their hands, but father and sister maintained hand holding with each other.

'Children.' said Pastor Bentley. 'Please, eat. Fenny. Tell us why you are late.'

'Yes, you said you needed to talk to us!' exclaimed Desiderata as, still clasping her father with one hand, she started to ladle the stew out into bowls with the other.

'I don't know if you have seen the news today, about Archbishop O'Driscoll being exposed as a killer by a man who then committed suicide on the Royal Mile.' asked Bentley, tucking into his stew with gusto, despite the anxiousness in his demeanour.

'I heard, yes. Shocking, if it is true.' answered Pastor Edward.

'I saw it too. Did he really have wings! Do you think he was an Angel?' interjected Desiderata eagerly, with wide eyed innocence.

Her Moons Denouement Max Hardy

'No Dessie, they were mechanical wings and as far as we can tell he was a lone loon. We can't find reference to any organisation, group or faction known as the Fallen Angels. That's not the thing we need to worry about.'

'Do we need to worry about something?' queried Pastor Edward.

'Yes we do Father. There is no doubt that O'Driscoll killed six of the seven women that he was alleged to have murdered. He can't have murdered the seventh. We know the seventh: Heather Scott. And somehow, the evidence we have from the Crime Scene today indirectly links me to her.'

'Heather was a long time ago. How could that happen Fenny? We are so careful.' queried Pastor Edward. Desiderata dropped her spoon into her bowl with a clang and clung onto her father's hand tighter, looking at him anxiously.

'At the minute, I don't know. It could be a total coincidence. It is possible that some fucker...' he started in frustration.

'Fenny!' shouted Pastor Edward. 'I will not have that kind of language under my roof!'

'Sorry Father. It's possible that the evidence has been mixed up. It's possible that someone is out to get me. Do you remember Rebecca Angus, the mental case who slaughtered her son a few years back? She went missing from the nuthouse a few weeks ago and may just hold a grudge against me. She could be involved in this. Either way, the case into Heather Scott's death will be reopened and I will probably be under scrutiny. That's why I think we should put our plans for Coleen on hold.'

'No!' screamed Desiderata, aghast. 'We can't. Everything is arranged. Everyone is lined up. We just needed the passport and you have that

Her Moons Denouement   Max Hardy

now. We can't Father. Please say we don't have to stop it.' she finished, clawing Pastor Edward's arm with her hand imploringly.

'Now, now Dessie. Keep calm. There's no need to halt our plans. Your sister is right Fenny. Everything is lined up. It is too late to pause things. And if you are going to be under scrutiny, it would be better to do it now so she is out of the way. You will just have to be extra vigilant. That is my final word.' Pastor Edward stated firmly.

Bentley dropped his spoon into a now empty bowl and sighed heavily as he took a passport from his inside jacket pocket and placed in onto the table.

Desiderata, all anxiety gone, replaced once again by excitement, grabbed the passport and flicked to the picture and the personal information. 'Carly Dawson. Coleen is now Carly. That should be easy for her to remember. She is ready for you Fenny.' said Dessie as she jumped up out of her seat and leapt over to one of the high gloss aubergine drawers. She pulled it open and grabbed a white carrier bag from inside and dropped it with a heavy thud onto the table in front of Bentley. 'It's all in there.' she finished, her eyes wide with anticipation.

'It's getting late now, time for Dessie and I to retire. You know what you need to do Fenny. And once you have, you need to tidy up the kitchen and it will be the cupboard for you tonight. Do I make myself clear?' Pastor Edward stated as he stood up and shuffled his portly frame out of the dining booth.

'I understand Father.' Bentley answered contritely as he watched Dessie and his father walk past him, hand in hand, into the hallway and up the stairs.

He sighed heavily and whispered 'Fucking bastard' quietly under his breath as he slowly stood up and grabbed the plastic bag from the table. He walked to the back door, at the rear of the kitchen, and

Her Moons Denouement   **Max Hardy**

opened it, stepping into a garage which was attached to the side of the house.

The garage was full of junk. Old rusting car parts festooned the floor. A menagerie of abandoned tools skulked on every available surface in between open topped paint tins with brushes left inside to harden.

He stepped instinctively through the junk on the floor to the back wall of the garage, to a clear area of floor in front of the bare tongue and groove slats. He grabbed the top edge of one of the slats and firmly pulled it, revealing a disguised door made from a dozen or so of the slats.

He reached inside the wall to the left and flicked a switch, illuminating a recess about a metre deep with a step ladder heading down into the ground. Bentley climbed onto the top rung and started to descend, the contents of the plastic bag tolling off the ladder as he did, cursing under his breath at every step.

At the bottom of the ladder, he pushed a door to his right, which opened into a dimly lit room no more than three metres wide, by the same length, the roof just above the height of his head. The walls and roof were solid granite, worn oak boards on the floor. Bentley ducked as he entered, and looked over to the single bed that stretched across the far end of the room. The only other pieces of furniture in the room were a white paint flaked wooden chair that sat beside the bed, and a small wooden table next to it with gouges in the surface and a half full glass of water on the top.

The bed was made with crisp white cotton sheets and a patchwork eiderdown, slightly ruffled from the woman that was sitting, back to the wall and knees pulled up to her chest, on top of it. The woman wore nothing on her feet, a pair of three quarter length jeans and a simple white vest top. This exposed the bottom of her legs, her arms, shoulders and neck. On every visible part of her skin were bruises, cuts

Her Moons Denouement Max Hardy

and lesions interspersed with the odd cigarette burn. Her face was equally bruised, her eyes bulging with swelling, the balls barely visible through blackened slits.

Bentley crossed the room and sat his large frame down in the seat next to her, compassion entering his grumbling countenance as he looked at her, smiling.

She smiled back at him nervously, her fingers shaking and fidgeting agitatedly on hands sitting on top of her pulled up legs, which were also shaking.

'I guess it's time.' she said with a croaky hoarse voice.

He fumbled around in the plastic bag that he had placed between his legs and pulled out a sealed syringe packet and a small phial of clear liquid. His own hands were shaking as he ripped the seal of the syringe and stuck the needle into the phial, sucking up the contents.

'Yes. Have you decided where? This is a local anaesthetic. It will dull the pain. Trust me, you won't feel a thing.'

'Look at my face. Do you think pain worries me?' she answered with acerbically before continuing. 'I have decided. My little toe.' she answered, pushing her shaking right foot forward over the bed, the chipped painted nails of the toes oscillating in and out of view as she clenched them.

Bentley put the syringe on his knee and thoughtfully rubbed his large, dirt-stained hands together, warming them, then reached down and with a tenderness that belied his heavy frame, he gently cupped her delicate foot. She didn't flinch, even though his podgy fingers slid over her naked sole. In his hands, the tremors of her nervousness began to abate. He picked up the syringe and brought it up to the soft flesh at the end of her little toe. He hesitated, looking up from the needle and into her wide, anxious eyes.

Her Moons Denouement   Max Hardy

'Last chance. Are you absolutely sure you want to do this?' he asked, his own features heavy with angst.

'Absolutely.' she said, clearly and concisely, without the slightest hesitation.

'Okay.' He murmured and then pushed the needle into her toe, depressing the syringe and offloading its contents. She flinched slightly, reflexes trying to draw the foot away, but Bentley gently squeezed and held it firm.

'It will take a minute or so to numb your toe. I'll take some blood in the same syringe. Left or right arm?' he asked, gently resting her foot on the edge of the small table.

'Right.' She answered, stretching out her forearm, showing him the throbbing blue vein in the crease of her elbow. He leaned over and gripped the arm lightly, sinking the needle expertly into the vein and drawing off a full syringe of blood. He dropped it back into the carrier bag and pulled out a half bottle of whiskey at the same time, unscrewing the top and taking a quick swig. He picked a roll of bandage out of the bag next and wiped the end of it over the top of the bottle before offering it to her.

'You might want to take a swig. Dutch courage.'

'I don't need it for courage. I'll take a swig though: to wish him hell!' she exclaimed, tensing, anger entering her eyes as she grabbed the bottle.

She relaxed slightly back onto the bed, taking comfort from the warmth of the whiskey as it lid effortlessly down her throat and stretched her foot out over the table, looking down to the curling little toe.

Her Moons Denouement

Max Hardy

'You might want to look away now.' Bentley advised as he unrolled the bandage underneath her foot and then reached back into the carrier bag.

'No a cat in hells chance! I want to see my pound of flesh. I have to see the part of me that will take all of him.' she replied forcefully with noticeable acrimony.

'Are you sure?' he reiterated, hand hovering within the carrier bag.

'Sure!' she stated, simply.

He shook his head slightly, lifting a large wooden handled meat cleaver out of the bag into view, resting one end in a well worn gouge on the table and the body of the blade over the little toe, up to the knuckle, levering it a few times to get the position right.

'Absolutely the last chance.' he said, looking imploringly into her eyes.

'Do it!' she hissed, taking a swig from the whiskey.

He slammed a fist down onto the top of the blade.

Chapter 10

Rapid eye movement caused her lashes to flutter frantically and caused the skin of the upper lid to ululate uncontrollably as the eyeball strained ineffectually to force open both lids, which were stitched shut. Tiny drips of blood oozed from the holes pierced through the lids, discolouring the black cotton thread of the stitching, making it glisten in the glow of flickering candlelight. Both eyes were cross stitched the same, the pattern parallel, done with fastidious precision. There were seven components to the symbol in the stitching. The first 'alif', the second 'hamzat wasl', the third and fourth 'Iam', the fifth 'shadda', the sixth 'dagger alif' and the seventh 'ha'.

Drops of blood meandered down the side of her nose in a river of salty tears that merged with beads of sweat pouring from open pores, all heading for her nostrils. They were trying to flare, but the stitching stopped them. They pulsed, along with the short frantic pants of her sobs, forcing a trail of clear snot through the tight thread that joined the effluence of her eyes and flowed down the philtrum to her mouth.

A mouth that jittered, muttered and mumbled, through lips ruddy with the blood of the puncture wounds from the needle that had pierced them, weaving an intricate hashed stitch that sewed them shut.

She was naked. Naked and strapped on her back into a wicker frame positioned in the middle of the room. The frame was woven in an arc, forcing her back to bend at the base of the spine, her torso angling down towards the floor. The arms continued that descent, to be cradled in the curve of wicker and then held tight by leather straps. Her head rested on a small support just before the floor, further straps securing her neck and forehead. Long black hair flowed back over onto the floor, exposing her ears. Ears also stitched closed.

Her legs were cocooned in wicker stirrups, positioning the thighs in the air wide apart, the bottom part of the legs bent down at the knees, back towards the floor. The weave encasement creaked as she tried to force her legs against it, the muscles of her flat brown stomach seething from side to side as she convulsed and strained against her restraints.

Gentle Anasheed chanting filled the air, flowing from speakers hidden behind long swathes of pure white silk that flowed out from a central ring placed directly above the wicker frame toward each corner of the room, where the flickering candles sat on marble stands. The floor was marble also, with an indented circle surrounding the frame.

He was naked too. Tall and lithe with a shock of black hair both on his head and face. He was whispering the same chants that were coming from the speakers as he viewed his handiwork on her left ear, plucking the stitches to make sure they were taut. She flinched when he did, the volume of her muted moans rising to the level of the chants.

He trailed a hand from her ear, up over her face, the tips of his fingers tickling the threads on her left eye, then pushed a thumb hard into the socket. Her whole body arched in agony, the pain she so wanted to scream just a guttural growl, lost in her restricted throat.

He walked down towards her open legs, one hand snaking over her breasts and down her stomach, the other dragging a small, stainless steel trolley behind him. He let his hand rest on her stomach, feeling the susurrations of her abdomen, before raising it, balling a fist and slamming it forcefully into her belly button.

Her Moons Denouement Max Hardy

She convulsed and urine spurted from between her open legs and liquid faeces dribbled out of her sewn up anus. His chanting paused as he watched the flow of liquid, a tongue snaking out of his mouth to lick his lips, young eyes full of fervour and desire, his semi erect penis becoming obviously more aroused.

He took a Musallah from the base of the trolley and rolled it out on the floor between her open thighs, a small niche at the top of the matt pointing directly to her exposed vagina. He knelt on the musallah and recited incantations, head touching the matt, before looking up, directly at her shaven pubis.

On top of the trolley was a gleaming scalpel, clean and unused. Sitting next to it were a number of used tapered suture needles, with one left unused. He picked up the scalpel in one hand and with the other, reached up and placed a thumb and forefinger on her clitoral hood, pulling the skin roughly back, exposing the glistening clitoris below.

She started to shake frantically, her body pulsing in its leather bindings, her legs twitching either side of his focused, determined eyes. His fingers pulled further back, leaving a few millimetres of flesh around the hood. He raised the scalpel to the top of her left labia majora and deftly sank the blade into the skin, the slightest trickle of blood oozing from the incision. She tried to move her hips as she groaned under the intensity of the cut, but his hand held her firm and with great dexterity, he cut a swathing arc all the way around her clitoral hood in one motion, blood spurting up onto her pubic mound and down onto her vulva. Suddenly, he leant his head over the gaping cut and sank his mouth over it, sucking in the flowing blood, taking the loose flapping skin between his teeth. His erection stiffened as he drank her life juices and then with one fierce jerk of his head, he ripped the semi severed mound from her clitoris.

Her Moons Denouement   **Max Hardy**

Muted screams streamed from her stitched mouth, strained in a throat with sinews stretched in agony, vibrating in time with the agitation of shock that overwhelmed her.

He whispered in time with the chanting, picking up one of the curved needles from the tray and running the tip of it through the smeared blood on his lips before dropping it down to her riven, bleeding flesh and pricking it into the exposed tissue, circling her most tender spot.

A red dot appeared on her belly button, then steadily moved down towards her pubic mound. He stopped the pricking, confusion entering his dilated, crazed eyes as mesmerised, he watched the dot move all the way down her bleeding vagina, lose itself for the briefest of moments in the gap between them, then reappear on his chest, stopping in line with his heart.

Panic quickly overtook the confusion as his eyes moved from the dot into the room, following the oscillating red beam that danced in disturbed dust all the way back to one of the flowing swathes of white silk which billowed gently, darkness swaying in its folds, a shadow morphing as he focused his eyes, a shadow holding a gun.

'Right now Imam, you have a choice. There is an AK-47 assault rifle fitted with laser targeting sights pointing directly at your heart. Stay perfectly still and we won't shoot you. Move even one millimetre, and we will.' came a voice from directly behind him. A female voice.

His eyes were darting between the shadow behind the silk, down to the needle he held pressed against the clitoris, to the scalpel he still held in his other hand, head not moving one iota as they did. Sweat started to pop on his brow as adrenaline coursed through his veins, controlling the panic, focusing his mind, focusing his thoughts, focusing his actions. His senses were now attuned and acute, and he could feel someone behind him and hear their rapid breathing above the timbre of the chanting.

Her Moons Denouement Max Hardy

'And what choice will I have after that?' he asked, eyes now back on the shadow that was moving closer to the edge of the shifting silk, the targeting light not budging from his chest as it did. He was imperceptibly clenching the hand that held the scalpel, the timed movement rolling the blade forward through his fingers, angling it upward.

'That choice will depend on your people and what they think of the atrocities you have enacted upon poor, defenceless women like Perdip Tousivuna who is lying there in front of you, mutilated. You do remember her name, don't you?' The voice was even closer now.

He smirked, still cajoling the knife forward in his hand as he watched the shadow step from behind the flowing silk, into the flickering candlelight. He saw the black laser sights of the AK-47 first, then the steady finger wrapped around the slightly depressed trigger, before taking in a tall, muscular dark haired man with a dark beard, dressed in a tight fitting Harlequin outfit, totally at odds with the Russian weaponry he held. He looked brazenly into the Harlequins unflinching, sparkling green eye that was levelled down the sights, staring directly at him.

'My brother, the infidel lover, traitor to his faith.' he sneered at the Harlequin before spitting in his direction.

'Do you think I ever forgot Perdip's name? Or the taste of Perdip's blood. Or the taste of Perdip's cunt. Do you really think my people will see ridding Allah's kingdom of one more whore an atrocity? I know Allah won't.'

'Allah might not, but I sure as hell do!' her voice whispered directly into his ear.

A flash of intensity shot through his eyes at the closeness of the voice and in an instant he was thrusting the hand that held the scalpel upward, towards his ear, towards where he thought her head would be. As he did he started to turn his body sideways on to the Harlequin in front of him, moving his chest out of the firing line and his shoulder into it.

There was an audible whoomp, over in an instant as a single shot was fired, the bullet smacking forcefully into the Imam's shoulder, skin, bone and blood spurting out of the exit hole left by the bullet as it thudded into the wall behind him. He screamed as the bullet hit, the impact knocking him backward, his still rising arm flying through thin air where he thought the voice was, before following his torso as it landed on the stone floor with a heavy thud. He tried to sit up as quickly as he had fallen but a black, leather heeled boot smacked into the side of his face, dazing him. A second later the same boot was thrust down onto the hand holding the scalpel, breaking all five fingers as it ground the hand into the stone.

Then the boots straddled him as the legs within, dressed in black and white silk pantaloons dropped down onto his chest. A heaving bosom in a white blouson, black pom pom's for buttons, leaned over him. A black ruffle framed a slender white painted neck that carried an elegant white painted face and green eyes made up black, a single black tear painted onto her left cheek, looked down at his squirming features in disgust. She thumped a hand encircled in a black ruffle cuff directly onto the bullet wound in his shoulder, leaning over his face as he once again screamed in agony.

'You believe your God would think that the mutilation and murder of five women was just, just because they were whores? Is that what you believe?' she spat into his face, her nose touching his, her simmering emerald eyes, full of anger, penetrating his shocked, agonised glare.

'It is his will, everything I do is his will. Everything I do is in his name. For Allah!' he answered, defiance entering his pain filled tone.

Her Moons Denouement   **Max Hardy**

'Understand this Imam. I do not fear you. I do not fear your god and everything I do, I do in my name. Never forget my name.' she growled, eyes shining as she sank her fist harder into his bleeding wound.

'My name is Madame Evangeline.'

Chapter 11

'Not here Chris, my boss is in the car!' Annie pleaded, standing on the doorstep to her flat, her boyfriend brooding in the doorway, his dark expression directed towards the beaten up Volvo parked up at the other side of the road, towards Bentley who was staring at him intently, listening in on the over loud conversation.

'You told me you were his boss now. Is that another lie? Another one of your convenient excuses?' he shouted over her head, pushing her hands off his sweaty running top as she tried to direct him back into the hallway.

'I told you I had been put in charge of the case. I didn't tell you I was his boss. He is still a DI. I know you are pissed I was out late again last night, but I explained that, you've seen the story on the news.' she whispered, pleading.

'Just excuses Annie, always excuses with you. Just do one.' he shouted, pushing her forcefully out of the door, causing her to stumble on the step and stagger into the sidewall between the houses. 'And if you can't be home at a reasonable time, don't bother fucking coming home at all. Have Fancy Dan over there put you up, or put one up you, if he hasn't already.' And with that last vitriolic slur, he slammed the door shut.

'Chris, don't be an arse!' she shouted at the unresponsive solid oak door, tears smudging her mascara, her eyes already puffed and panda.

Her Moons Denouement   **Max Hardy**

She knelt down and picked up the contents of her bag from the path where he had thrown it earlier. She gave the flat one last forlorn look, then, arms crossed protectively across her chest, she turned and walked toward Bentley's car, opened the passenger door and slouched into the ripped and dirty leather seat, sighing in time with the rustle of the empty crisp packets she sat on.

'I'm sorry about that Sir.' she said apologetically, not looking at him, not able to, but searching out a tissue from her dishevelled bag.

'It he usually that much of a twat?' Bentley asked conversationally as he started the car and pulled out of Great Stuart Street with its precise and well kept rows of Georgian Houses and into the arc of Randolph Crescent, a semi circle of even more opulent buildings, some converted to flats, most offices and consulate buildings.

'It's not his fault. I should have called him.' she answered, flipping down the dirty sun visor, which fell off at the hinge and plopped into her lap. She looked at Bentley wide eyed and surprised. 'I am so sorry about that!' she continued, lifting the visor and clumsily trying to fix it.

'Don't worry about it, just use the mirror like that. It's a bit cracked and probably a bit dusty. Part of the job, being out late. Does he not understand that?' Bentley asked as he turned right onto the A90 and headed off towards the Police Headquarters on Fettes Avenue.

Annie raised the visor to her face, trying to gauge from her reflection how much of the smearing around her eyes was her makeup running and how much was the dirt on the mirror. She started to dab at the makeup anyway.

'He's just a bit jealous, that's all. It doesn't help when I don't let him know what I am doing. He tries not to be jealous and we are working on it.' she replied, most of the smudged makeup now rubbed away.

Her Moons Denouement   Max Hardy

'Really? I think you need to grow a pair and tell him how it is. Tell him to get over himself. Can't abide fucking pussies.' Bentley replied, his features thoughtful, watching her straighten her face out of the corner of his eye.

She sat back abruptly in her seat, slightly taken aback at the candour in his comments and looked over to him. He turned to look at her, his face still thoughtful.

'Don't let him bully you. Whatever he does, you make sure you stand up to him. You're a fucking police 'person'.' he sneered with sarcasm. 'Start fucking acting like one.'

Annie stared at him wide eyed for a second, head nodding as she took in his words and let her mind ruminate on them.

'Alright Bentley. I'm not quite sure who the biggest twat is, you or my boyfriend, but if that's the way you want to play. What did you find out at the club last night?' she asked curtly, thrusting the dirty hanky into her bag and dropping the visor into the footwell.

'Better, much better.' he said, flashing a wink as he continued, 'Our Elvis seems to be a bit of a loner. He's got a regular list of 'clients' that he hooks up with but doesn't hang out much with the 'staff' at the club. I talked to half a dozen of the 'staff' and none of them could even tell me where he lived, let alone who his friends were. No one had heard of an organisation called the 'Fallen Angels'.'

'Did you get a list of the 'clients'?' Annie asked innocently.

Bentley burst out laughing, a huge raucous guffaw that shocked Jackson into barking. 'God girl, are you really that raw. This is a fucking illegal S&M gaff we are talking about here, they don't have frigging lists, they don't even have bloody 'clients', just people who turn up there and fuck in a hundred depraved ways and somewhere, somehow, money changes hands. You won't get a single member of 'staff' to tell you who those people are.'

'Even if we bring them in?' she retorted.

He looked over to her with wide, flabbergasted eyes. 'That's the one fucking sure way to shut them up tight and lose any kind of trail there may be. And I told Shankers that I thought you were smart. What a dick I am.' he finished, shaking his head as he pulled into the headquarters car park and killed the engine.

'So there was a lead then?' she pushed, sitting up and leaning into him slightly, ignoring the insult.

'You're learning. I didn't get a list, but I managed to get them to point out two 'clients' who were in there last night. I talked to them. They would mainly meet him at the club or occasionally at hotels, depending if they wanted to do anything even more debauched. Stupidly I asked how debauched. One of them was into sexual asphyxiation and our Elvis seemed to be a something of an aficionado on that particular perversion.'

Bentley climbed out of the car, pushing the rear passenger window down and throwing Jackson a dog biscuit out of his jacket pocket. Annie climbed out as well and hurried to catch up with him as he slouched towards the station.

'So what does that mean? That he was in on the killings with O'Driscoll? Why would he expose him if that were the case?'

'I don't think so, that wouldn't make sense. None of his rhetoric suggests that he was involved. Perhaps it's how he found out about O'Driscoll though. Something to consider.'

They walked into the station entrance and the Duty Sergeant shouted after them as soon as they came through the door.

'Bentley, she's after you. Wants you up there straight away. You too Tait.'

'Oh fucking joy of joys, whoop de do. Thanks Bob.' Bentley answered sarcastically as he trounced off towards the stairs, Annie in tow.

'Did you talk to anyone about Rebecca Angus?' she asked, a step behind his broad frame, not able to walk alongside on the narrow stairwell.

'Aye. No one admits to seeing the psycho recently and no one can recall if she knew Elvis. How did you get on at his flat? How far away was it from her place?'

'It was a couple of streets away. Close enough to be there in a few minutes. Much like you, not really a lot there. The flat was sparsely furnished. A table with a single chair in the kitchen, a painting of some flowers on the wall above it. Nothing in the living room and a single freshly made bed in the only bedroom. To be honest, it didn't even look lived in. Forensics have been through it thoroughly and found next to nothing. No prints apart from his, even on the front door, which is odd. You'd expect at least the postie's. No mail or any other documents at all in the place. Not even any clothes. Only thing they did find was a photograph on the kitchen table, a picture of O'Driscoll with another man. The two of them dressed in some kind of uniform, smiling at the camera while clanking pints of Guinness.'

'Feels like a fuck hole. Somewhere he takes people to do the deed rather than somewhere he lives. Where's the photo?'

'It's with forensics. They are scanning it into the system to see if we can get a hit on facial recognition.'

'Or they could have just shown it to us old farts who might recognise who it is! That's two fucking days wasted and they won't come back with anything, never bloody do.'

Her Moons Denouement   **Max Hardy**

He stopped at Cruickshanks office door and stepped to one side, letting Annie past.

'Sir?' she said as she stepped past him, perplexed.

'First off, don't call me Sir. You're the fucking officer in charge. Second, you're the fucking officer in charge, so you go in first!'

She stared at his worn, haggard expression, looking for a glint of his normal weary cynicism but only saw helpful impatience in its place.

'Thanks Bentley, I appreciate that. By the way,' she said, reaching into her bag and taking out a photograph, 'I have a copy here. Do you recognise him, you old fart?'

Bentley took the photograph and studied it intently, shaking his head slightly as he examined the faces. 'No, don't recognise him. Hold up.' He paused, bringing the photograph closer to his face, looking fastidiously at the lapel on the fatigues O'Driscoll wore. 'Fuck, 'Óglaigh na hÉireann', that's an IRA badge he's wearing. Jesus. Head of the fucking Catholic Church in Scotland, Serial Killer and member of the bloody IRA. Storming CV he's got.' He handed the photograph back to Annie.

'Better tell Shankers then.' Annie said, and knocked on the door.

'Come.' Came the bellowing reply. Annie opened the door and walked into Cruickshanks office, Bentley lumbering in behind her.

'Tait, this is DI John Saul, a colleague from our Northumberland patch. Bentley, the two of you have already met I gather.' introduced Cruickshank, formally.

Saul stood up slowly from where he was sitting opposite Cruickshank and offered his hand to Annie as she approached him.

Her Moons Denouement   Max Hardy

'DC Annie Tait.' she started, smiling with sympathetic nervousness, taking in his tall, well groomed figure and noticing the small plaster in the palm of his hand as she shook it. 'So sorry to hear about your loss.' she stepped slightly to the side and Bentley shook Saul's hand firmly, visibly causing him to grimace.

'See you've ditched the Tuxedo then?' Bentley commented as the three of them sat down.

'It was a rag by the end of that day, sweat and blood were the only things holding it together. And dog piss.' Saul answered with sardonic joviality.

'Aye, heard you had a bad time of it. For what it's worth, sorry for your loss. Jackson tends to get pissed off when people make me angry, then pisses on them. What can I say; better than having him bite you. What brings you north of the Border?'

'When I was nailed naked to a chair and just about to have my heart ripped out by your friend Gordon Ennis, a man saved me. I don't have a clue who that man was. He could be called Rob Adams, could be Ben Hanlon, he could even be the twin brother I never knew I had. What I do know is that he saved my life and his parting words to me were 'Think on one thing, Even Fallen Angels Have Wings.' The same words that Elvis Aarons used yesterday just before he committed suicide. Now what I want to know is are they the same person, and if not, what's the connection?'

'He was no friend of mine, how the fuck was I to know he was ten bricks short of a hod! Still had that nutter Angus pegged right. You know what they say. Takes a psycho to know a psycho.'

'Bentley!' Cruickshank admonished sternly.

'Sorry Ma'am.'

Her Moons Denouement Max Hardy

'I take it you still think Madame Evangeline was a figment of Rebecca's imagination.'

'Oh fu..flip, here we go again. Okay, she might not have mutilated her son, but she sure as hell still shagged him, was there when he tripped and died, and there is no evidence whatsoever to corroborate the existence of Madame flippin Evangeline. I'm telling you, the bird is all in her sick, twisted mind.'

'Gentlemen, I don't think that's really helping us and I don't think it's what we should be focusing on at the moment.' started Tait, her voice still full of nerves, but tinged with authority. 'The important thing is there are potentially two people divided by two weeks and a hundred miles that have used the same phrase. Calls the theory that Elvis was a loner into question straight away.'

Cruickshank nodded approvingly 'Quite right Tait. You two stop the pissing contest and Saul, please tell us everything that you know.'

There was an urgent rapping on the office door and it was immediately pushed open, DI George McCalvey striding into the room, an open laptop in his hands.

'Sorry for interrupting Ma'am but you really need to see this.' McCalvey said, placing the laptop on her desk. 'We got it through from the BBC about ten minutes ago. They received a video clip. It's from the Fallen Angels.'

Chapter 12

I really need to get a grip. It's every woman, every bloody woman. Half an hour ago it was Gaynor Cruickshank. I'm looking at her and thinking, 'Is she Jess, in disguise.' The fact that she is a foot smaller doesn't even come into it. I saw the curve of a jaw and my mind suddenly went there. The same with Tait. I can smell her and it reminds me of Jess. And Jess is smiling in my mind. Same height, same build, but totally different hair, colour eyes, protruding teeth, personality, everything.

Same with Bentley. Is he Hanlon? Still the same narrow minded superficial twat I recall from two weeks ago, but that could all just be a front. At the minute, it's difficult to know what to believe. It's difficult to know who is who. I just need to get a grip and focus. Not sleeping isn't helping at all.

'Have the BBC run the story?' Cruickshank asks McCalvey.

'No Ma'am. They forwarded it straight onto us. They want to talk to you about when they can show it.'

'Well, they can wait on both counts. Call legal straight away and get it embargoed. No backscratching on this one, I want it out of circulation for at least forty eight hours.'

She didn't even flinch, straight to the point and decisive. Tait looks surprised at that news, I can see the cogs whirring as she leans in

Her Moons Denouement   **Max Hardy**

toward the small screen. She is copying Cruickshank, arms crossed on the table, back straight. Bentley is thoughtful, slinking further back in his chair as McCalvey presses the play button and then leaves.

'Demi Simpson, Shelley Crabtree, Josie Richards, Kelly Pieterson, Rachel Lavery and Briony Williams.'

A female voice reading out the names, very clipped and precise, a deep husk to the tone. Quick images flashing up, headshots of mainly happy faces imposed on graphic scenes of the women spread-eagled over alters, O'Driscoll in the foreground, his privates pixelated. I thought there were seven. Did they not mention seven women on the news last night?

'All masochistically murdered by this man, Archbishop Liam O'Driscoll, a paragon on the Roman Catholic Church.'

An image of O'Driscoll fills the screen. He's dressed in ceremonial robes, standing in front of a font at a baptism, holding a baby. The image starts a slow zoom in on his face as an anger enters her voice.

'He would have you believe that these women were possessed by evil spirits. He would have you believe that his faith compelled him to rid the world of these evil spirits by killing them. He would stand in front of each and every one of you, Christian, Muslim, Bhuddist, whatever your religious persuasion and tell you that in the eyes of his God, your world is a safer place without them. Look into his eyes, look deep into his eyes. Do you see empathy, compassion, kindness, warmth, friendship, love?'

I don't. They are hard and heartless. I notice the baby in the picture is crying. I see that his hand is holding its arm tightly, just as it goes out of shot, the screen now filled with his face.

'Do you see madness, insanity, evil, even the devil staring back at you?'

Her Moons Denouement   **Max Hardy**

His face is gone, the whole screen now filled with his brown eyes, tributaries of blood vessels snaking into the white, making them bloodshot.

'Or just a man, like any other, a person, like you: or like me.'

Just the brown of the irises fills the screen, then their colour changes to green and the pupils morph from a dull lifeless black to be full of reflected light, moving as they dilate. The camera starts to zoom out. Heavy black mascara and eyeliner around the emerald eyes. White makeup applied around the sockets and into the face. It's the woman who is speaking, I can see the muscles of her cheeks as they come into view, they are moving in time with the words.

'Look into my eyes. Do you see the devil staring back at you?'

No, I see Jess. It is Jess. Not just the eyes, but also the curve of her nose, the high cheekbones. It is definitely Jess. I lean closer into the laptop, raising a finger to the screen, tracing the contours of her face.

'Are you alright Saul? You might want to move back from the screen so we can all see.'

Cruickshank's tone was forceful and it broke through my obsessive compulsion that every woman I see is Jess long enough to bring me back into the room with the other occupants, to see their perplexed faces. I decide against telling them what my mind is thinking for the moment and lean back from the screen, apologising.

'Or do you see a clown with a sad face. Does a clown make you laugh, or do you fear it? And if you fear it, why?'

Her full face is on the screen now. It is Jess. Jess made up to look like Pierott. What's the relevance, what has that got to do with Fallen Angels? What's that got to do with O'Driscoll? Oh shit, that picture coming into view behind her head, it's a Cezanne. Another Cezanne.

Her Moons Denouement Max Hardy

This is Jess. This is Madame Evangeline. She lifts a wet wipe to her face and rubs the white face paint off one cheek.

'Underneath whatever face we paint, whatever mask we wear, whatever god we act in the name of, we are human, first and foremost. Humans with a propensity for good and evil in equal measures. Humans with a propensity to use faith and fear as weapons to control other humans. Humans with a propensity to use faith as an excuse for our own depravity.'

Her whole torso is in view. She is sitting behind a desk. What kind of desk is that? No windows in the room, just blank white walls, that single Cezanne behind her head. Nothing to give a clue as to where she is. Hands, damn, she is wearing gloves. Think John, think, what are her other discerning features.

'We are the Fallen Angels. We aren't gods, we aren't supernatural. We are humans. Humans who have a belief. Humans who have a faith. Humans who fear a lot of things, but not our faith. We bleed, we cry, we hurt, we die, just the same as you. I am not here to ask you to believe in us. I am here to ask you one simple question. Why do you fear your faith?'

Jess, Madame Evangeline. She led me into temptation. She put me in a position where I had to make a choice. Why did she do that? Did she want to see what I would do? Was she testing me? Why was she testing me?

'Don't just think of that question in isolation. Look at these images of the beautiful women Archbishop Liam O'Driscoll murdered and as you look into their eyes, ask yourself, 'Why do I fear my faith.'

The girls again, smiling faces, dead bodies, flicking through them at pace. Powerful images, a powerful thought. Stop. A picture of a different woman, her eyes, nose and mouth sewn up, face bruised and bleeding around the stitching. She looks in agony.

Her Moons Denouement Max Hardy

'Just in case you think the atrocities carried out by Archbishop Liam O'Driscoll are an isolated incident. Just in case you think using fear and faith as a weapon is confined to Christianity. Just in case you think we are extreme in our actions, look at this poor woman's face. At midday today, somewhere in the city, we will tell you all about the religious leader who exacted this brutality upon her and many other women. It gives me no pleasure at all to say even that won't be the end of our revelations.'

Symbols in the stitching. Islamic symbols. 'Praise Allah.' A muslim religious leader. It's going to be a mosque. Symbols. Fallen Angels and Clowns. What's the link. One kicked out of heaven for disagreeing with God, the other fall guys of kings. Is that it? Both with the inside track on leaders. The significance of removing the face paint. About a quarter of the facepaint. Does that signify three more revelations?

'Think on one thing: Even Fallen Angels Have Wings. I am Madame Evangeline and we are the Fallen Angels.'

Yep, who the hell else was it going to be. She might look like Jess, but that's not her voice. We can check that. There's not enough of the face to tell. She could just as easily be Rebecca. Bottom line is, here is someone on video claiming to be Madame Evangeline.

'Well Bentley, what was it you were saying about Madame Evangeline not being real. Up there with your other exemplary police work. You are a waste of space. Don't bother protesting either.'

He's very subservient to a dominant woman, very aggressive to men and unusually supportive to Tait. I can see he wants to scream at me.

'Ma'am, could I just get onto a web browser on this laptop please? The symbols in that stitching are Islamic. 'Praise Allah.' We need to check how many mosques there are in Edinburgh.'

Her Moons Denouement   Max Hardy

'Go ahead Saul.'

'Thanks Ma'am. OK, so google 'Mosque's Edinburgh'. There are nine. Where are they, lets map them. Dotted all around?'

'That one!' Tait shouts as she stabs the screen. 'That's the Central Mosque, just off the Royal Mile. It's a Fringe venue as well. My guess would be that one!'

'Based upon the information to hand Tait, I would agree with you. However, the information we have to hand is very light. While the symbols on the eye suggest Islam, there's nothing to suggest it would be at that Mosque. Bear in mind Madame Evangeline said 'somewhere in the city', so we can't exclude the other Mosque's from our thinking. But I would agree, we prioritise that one. Tait, Bentley, rally the troops and get them down to the meeting room now. We've got just over two hours to work out where the hell in the city this is going to happen. We cannot have the public or the press around when it does. This has to be contained. Saul, you stay here please.'

Bentley fires me a furious glare and stands to leave. I can get that, he's been shown up and belittled and it was me arguing the toss about Madame Evangeline. God, it's good to see the naïve enthusiasm in Tait's eyes. I was like that once, still with a hunger when the chase was on. I know what Cruickshank is going to say.

'Saul, I'd like to thank you for coming up and letting us know about your experience and the possible link between Hanlon/Adams and our case. As you can see, things are progressing and thanks also for that last bit of insight into the symbols, it was really timely. However, you know that I can't let you be involved in this investigation. You are signed off. I have had clear instructions from DCI Strange to tell you to go home and rest so I would suggest you do that. Do I make myself clear?'

How the hell does Jerry know I'm up here! Harry bloody Massah!

'You do Ma'am. I can't promise to go home. But I can promise I won't knowingly get involved in this investigation. I just need to answer a few questions for my own sanity. Could I ask you just to consider one thing?'

'Just understand one thing first, knowingly or unknowingly, if you interfere with this investigation, you will be for the high jump. What do you want me to consider?'

'Rob Adams, Ben Hanlon, Jessica Seymour and Madame Evangeline. No one knows who they really are. However, for them to know the things they do, for them to have the insights they seem to have about these murderers, they must have eyes somewhere within the force. From my own bitter experience, that could be someone you know, that could be someone on your team.'

Chapter 13

The sun shimmered, beaming lonely in a cloudless sky, talons of sunlight shining off the darkened glass of the office buildings surrounding Edinburgh Central Mosque on Potterrow, just off the Royal Mile. The stone building, with its tall, dominant prayer tower looked clean and crisp, only the brown bricked symbols halfway up the towers breaking the uniformity. The entrance was a large rectangular stone surround, half the height of the prayer tower with inlaid arches ever decreasing to the thirty foot high doorway into the building.

There was an eerie silence on the streets and the open area in front of the Mosque, not a single vehicle on the roads or anyone at all wandering around. Further down the main road, about a hundred metres in either direction, flashing blue lights signified the boundary setup to secure the area, police vehicles blocking access. On the road up to the Royal Mile, the police vehicles were parked below a scaffold frame built over the road that was supporting large banners advertising the Edinburgh Fringe.

A smaller door inside the larger Mosque door opened with a groan and a solitary policeman came out, quickly running across the concourse and road, footfalls echoing in the emptiness, towards the cars parked below the scaffold.

Her Moons Denouement Max Hardy

'All secure Ma'am. There is no one in there.' PC Campbell said, slightly out of breath as he arrived at the small group of colleagues standing in front of an open van. A line of police officers stretched right across the road, facing outward and controlling an ever growing inquisitive crowd of Festival revellers, tourists and a large contingent of press. A mirrored line of police officers stood in front of the vehicles, facing the Mosque, ready to mobilise into the empty area.

'Thanks Campbell. Join the line and keep an eye on the crowd.' Cruikshank said as she raised a walkie talkie and started to speak into it while scanning the rooftops of the perimeter buildings. 'ARO's call off one through ten and just to reiterate, absolutely no engagement without my explicit order.' The walkie talkie crackled and ten voices, one after the other called off their readiness, hands raising in the air from the rooftops as they did.

'Excellent. Tait, is everyone in position at the other locations?' Cruickshank asked, turning back to the Police Incident Van behind her, where Annie was sitting at a small communications bench inside it.

'Yes Ma'am, all eight teams have reported back. Perimeters in place, exclusion zones clear and Mosques are now empty. Just a matter of waiting.'

'Well, we've only got a few minutes to find out where it will be. Let's pray we've read the Islamic signs right.' Cruickshank stated as she paced impatiently in front of the van.

A loud screech of feedback seared through the relative silence of the scene outside the mosque, emanating from the speakers at the top of the prayer tower.

'I thought you said there was no one in there Campbell!' Cruickshank shouted down the line to the Police officers receding figure.

Her Moons Denouement   **Max Hardy**

'Allahu Akbar, Allahu Akbar, Allahu Akbar, Allahu Akbar.' followed the screeching out of the speakers.

'That's the start of the Adhan.' Cruickshank shouted, confused. 'Is that on a timer set for midday or is someone in there!' she demanded, looking sternly at the approaching figure of a panicking Campbell.

'It's not automatic Ma'am. I checked with one of the Imam's before we emptied the Mosque. They don't automate Adhan.' Campbell answered with pained anxiety.

'Well that must mean someone is in there. Men, lets walk forward slowly towards the Mosque entrance. Tait, any news from the other locations?'

'No Ma'am, all quiet.'

'God is great, God is Great, Is God Great? Is your God really Great?' Blared out from the speakers, the change in the order of the words accentuated, the last question pointed.

'Right men, keep your eyes peeled on every doorway, window, alley, manhole cover or cubby hole that someone could hide in. This is happening here and now. That's not the Adhan, someone is starting to make a point.'

'Is your God, who would let his followers, let his leaders, let his Imam's torture, mutilate and murder innocent women really great?'

Cruickshank walked in front of the advancing police line, her eyes darting around the concourse, looking up at the prayer tower, delving into the shadows of enclosed alleyways.

'Or is he another false god that uses fear to instil faith. In whose faith is your fear founded. What mortal flesh would you divest to appease your saviours wrath, who's pious wrote would you impress while seeking raptures righteous path. What mortal flesh would you divest!

Her Moons Denouement

Max Hardy

The skin of a woman's labia ripped off with bare teeth! Extreme Genital Mutilation. Orifices sewn shut, bodies beaten for fun! All in the name of a God who is great!' The voice soared and echoed around the open space, the crowds gathered behind the police barriers silent in anticipation, the police lines quietly moving, intently scanning their surroundings.

'One through ten call off, do you see anything!' Cruickshank whispered into the walkie talkie, holding it to her ear as ten negative replies rang out. 'Shit, where the hell is he?'

'Raise your eyes to the sky, see the blasphemy of his god, witness not just the words of his travesty, but the impact of his actions, not from my lips, but from those of his victim.'

A loud, piercing rip sounded out from behind Cruikshank, causing her to turn and see the large festival banners peeling away from the scaffold beam spanning the road behind her to reveal three people on a small platform. The crowd jostled backward, the police line underneath forward and everyone looked up, a collective disquiet spreading through them as they saw the occupants of the platform.

One man, the Imam, was bound naked to a scaffold post, his hands raised above his head and tied tightly with rope, as were his feet. Barbed wire was wound tightly around his body from toe to fingertip, biting into the bleeding flesh. He looked sedated. A second man, the Harlequin, stood beside the Imam, holding a microphone in one hand and a pile of pictures in the other. His back appeared bulbous and around his neck was a noose, the rope of which was tied tightly to the scaffold cross beam above him. A woman leaned against him, holding onto his arm. She was wrapped in a white sheet blotched with blood stains, the most pronounced of which was around her crotch. Her eyes, nose, mouth and ears were dotted with bloody, bruised pinholes. The Harlequin raised the microphone to her lips.

Her Moons Denouement   **Max Hardy**

'I was scared.' she started nervously, her voice broken and weak, each word obviously causing her damaged lips pain. 'He was so charming, so supportive. I am a good girl. I pray every day. I know my place and I just needed guidance. I was scared because I liked a boy who wasn't a Muslim. I know what Allah says about that and I came to the Imam for advice. He kept asking me if I had sexual thoughts about the boy. He told me that was alright, that a woman was allowed to have those feelings and that it was only wrong to act on them. So I told him that I had because it is wrong to lie. He was still very considerate, offering me a drink of water, seeing I was terrified. I drank the water as he started to talk to me about Infidels and then I must have fallen asleep. I awoke strapped naked into a basket frame. He was naked too and started beating me and screaming at me, calling me a whore. He then started to sew my ears up. It was agony, and I screamed and pleaded for him to stop. I pleaded to Allah to forgive my sordid thoughts. He kept stitching: my lips, my nose, my anus, my eyes.' she paused, tears streaming from her damaged eyes, her breathing frantic as she relived the Imam's actions. The Harlequin wrapped a comforting arm around her and whispered something into her ear. She nodded.

'Campbell, get me a megaphone, quickly.' Cruickshank ordered as she walked earnestly back toward the gantry, lifting the walkie talkie as she did. 'ARO's, get your weapons trained on the Harlequin. Tait, stand down the units at the other site and get them here as fast as you can and for god's sake, see if we can jam that bloody microphone signal.'

'Then he gouged at my eyeballs and hit me hard in the stomach, before cutting me down below and ripping the loose skin off with his teeth.' she said, her voice rising in intensity, full of terror as she loosened the sheet around her and let it fall to the platform, leaving her standing naked, the gaping wound of her mutilated vagina visible for all to see.

A loud gasp escaped those in the crowd that could see the detail of her injuries, blaspheming and angry shouting following.

Her Moons Denouement Max Hardy

'He would have stitched me down there too if I hadn't been rescued by this man. And then he would have killed me, like he has so many others. I wanted help. I was afraid and I wanted help. All I wanted was his help.' She started to cry and the Harlequin stooped and raised the sheet back over her body and cuddled her tightly into him. He took the microphone back.

'This is Imam Veron Mann. He is my brother and he has mutilated and murdered five women. Perdip would have been his sixth. We were fortunate to find her just before he killed her, just before he carried out this further atrocity upon her.' he finished, throwing the wad of pictures in his hand into the air where they caught on the thermals and floated delicately down to the ground, grotesque glimpses of ravaged torso's, ripped and riven, the internal organs missing, flitting in and out of sight.

Hundreds of pictures fluttered to the ground and Cruickshank grabbed one as it wafted close to her. She looked at the atrocity on the photograph, the name of the woman and the date she was murdered typed on the bottom, and physically convulsed.

The crowd started grabbing for the photographs too, shouts and screams breaking out amongst them, some people pushing back to get out of the area, some pushing angrily forward to get closer to the Imam, hurling verbal abuse in is direction.

Campbell arrived next to Cruickshank and handed her the megaphone. 'Start collecting these up and get that line to push the crowd back. Try to get the photographs off them too.' she ordered, thrusting the photograph into his hands. She raised the megaphone to her mouth and directed it upward, toward to platform.

'That is tragic, absolutely tragic and I would like to thank you for bringing these atrocities to our attention. What do we have to do to ensure that there isn't another life wasted here today? Can you help me with that? I am DCI Gaynor Cruickshank and I am here to listen. What's your name?'

The Harlequin smiled, hugging Perdip tighter as she shook beside him, looking out over the rooftops to the Armed Response Officers, their weapons pointed at him. 'DCI Gaynor Cruickshank. There will be no other life wasted here today. There will only be a natural end, a conclusion, a denouement. We will no longer stand by and let these atrocities take place under the fear of faith. We will no longer stand in the shadows of your gods and let Angels Bleed in the ignominy of his seed.' His voice was rising, calmness being replaced by fervour as he tenderly assisted Perdip to sit down on the platform, the large bulge on his back rippling, a rip of Velcro searing out through the microphone as he stood back up, stretching his arms out.

'Shit, he's getting ready to jump. ARO's, if you have a clear wing shot -and I mean wing shot- and it does not jeopardise the safety of the woman, then you are authorised to shoot now.' Cruickshank hissed into the walkie talkie.

From behind his back, two large feathered wings rose in tandem with his arms, reaching out beyond their fingertips. The crowd gasped in unison, as a myriad of cameras flashed in time. 'We will no longer let the innocent be used as pawns in their game. The weak, the vulnerable, those who believe because they know no different, because they are led. We will expose the bloody malevolence of their leaders. Even Fallen Angels have Wings.'

A single shot rang out through the square, hitting the Harlequin on the left shoulder, forcing him to stagger back on the small platform, forcing him to fall backward into the air, the rope tied to the cross beam unravelling. A look of pained euphoria ingrained itself on his face as he fell, shouting into the microphone, 'We are the Fallen Angels.' a split second before the slack in the rope ran out, jerking his body viciously and breaking his neck instantly.

Her Moons Denouement **Max Hardy**

Chapter 14

Well, there is no doubt at all now that there is someone called Madame Evangeline. Who she is though is a different matter entirely. Logically I know that there is still not enough evidence to prove that Jess is Madame Evangeline. Even that video from the Fallen Angels isn't conclusive. A painted face with similar features and a voice that is totally different. I know part of me wants to believe it is her and part of me that it isn't. I know Jess is alive and I know I have to link the two of them together in some way. I need to find out how the hell she managed to get out of that hotel room on New Years Eve. If she did come up to Edinburgh on a train with someone who looks like me, I need to find out where they went. How can I find that out without using contacts in the force? How can I….hold on. What about Harry? He might have contacts? No, he'll go running straight back to Jerry and tell him what I am up to. Possibly not if I confront him about that first. It's worth a try.

I limp down Princess Street, weaving through the shopperati dipping in and out of the stores to get a hit of their consumer fix. Life goes on, ever moving, even though someone not a mile away has just died, a killer has been found and a world of pain has been exposed. Couples, smiling and tactile, kissing and cuddling pass me by, oblivious of my pain, oblivious of what is happening in their city. I shuffle on and call Harry.

'Harry. It's John Saul.'

Her Moons Denouement   Max Hardy

'Hello Mr Saul. How are you today? What can I do for you?'

'I'm a little perplexed to be honest Harry. Thanks for your time yesterday, it was really helpful. Crystallised a few things in my mind and opened up a few other thoughts. I was wondering if you could help me. I am in Edinburgh at the minute, following up some leads. The DCI I was talking to appeared to know that I was coming and had explicit instructions from Jerry to order me home to rest. You wouldn't know anything about that would you?'

Silence for a moment.

'I could try and lie. I could, but I won't Mr Saul. I saw Jerry last night when I was picking up the girls from Pony club. He asked me if you had been in touch. I told him about our meeting. He does have your best interests at heart, you do know that don't you?'

'Harry, I know Jerry is trying to look after me and I know he would have found out in one way or another what I was up to. I guess there is probably only one way that you would treat our conversations as confidential and not go reporting back to him.'

'Mr Saul, it's not like that, honestly. I feel conflicted. Jerry recommended me to your wife and really she was my client. As a friend he just asked me to let him know if you had been in touch.'

'That's alright Harry, I don't blame you, I just need to get past that. I would like to hire you to work for me on something. Hopefully that will dispel any conflict you might have.'

'Well, if you hire me, then that's a different thing entirely. What is it you want me to do?'

'The two train journeys that you photographed Jess and the other me making, do you think you could find where they went to when they arrived in Edinburgh. See if you can find any CCTV footage of them getting off the train, figure out if they got taxi's or lifts anywhere after that?'

Silence again.

'Look Harry, as far as the police are concerned Jessica Seymour is dead. They will not and I don't expect them to put any effort into finding out what a dead person did in the weeks leading up to that. For my own sanity I am trying to piece together something that has ripped my world apart. I can't do that on my own, I don't have the contacts or the bandwidth to do everything. I need some help and you definitely have a starter for ten with regard to knowing what Jess was up to over the last month. Will you help me, please?'

'Okay Mr Saul. Leave it with me and I'll get back to you as soon as I have something. Is this the best number to call you on?'

'Thanks Harry, I really appreciate this. Yes, just call me back on my mobile any time, day or night. Sleeping seems to be escaping me at the moment.'

I hang up just outside the hotel entrance, and look up at the multi windowed façade. Probably about ten feet between each window, with a very narrow ledge just below the window sills. Wide enough for someone to walk along? I'll soon find out.

The hotel reception is quiet as I enter, the heady odour of orange pot pourri invading my nostrils. It triggers a memory of Jess and I, still sweating from the 10k we had done, pushing each other away, laughing as we drank in the scent and teased one another about our own body odour. We ended up fucking the second we got through the hotel room door, she ripping my pants down and climbing straight onto me where we stood. The receptionist smiles as I approach and introduce myself.

Her Moons Denouement   Max Hardy

'Ah yes, Mr Saul. You wanted rooms the two rooms next to each other. They are all ready for you Sir. Do you have any baggage to take?'

'No, not at the moment thank you.'

I take the key cards and head for the lifts, scanning the reception area. CCTV pointing out from the lifts to the main entrance. No CCTV in the lifts. Third Floor, CCTV cameras just outside the lifts, one pointing in each direction down the corridor. I turn left and head toward the room Jess and I shared, walking past it to the next room, the one where the booted foot came from. Damn, no other camera's at this end of the corridor. I unlock the door with the key card and enter the room. Lights automatically illuminate, adding an unnatural lustre to the natural sunlight streaming in through the netted sash and case windows.

The part of my mind that is creative had expected to see a black leather cat suit lying on the bed, thigh length leather boots next to it, a big flashing light above beaming 'She got dressed here!'. Instead it was just a normal hotel room, slightly upmarket, very much the same as the one next door, just reversed, but...

Why is the analytical part of my mind not surprised? But with a Cezanne painting above the bed. I walk over to the window and raise the bottom half, the nets billowing in the breeze. I then leave the room and go into the one next door, deliberately focusing, not breathing, moving straight to the window, ignoring the furnishings and décor and memories of my time with Jess that are pushing for prominence. I open it, thrusting my head out, breathing again, breathing in the air filled with fumes from the cars heading out over the Waverley Bridge to my right. I look to my left, to the netting blowing out of the open window in the next room and then down to the narrow ledge between them. It's about twenty centimetres wide and there are a couple of gaps in the stonework around head height which look like reasonable hand holds.

I climb onto the window sill, smarting as I stretch my groin, and swing both legs out, resting them on the ledge, the breeze ruffling my trousers. I can feel my heart thumping in my chest, adrenaline coursing through my veins as I look down to the people passing by three floors below. The inevitable movement of time. Everything progresses. Everyone gets on with life, in spite of the agony, in spite of the sheer aching numbness. Even I do. I could jump now. I could jump and end the torture, throw a ripple in the rivers of the throng below. But I won't. My death of choice is by revolver. That doesn't mean that I might not accidentally slip, and the height and precarious position is certainly making me scared. So I look straight ahead, to try and distract my mind from the height. Straight ahead to the offices across the road. Straight ahead, focusing on a window in the office across the road. Straight ahead, at the redhead standing in the window of the office across the road. At the redhead looking directly at me, smiling.

At the red head who looks remarkably like Jess.

Like Jess.

I duck under the window and throw my legs back over into the room, hitting the floor in a run. Third floor, sixth window from the left, redhead, head high rubber plant beside her. I sprint out the door and down the corridor, my heart racing, my groin and feet screaming at me in agony as I reach the lift and continually bang the button impatiently. The doors open and I dive in, being as animated with the button on the inside. I can't stand still as the lift descends: nerves, pain and frustration. Why is she taunting me? It is sheer mental torture. If she is part of this religious 'cult' that is the 'Fallen Angels', I'm not convinced about them if this type of mind games is part of their ideology. Twenty Three seconds.

Her Moons Denouement   **Max Hardy**

The lift doors open and I career out into the lobby, my brogues slipping on the polished tiles, almost sprawling headlong. Almost. I slow slightly and adjust my footing, open my gait into a run rather than a sprint and head out onto Princess Street, every one of my wounds now burning. I weave through the afternoon crowd, quickly looking right, quickly judging the gaps in the traffic coming out of the junction with North Bridge. Fifty one seconds.

I shuffle between an Edinburgh Tour bus, a taxi and an irate old woman who beeps her horn maddeningly at me as she has to brake, but make it to the other side unscathed, not pausing as I reach the entrance of the Waverleygate offices where I saw Jess, slowing to a walk as I see a security guard sitting with a receptionist at the main desk in the lobby. Four floors, third one empty, six businesses on the other three. Think. Who could I be? Just need to act natural. Head for the lifts. Pretend I am from 'Bailiss', a company on the 4th Floor, if they ask. Seventy nine seconds.

They don't ask, just smile at me politely. I return the pleasantry, reaching the lift, casually calling it, my heart thumping, sweat beads starting to form on my face from the exertion. The lift opens and I slowly walk in, pressing floor 3. The second the doors close the façade of calmness disappears and I start banging the 3rd floor button erratically. Right. Lift is facing the front of the building so I will be going left when I get out. Come on! Ninety four seconds.

The lift bings, the doors open and I sprint once again, straight to my left, into an empty corridor. CCTV facing right down the short corridor at me. The guard will see me running. Too late to worry about that. I barge through double doors at the end of the corridor into an empty open plan office that stretches the full length of the building wing. Count windows. No need, there's the one with the rubber plant. Can't see past it. Can't see if she is there. One hundred and one seconds.

Her Moons Denouement   Max Hardy

I slow as I approach the plant, the adrenaline ebbing from me as I see an empty space at the far side of it. Fuck. Fuck. Fuck. I walk to the window, spinning around, my stomach heaving with desolation as I look for her frantically. No one. The floor is empty.

'Fuck!' I scream, taking a deep breath to counter the sobs of frustration building in my throat. A deep breath that fills my lungs with as scent. Coco Chanel. Oh my God, Jess. Your scent. I breathe deeper, luxuriating in her odour, letting it engulf me for a moment as I step toward the window sill where she had been standing, my attention caught by a card precisely placed at the centre of it.

I pick it up. A black card with red writing, 'Sodom and Gomorrah', the 'S' and 'M's' embossed. The club where Rebecca met Madame Evangeline. I turn it over. 'Meet me at nine. Booth eight.' in the centre of a lipstick kiss. My stomach leaps, the desolation of losing her again in under two minutes usurped by the thought that finally, there may be some answers.

I look up, out of the window, back across to my hotel room.

Where Jess is sitting on the window ledge, smiling at me, her long red hair billowing in the breeze. She stands and pirouettes along the narrow ledge gracefully and quickly, sitting down on the ledge of the other open window within a second, looking straight at me again. She smiles, blows me a kiss, falls backwards into the room and is gone.

There is no doubt now. Jessica Seymour is Madame Evangeline. No doubt at all. I chose her: I chose her and killed my wife and son in the process.

Chapter 15

'Another suicide. Another mass murdered revealed. Another PR fiasco with the press having live footage of the whole sorry mess. It is not good enough girls and boys, not good enough at all. We were handed information on a plate on where and when todays events were going to happen and we still found ourselves outwitted and quite frankly, made to look inept and incompetent. We need to get on the front foot. We need to start seeing the patterns in what is going on, we need to start delving into the evidence and working out who the hell is involved in this and how the hell they have the upper hand. One thing we know for definite is that today was not the end.'

Cruickshank stood at the front of the Incident Room, hands thrust firmly down the sides of her perfectly ironed skirt, the fists flexing in frustration, knuckles angry, her countenance a vista of furious disappointment as she boomed out the tirade. Dozens of Detectives looked anywhere apart from directly at her, their expressions beaten and sheepish.

Apart from one. Bentley wasn't paying attention to Cruickshank's rant. He was looking through the case notes in front of him. At the names of the Imam's victims. At a name he recognised.

Cruickshank honed in on DI Barry Trentor first, glaring at the angular faced Detective who tried to busy himself in his notes under her piercing eyes. 'So Trentor, an update on the O'Driscoll murders if you please. Hopefully with some insight as to how our friend Elvis knew all about them and we didn't!'

'Well Ma'am, we have managed to corroborate all of the forensic evidence back to O'Driscoll's confession....' Trentor started but was immediately cut off by Cruickshank.

'Baloney Trentor. Did you listen to what I asked you? Insight into how Elvis knew about them. We know he's bloody confessed, we know we have the forensic evidence. That doesn't help us at the moment.' she shouted in frustration.

Tait nudged Bentley in the arm. 'Did you tell Trentor what you found out about Elvis?' she whispered over to him.

He didn't look up, engrossed in the evidence file in front of him, his features drawn and pallid.

She nudged him again, harder, her question louder. 'Bentley, did you tell Trentor about Elvis?'

Bentley looked up at her with a haunted expression, not registering her face for a second before his countenance changed to one of recognition, then anger. 'When the fuck have I had time to tell him that.'

'Tait, Bentley!' Cruikshank's words seared across the room, stopping Trentor in his mumbling tracks, causing everyone in the room to turn in the direction of the two Detectives. 'Are we keeping you from something, some private assignation? We are in the middle of a serious briefing here so your attention and focus would be greatly appreciated.'

'Sorry Ma'am.' Tait answered immediately, embarrassed under the admonishment. 'In the speed of everything that has happened today I forgot to update DI Trentor on information we gathered from our conversations at 'Sodom & Gommorah' last night. Would you mind if I spent a minute doing that now? I think it is relevant to your question.'

Bentley's expression turned from anger to surprise then awe as his colleague consciously took the blame for his forgetfulness.

'When you say 'I' forgot, is that who you mean?' Cruickshank pointedly asked, probing eyes darting between Tait and Bentley,

'I am the lead officer on this part of the investigation Ma'am and as such it is my accountability to ensure that all of the relevant information gets logged and passed on to the correct Detectives. So yes, 'I' forgot.' Tait answered with controlled nervousness, holding Cruickshank's glare with wavering determination.

Cruickshank returned the gaze for a full five seconds, then with an almost imperceptible wry smile, continued. 'Come on then Tait, you have a minute.'

'According to his employer Elvis Aarons was very much a loner. We did find out that he had a regular pool of 'clients' that he associated with. We managed to talk to a couple of them who were there last night. One of the things they told us is that Elvis has a particular fetish with regard to sexual asphyxiation. It is possible Elvis may have come across O'Driscoll because of that Ma'am.'

'Good, definitely worth a minute of interruption. However, at the moment it is just conjecture. Trentor, can you build that into your next interview with O'Driscoll. If he can corroborate that, then we possibly have a source. Purves, look at that with regard to the Mann investigation. I know things are fresh on that but where are we now?'

DI Rosamund Purves, a middle aged woman with long, flowing dyed blonde hair, grey at the roots, flicked through the notes in front of her, taking a second to compose her thoughts in the light of Cruickshank's mood.

Her Moons Denouement   Max Hardy

'We have five dead victims Ma'am as well as Perdip Tousivuna. The names and pictures are all on file. We are currently checking into the background of them all. We have carried out an initial interview with Perdip. She is still deeply traumatised by events and is in hospital having her wounds dressed. She was very lucid however and has given us some interesting leads. As well as the Harlequin referring to Imam Mann as his brother, Perdip also said that the Imam referred to the Harlequin as 'Brother' too. So we are checking out a biological connection. Perdip also said that she only ever saw the Harlequin but that there was also a woman present at her rescue. We want to play her the video of Madame Evangeline later to see if she recognises the voice. She was able to give us the location of where she was held captive and we have a team heading over there now. She then told us that the three of them had been up on the platform for about half an hour before the police started to arrive. They climbed on from one of the windows of the building the scaffold was secured to. We are looking at CCTV footage to try and see when they arrived at the building. One thing to note Ma'am, she is extremely reluctant at the moment to answer any specific questions about the Harlequin. At the moment, she is viewing him as her saviour.'

'Understandable, but she has information which could be crucial to us, so think carefully about your interview strategy. Get personal. We need to show that kind of intimacy and empathy that the Harlequin and the 'fallen Angels' seem to have demonstrated to her. Some good leads there Purves, chase them down as quickly as you can. When are we expecting news from forensics on the identity of the Harlequin?'

'It's due in the next hour.'

'Keep on top of them. That's one of our more crucial lines of enquiry. Has the Imam said anything yet?'

'No Ma'am, he is still coming around from sedation.'

Cruickshank turned and addressed an extremely tall, skinny man next, the handlebar moustache he wore warming the rim of the thermos mug he was supping from.

'Gregory, have you found out anything at all about Heather Scott that can help us with this case?'

'Apart from Bentley's dog being the Prime Suspect.' he joked, his initial smile turning rictus at the steely glares and shakes of disapproval that came from just about every other Detective in the room. No one had to say anything.

He coughed, cleared his throat and got serious in a second. 'The case files were brought up from storage this morning Ma'am and we are currently reviewing the key evidence that was presented at the time. At the moment, there is nothing to suggest anything different to the conviction that was made. Given the religious slant that events have taken, we are trying to find out if Heather belonged to any particular denomination. Nothing so far. We may need to go and check with relatives.'

'Just think carefully about how you handle that. I wouldn't want relatives to think we were questioning a conviction when we have no evidence of anything different happening. It will cause concern. It doesn't mean you don't ask, it just means be discreet. Thanks Gregory.'

Cruickshank looked down at her notes and sighed heavily, shaking her head as she read through them. 'Intel back from GCHQ reports no chatter at all out there in the wild about any organisation, cult, sect or faction called the 'Fallen Angels'. Nothing at all from the National Counter Terrorism Security Office either. Not a jot. Both are now actively scanning and will keep a watching brief on our investigations.' She sucked in her bottom lip and muttered under her breath, musing.

Her Moons Denouement Max Hardy

'Where do they come from and where do they go. They hide in plain sight.'

'Ma'am, I think there is one thing that we should consider exploring.' Tait said, breaking the silence of those watching the DCI pondering.

'I'm open to suggestions Tait, so fire away.'

'Well, the only link we have seen so far in events is the club where Elvis Aarons worked, and the fact that someone called Madame Evangeline may have also frequented that club.' she paused, waiting for a rebuke, feeling Bentley's eyes glaring into her, but instead saw a nod of encouragement from Cruickshank. 'It can't be coincidental. Why don't we raid the club? It is an illegal establishment anyway so we wouldn't need a warrant?'

Cruickshank visibly ruminated over Tait's idea, her head bobbing in time with her obvious thoughts. Eventually her eyes raised and an expression of affirmation morphed onto her stern features. 'Excellent idea Tait. You have whatever you need to make it happen. We will still need to inform the Superintendent. What time do you propose and I'll get it cleared?'

Tait baulked at the question, not having thought the DCI would agree to it and not having thought through the practicalities. Bentley saw her struggling and interjected, obvious annoyance in his voice.

'There's no point going any time before eight, there'll be no one there. You should have a decent crowd about nine. Still plenty of time to arrest and process before the nights out.' He answered, scowling at Tait as he did.

'Nine it is then. Right everyone, the day is still young and we have a ton of evidence still to process. Remember, focus on the things that will help us identify the connections in this. We need to find out who the 'Fallen Angels' are. We need to work out why they are doing this.

Her Moons Denouement Max Hardy

We need to understand the significance of Heather Scott. Now back to it.'

With moans, groans, screeching of chairs being forced back and a general return of related chatter, the Detectives started to leave the Incident Room. Tait stood up to leave, expecting Bentley to follow, but he sat still, attention fully engaged on the notes in front of him again. She sat back down next to him, concerned.

'Are you alright Bentley? You seem worried? Is there something in the files troubling you?'

He let out a long sigh, then leaned back in his chair, putting his hands into the pockets of his stained, hair covered Mac and pulling it tight around him.

'You shouldn't have done it, but thank you for taking the flack on that. Shankers doesn't need an excuse to bollock me at the best of times. That might just have tipped her into kicking me out of the door.'

'First off, I'm the fucking officer in charge, so if my team screw up, I screw up. Secondly, I'm the fucking officer in charge, so I put my team first.' she retorted with an affectionate smile.

'Touché, as the French twat would say. You are learning girl, you are learning. Quickly on some things, not so fast on others. I told you the raid was a bad idea. They will just close ranks and we won't get anything out of them, but give it a go. At least it is a lead and we might figure out if Rebecca Angus fits into this somewhere too.'

'I'm just following my gut on that, I don't mean to belittle your advice, but I think we have to try: and less of the girl, it's Ma'am to you.' she jibed before continuing more seriously. 'You sure you are alright?' she finished as her mobile bleeped in her pocket. She fished it out and scanned a text message as Bentley answered.

Her Moons Denouement Max Hardy

'Just thinking it all through Ma'am, just thinking it all through. What do you want me to do in organising the raid?' he asked. It was Tait's turn to be distracted now as she read the text.

'Is that bugger lugs boyfriend giving you grief again?' he asked instead when she didn't answer his first question.

She looked up with a vacant expression on her face. 'Sorry. Yes. No, don't worry about it. My problem. It's like looking after a petulant kid.' she answered, still distracted as she turned her back on Bentley while texting a reply.

Bentley's phone buzzed then also. He rummaged around in the pocket of his grubby Mac and pulled it out. It was an old battered Nokia 3330, grey with a small green screen, the words 'New Text' displayed. He clicked on the 'Messages' menu, a puzzled look crossing his features as he saw the message line with no phone number next to it. He clicked on the message and opened it.

All colour drained from his already pallid face and almost instantly beads of cold sweat popped out of his brow, sidling down his forehead. His top lip started to quiver in tandem with the hand holding the phone, the words on it shaking to a point where they were almost unreadable. Almost.

There were only two words: 'We Know.'

Chapter 16

Jacob and Sarah, Sarah and Jacob. Their images are just swirling around my mind. Snapshots of moments, different times, some good, some bad, but all with eyes that are accusing. I know it is my own guilt. Now I know that Jessica is Madame Evangeline, they are reminding my mind, they are screaming in my mind. It's not just the guilt of knowing I have killed them. It's the guilt of knowing that I have thought of just about nothing else other than Jess and they have been on the periphery for the last two weeks. I'd like to think that it is because the pain of losing them is so great that my mind is distracting me from thinking about them. I'd like to think that. But I know it is not true. The reality is I felt more pain in losing Jess, I feel pain still at the thought she is still alive. My mind just wants to know why. No, sorry, my mind *needs* to know why. They are still on the periphery, accusing me.

I knock on a nondescript black door up a side street in Leith, the entrance to 'Sodom and Gomorrah'. A small hatch opens about head height and a guttural voice from an unshaven mouth asks 'Card'. I pass it through the hatch and after a second the door is opened. A rotund black suited man looks me up and down, taking in the leather trousers, white t-shirt and leather jacket I am wearing. I must pass muster as he steps to one side and lets me past. Behind the door there is a coat rack and in front a corridor about five metres long with another nondescript black door at the end. There is a small opaque pane of glass in it at about head height, strobe flashing through it. I

Her Moons Denouement   **Max Hardy**

approach the door, an audible bass vibrating the handle as I open it, the full crescendo of a disco tune battering my eardrums as I enter the club.

Dry ice floats thickly around the floor, diminishing in intensity the further up in height but still blurring the large room. Apart from the strobe flashing, all other lighting is very subdued, almost non-existent, only the outline of things and people visible as my eyes adjust.

Then my eyes adjust. It is just as Rebecca described it. Goth Disco. Naked people everywhere, in every conceivable state of copulation. Why the hell haven't they closed this place down? I walk through the writhing bodies, paying them little attention. I know where I have to go, to the booths out the back, past the bar. A woman, petite, blonde and naked approaches me. I avoid eye contact, but that doesn't stop her throwing her arms around my neck.

'Darling, long time no see, how have you been!' she slurs, obviously drunk as she forces her pert breasts into my chest. I take a step back, gently grabbing her hand from my neck and firmly directing her back off me.

'Sorry, I think you have the wrong person.' I answer, pirouetting around her, leaving her standing, confused.

'Wrong person? Sorry. Could have sworn you were Adam.' I hear her mumble after me as I step through the curtain into another dimply lit corridor, curtained entrances down the right hand side, neon numbers above each. Why would she think she recognises me? Is this somewhere my doppelganger frequents. Is he called Adam? Adam and Evangeline. Adam and Eve. Forbidden Fruit. A Serpent and temptation. What the hell has she tempted me into now?

I stop dead, looking down the corridor at the number eight, at the distinct tones of black and darkness brought to life by the glow of the neon. I panic. Jesus John, what are you doing? Have you even

Her Moons Denouement   Max Hardy

thought that this is another trap, another temptation? Have you thought of anything practical, such as what you are going to say to a dead woman who has been haunting you for the past two weeks? Have you? Or are you just bothered about why me? Poor me, why did you do it to me? Why?

There's a bigger picture here John, a much bigger picture and you aren't seeing it. You aren't letting yourself see it. No I'm not, because the woman I loved -no love-, the woman I thought was dead is behind that curtain. The most important thing now is to talk to her. The most important thing now is to try and understand. Get a grip John.

Anxiety eats away at my stomach causing it to churn while approaching the curtain, the sound louder than the dulling beat of disco as I stop in front of it and take a long, deep breath, trying hard to regulate my breathing, to calm my fractured mind.

I pull the curtain back and step into a small space with a red faux suede chaise lounge sitting in front of a glass window looking into a small room, the whole floor of it taken up by a bed. A bed with a woman in a black leather catsuit sitting on it in the lotus position, legs crossed, hands resting on the knees palm up. A woman with red hair, her head tilted down slightly, obscuring her face from my line of vision.

'Jess?' I question timorously, my voice breaking on the 'ss', sounding sibilant. I walk around the chaise lounge and sit down on it, now at the same height as the woman. I am able to see more of her face. Her eyes are open, her emerald eyes, looking down at a point on the bed in front of her. Her face is heavily made up, a thick coat of foundation, very dark mascara and shining cherry lipstick. Her lips move.

'The first time I saw her was on that Chaise Lounge. I was masturbating, watching two women on this bed pleasuring themselves. She pulled the curtain back, stuck her head in the room and watched me play with myself in the windows reflection. Then she

Her Moons Denouement   Max Hardy

came in and pleasured me and in that moment, my life changed forever.'

Her head rises, contours and angles of her features morphing as they move through the shadows and she looks so much like Jess, but I see slightly sunken cheeks, echoes of scarring under the makeup and as I look down at her upturned palms, the ravages of her self harm are all too evident. Rebecca Angus. Anxiety washes away, to be replaced by crushing disappointment married to instant curiosity.

'Put your palm on the window John.' she instructs, staring straight at me now, warmth and compassion flowing from her sparkling green eyes. She looks so alive and vibrant as she leans forward and puts her hand against the window. I do too, my shaking digits matching up with hers. She looks at the plasters on my injuries, head tilting to see.

'Together, we wear the scars of her love, for all the world to see. What they don't see are the scars in the mind. What they don't see is the torment. What they don't see is the dichotomy. She took us both to a place where we lost everything, where the only way to cope with the utter devastation is death itself: yet we still love her.'

My lips quiver, emotion welling up from deep inside, devastating pain I have kept buried, knowing I can't cope with it. Her words, simple words, resonate through my whole being. She knows exactly how I feel. She knows exactly how I feel because she has been there too. Tears flow from my eyes, snot from my nose and I cry, uncontrollably.

Rebecca is crying too. She uncrosses her legs and moves closer to the window, pushing both hands hard against it. I fall to the floor and do the same, clawing at the glass to try and hold them, to touch her, to physically share the grief.

'I need to understand why she did it. I need to look her in the eyes and understand why. I hoped she was alive, I thought you were her. I thought that I would be asking her those questions right now. But I

Her Moons Denouement Max Hardy

guess all those times I thought I had seen her, it has been you? It was you at the hotel this afternoon, it was you in Jacob's bedroom yesterday and it was you in the crowd in Newcastle. All you?'

'All me. But don't for one second think that means she isn't alive. Don't for one second think that while I have been watching you, she hasn't been watching you too. That she hasn't been watching both of us. That they haven't been watching both of us.'

'They?'

'I know him as Ben Hanlon. You know him as Rob Adams, or perhaps the 'Unknown Caller', or possibly your twin brother?'

'How do you know that, about the twin brother thing, that's not been on the news? I only found that out yesterday.'

'I've been inside your house, I've read all the evidence on your studio walls. I've seen all the tapes you have, of the time I spent with Ben Hanlon. You even have the white mobile she gave to me. Why didn't you hand those things over to the police? Why didn't you tell them about the tapes he made?'

I take a hand off the window and wipe the snot and tears from my eyes with my t-shirt, quickly returning it to partner hers, not wanting even the illusion of contact to be broken. Do I tell her why? Can I trust her? I don't really know who the hell she is, as much as we share a common pain. Am I letting emotion overwhelm my judgement again?

'You don't have to tell me John, it's not important. I realise it may be hard for you to trust me, after all, I am still officially a murderer and a fruitcake on the run from the police. I could still even be Madame Evangeline.'

My face must look guilty as hell right now. How did she know that was what I was thinking? I know she isn't Madame Evangeline.

Her Moons Denouement   Max Hardy

'I know you aren't Madame Evangeline. I have seen all of the tapes Hanlon recorded. I have seen what you went through. I know that you were played. The same way I was being played. This is personal. I don't know why it's personal and I believe that the police won't fully investigate the things I have seen because of that. They have no reason to. At the moment, they think she is dead. There is no official record on any system, anywhere of a Ben Hanlon or a Rob Adams as we knew them. To the rest of the world, they never existed. It's down to me to find out why.'

'Down to us. I'm in the same position John. I have no idea why she turned me into this person you see in front of you: a Madame, a dominatrix. I have no idea why she made me fuck my son. I have no idea why Ben Hanlon led me on a road to redemption, why he took the time to bring me back from the brink. I want to know, I really want to know. More than that, I want to know why they are still watching us, why they are still playing us.'

'What do you mean, still playing us?'

She doesn't answer, but moves her left hand off the glass slightly, leaving a finger touching, which snakes down the glass, tracing a line on the reflection of my forearm. She circles at a point and then stops it.

'Press the flesh of your arm about there.' she instructs.

Bemused, I do as she asks, pulling up my jacket sleeve and pressing my thumb into the soft of the flesh.

'Can you feel anything? It will feel like a small lump, gristly with a bit of give.'

I can. I push it around slightly to see if it is just a caught nerve, but it moves with my thumb.

Her Moons Denouement Max Hardy

'I have one too. I found one in my arm a few weeks ago, just after Ben left, just as I was deciding whether to give myself up or try and find out who he was, just as I was self-harming, again. I didn't know what it was at first, but I had it checked out. It is how they know where we are. It's a tracker.'

How? How the fuck have they managed to get that inside me. I stare at the imperceptible lump with incredulity. My mind reels, literally, images of moments start to flash through rickety doors, of sterile white rooms, of metal beds with crisp cotton sheets, of sharp needles, of white wimples. Through the images I hear screams. Rickety doors start to crack. Of injections, of incisions. Thumping of running footsteps join the screams which are getting louder, people rushing past outside the curtain. Of pain, of excruciating pain.

Someone yanks back the curtain forcefully. I turn, surprised to see Bentley rushing into the room, Tait just behind him, both of them wearing Tactical Response Vests. They both stop suddenly, equally as surprised at seeing Rebecca and I in the room.

'Don't move, this is a raid.'

Chapter 17

'Shit that's her. That's Rebecca Angus!' Bentley shouted, striding toward the window as Rebecca smiled from behind it, blowing a kiss towards him as she started to retreat out of the room.

'Get around the back and stop her getting away!' Tait ordered, Bentley caught in two minds for a second, one part ready to thump the glass, the other to thump Saul. Instead he fronted up to Saul who was standing and putting his hands in the air.

Bentley thrust his head into Saul's face, noses a millimetre apart, spittle forming on his angry lips. 'Red hair, leather catsuit, S&M Club. Rebecca Angus. Now try telling me she is not fucking Madame Evangeline!' he spat vehemently.

'Bentley, this isn't the time for a pissing contest, she is getting away. Now get after her.' Tait screamed the order, grabbing Bentley's arm, yanking him away from Saul.

'I should punch your fucking lights out right now.' Bentley finished, Saul standing calmly and taking the abuse. 'Stuck up cunt!' he finished as Saul refused to react.

He turned and ran from the room, shaking Tait's hand off his arm, shouting at her as he did, 'I'm going, you just make sure you cuff this fuck.'

Tait approached Saul, her demeanour forceful, her tone stern. 'Turn and face the window Sir and put both hands on your head. You have some serious explaining to do.'

Saul did as instructed and Tait took one hand after another from his head and handcuffed him behind his back. She grabbed the cuffed hands and pulled him unceremoniously forward, pointing him towards the entrance to the room.

'Fairly easy to explain. I take it you are raiding the place to try and find out if there is anyone here who knows about the 'Fallen Angels'. It's a good shout. Elvis Aarons worked here, you have connection with Madame Evangeline. By the way, Bentley is so wrong about that. Rebecca is not Madame Evangeline.'

It was chaos in the corridor. Naked people were being chased by police, some had been caught and were either forced against walls being restrained, or pinned to the ground. Screaming and shouting permeated the confined space. Tait walked Saul through the terrified clientele, into the main room, where the vista continued, couples being decoupled from copulation by embarrassed police officers, blankets being handed out to those already restrained. More still being chased. She joined a procession of Officers leading those already captured out of the club and into waiting police vans in the alleyway.

'Whether she is or she isn't is not the important thing at the moment Saul. Why you were here meeting her is much more important given that she could be a prime suspect in our case. Now, get in the car, I'm sure Cruickshank will want to talk to you personally.' Tait opened the rear door on the car and forced Saul's head down over, pushing him into the back seat.

Tait turned and looked up and down the alley, through the multitude of flashing lights, through the myriad of police officers trying to force protesting, blanketed people into the vans, to try and see Bentley. She cursed under her breath, not seeing him anywhere.

'Good work everyone.' she said to the officers who were starting to gather around the vans as they deposited their suspects. 'Now, let's start getting them back to the station and get them processed and questioned. There are ten interview rooms and a dozen detectives ready and waiting for us. Campbell, make sure you lock down the club as soon as everyone is out and leave a team here until forensics are finished. They should be here any time soon.'

The officers started to disperse, jumping into the full vans and heading off to the station. Tait scanned the alleyway again, then saw Bentley struggle around the corner at the far end, bent double, holding his chest. She ran towards him quickly, concern screaming across her face.

'Bentley, are you alright? Did you get her?'

She reached him and helped him to stand, his face ruddy and sweating, his body shaking in the aftermath of exertion. He was panting heavily, not able to gain his breath and certainly not able to speak. He shook his head vigorously, waving a hand back around the corner and tried to string a few words together.

'G.t .w.y. She .ot .way!'

'She got away?' Tait repeated.

Bentley nodded. 'B.tch g.t away. T.o f.st f.r me.'

'Fuck!' she shouted, her expression crestfallen. 'Shankers isn't going to like that. She is going to want someone's balls. Come on, let's get back to the station and I'll give her the good news.'

Tait supported Bentley back to the car slowly and helped him into the passenger seat. She climbed in and gunned the engine then reversed the car out onto Baltic Street and headed off towards the centre of Leith in the direction of the Headquarters.

'Take deep breaths and just relax. Open the window and let some cool air onto your face.'

Bentley did as instructed, head back against the neck rest, taking deep gulps of the Edinburgh air, looking out of the window, watching the evening wear darkness well, searching every doorway, every side street, every window for a black cat suit clad woman.

'Sorry Tait, she was just too fast for me.'

'I thought we had positioned officers at the back door to stop anyone getting out.'

'We did. She just slammed the door into them, knocking them down and legged it. She was out of sight in a minute, over a fence and down a backstreet and when I got there, she was gone.'

'It's not your fault. I should have gone after her. High speed pursuits for an old fart like you are well and truly over.' she replied with strained humour.

'No, if I hadn't butted horns with fuckface back there, I would have had time. It's me who has let you down, again. Has he said anything?'

'Only that Rebecca is not Madame Evangeline.' She saw Bentley try and turn in his seat, anger bleeding into his already ruddy face. She slapped an arm over his chest and pushed him back into the seat. 'Leave it Bentley. Let's do this by the book. Don't let me down again.' She instructed, her eyes throwing daggers at him. He relaxed back into the seat.

'Right, can I trust you to check him in and bring him up to Shankers office? She will want a word before we officially question him.'

Her Moons Denouement   Max Hardy

'You can trust me.' Bentley answered as they pulled into the Headquarters car park. Tait and Bentley got out of the car in tandem, Tait proceeding to open the door for Saul.

'Right Saul, Bentley is going to check you in and then Cruickshank will want a word. I'll see you there in a few minutes.' she said, pushing him forward towards the building as he stood. Bentley grabbed the cuffs as Tait headed off in front of them.

Bentley slowed his walk, waiting for her to get out of earshot, then twisted Saul's cuffs until he grimaced in pain. He walked close in to Saul's back, and put his head right up to Saul's ear.

'What do you know Saul? What do you know about me?' Bentley hissed into his ear, pushing him forward towards the entrance of the building. Around them, other officers were also leading those arrested at the club from the vans into the headquarters.

Saul looked perplexed in amongst the pain of the tightened cuffs. 'I know that you are a bigoted, bullying twat with no real comprehension of proper police procedure if that's what you mean?' he answered, smarting as the cuffs tightened again.

'That's what I mean, that's exactly what I mean.' Bentley said, his words sounding empty and deflated as he loosened his grip on the cuffs, stepped back from Saul slightly and directed him into the building, towards the Duty Sergeant. Towards a long line of people being booked in by the Duty Sergeant. Bentley pushed past them all, right up to the front of the queue.

'Come on Bentley, you know how this works, first come, first serve, back of the queue.'

'Sorry Fred, Shankers wants to see this one straight away. Can you do basic info and I'll bring him back down for full processing.'

Her Moons Denouement   Max Hardy

'As long as you bring him back, I know what you are like.' Sergeant Fred Calvey replied. He took Saul's personal information. Bentley then walked Saul up to Cruickshank's office in silence, his features lined with worry, his head downturned and his body slouching as he shuffled behind.

Cruickshank's office door was open as they approached. The sound of raised voices echoing down the corridor.

'It just isn't good enough Tait, do you hear me. I would hate to think his incompetence is rubbing off on you!'

Bentley pushed Saul into the office, a spark of fire entering his tired eyes as he saw Tait looking small and vulnerable under Cruickshank's verbal onslaught.

'I don't know what she has told you Ma'am, but it was my fault that we lost Rebecca Angus, not Tait's. If you want to have anyone's bollocks, then have mine. They'll go nicely with your own.'

'Nice try Bentley, but Tait was in charge of the operation, Tait was accountable for ensuring that the correct resource was doing the correct job, so Tait is accountable for any bloody cock ups. Trying to antagonise me doesn't help her either. It just shows me she has no control over you. It shows me that perhaps she doesn't have what it takes to make it as a DS. Now, can we stop washing our dirty laundry in public and see why the hell DI Saul here was at the club!' Cruickshank finished angrily.

'Sorry Ma'am.' Both Tait and Bentley said in unison, both of them sitting down, Bentley directing Saul to sit as well.

'Well Saul, what do you have to say for yourself? Bear in mind our very last conversation. I thought that I was very clear about not wanting to see you anywhere near our investigation and here you are right in the thick of it talking to an escaped criminal, someone who could be our prime suspect.'

Saul sat calmly in his chair and looked Cruickshank directly in the eyes, holding her infuriated glare.

'Sorry Ma'am, as I told you earlier, I am just trying to find out what happened to my life. I went to the club because it was somewhere that I knew Jess...Madame Evangeline had been. I wanted to find out if anyone knew anything about her. I was searching the rooms and came across a woman who looked like Jess. It was Rebecca Angus.

'And you expect me to believe that do you, that you were both in the same place at the same time? Bullshit, you are going to have to come up with something eminently more plausible if you don't want me to charge with you with obstructing an investigation at least, being complicit in the whole thing at worst.'

Saul said nothing for a moment, just held Cruickshanks unwavering, challenging glare. In the silence running footsteps grew in velocity from the corridor, the slapping feet getting closer to the office until PC Campbell came running in, slightly out of breath.

'Ma'am. Sorry for interrupting but we need you urgently.' he puffed.

'What is it Campbell, you better have a bloody good reason for interrupting.'

'I think you want to know about this Ma'am. It's the people we have arrested.'

'Yes, the lowlife scum who frequent illegal sex clubs, what about them.'

'Well Ma'am, that's just it. They aren't lowlife scum. There are seven politicians, three gentry and another ten high profile business people in amongst those we arrested. There's an army of first class lawyers just about to descend on us.'

Chapter 18

Moonbeams stream in through the open window, teasing the darkness, scaring it to scurry away from the sullen light. I watch the shadows crease and fold, shifting with the movement of clouds in front of the moon, with the movement of the netting at the windows swaying in the breeze. All of these things inspiring the darkness to live, to have form, shape and substance, showing me glimpses of the time Jess and I spent in the room. My thoughts live in those folding shadows, mostly dark, sometimes grey and occasionally light.

A beam strays towards the Edwardian chair I sit in, rolling shadows over the table top in front of me, chasing them past the open whisky decanter and the dishevelled pile of notes to pause for a second on the revolver beside them, before being absorbed by the darkness once more.

A noise from outside the window distracts my mind from painting with shadows. A larger shadow, a head, blocks out some of the moon and then a body climbs over the sill and strides silently over the floor towards me.

I pick up the decanter and pour a shot of whiskey into an empty, waiting glass and place it opposite me, where the curvaceous slice of darkness sits down, her face enlivened in a moonbeam.

'They let you out then?' Rebecca asks as she picks up the glass and takes a sip of whiskey.

Her Moons Denouement   Max Hardy

'Eventually. Although there was a lot of waiting around while everyone was being processed. The DCI isn't stupid. I told her in the end that I had been left a card asking me to meet someone at the club. I gave it to her and then got summarily bollocked for withholding evidence. She believes that I didn't know it was you. I didn't tell her what we talked about. I said as soon as I got there, they arrived. I think she believes that.'

'Did you hear anything on the grapevine or in the cells about Madame Evangeline or the Fallen Angels?'

'No. The police have you tagged as possibly being Madame Evangeline. It didn't help that you were there while they were looking for her.'

'I don't think that will ever stop until they see us in the same room together.' She tilts her head. 'Even for you?'

There she goes again, reading every thought flowing through my mind. I'm back in a world where there is what I know and what I feel and at the moment both are dancing in the shadows, trying to avoid the light. She picks up the gun from the table as she waits for me to answer and watches me weigh her up.

'I've watched all the video's Dr Hanlon made. Everything I saw in them tells me you are not Madame Evangeline. In the earlier ones, he had to talk long and hard to convince you not to try and kill yourself, to bring you back from the brink. You are here, sitting in front of me now. How did he do it? How did he convince you to want to live, to not let the darkness consume you?'

She raises the gun to her eyeline and pops the barrel, taking out the single bullet and holding it up in front of me.

'He walked me through everything that had happened. He made me confront my fears. He put a weapon in the hands of a psychopath and gave me the choice either to use it, or to walk with him on a journey of redemption. He made it absolutely crystal clear that if I chose to use it, it wouldn't trouble him in the slightest. And I believed him when he said that.'

She puts the bullet back in the gun, spins the barrel and instantly smacks her hand on it to stop it, then holds it out to me.

'Tell me the worst thing that has happened to you. Tell me how it made you feel and I will tell you if I think it is worth a shot.'

I stare at the gun in front of me and stare up into her wide challenging green eyes, my mind in turmoil. What is she doing? Tempting me? Testing me? Teasing me? Or trying to help me? The worst thing? How do you quantify what is worst: losing your son, your wife or your lover? It is all the worst. I take the gun from her and run my fingers along the barrel, thinking. A tear springs to my eye as I speak.

'Betraying my wife and son. The worst thing that has happened to me is betraying them and watching them die at my hand. With the seconds counting down to their inevitable destruction, knowing that it was me who had put them both in that position, knowing that it was me who killed them. It made me feel like a murderer, like a monster, like I should be dead.'

I thrust the gun into my forehead and pull the trigger.

Click.

Sixteenth time, chance is still with me.

She looks at me impassively, studying my features.

'You didn't blink. You didn't think for one second what the impact of blowing your brains out in front of me would be. Neither did you wait for me to tell you if I thought it was worth dying for.'

Her Moons Denouement   Max Hardy

'Was it?'

'Yes it was, but I don't think it was the worst thing that has ever happened to you.'

She reaches over and takes the gun out of my hand, not taking her probing eyes off mine.

'I fucked my own son and at the time it was happening, I absolutely loved it. I sat astride him, taking the full length of his throbbing cock into my tight wet cunt and it was sheer ecstasy. He was the first man I had ever had and it was heaven. Then Madame Evangeline took off his mask and showed me who he was and my world exploded. In that second, in that instant I felt like scum, like a maggot, like the scourge of the earth and I wanted to be eradicated from all existence. I didn't just want to die, I wanted that whole experience to be wiped from the whole of eternity. Is that worth a shot?'

Tears stream down her cheeks, the heavy make up running in rivulets, exposing the scarred face below. I can't even comprehend what that must be like, to find that you had done that, to know that you had enjoyed it. I nod my head.

She puts the barrel of the gun into her mouth, sucking it in with her lips, watching me intently as she pulls the trigger.

Click. She didn't blink either. Seventeen.

Is this chicken? Is she testing me? Trying to show me that whatever might have happened to me, she has had it worse and is still alive? She's right, I didn't think about her. I'm not thinking about anyone but myself. I haven't been for a long time, a very long time.

'I betrayed my wife, the woman I had loved since we were at Uni. The woman who I had given my solemn oath to be faithful too. I did that because I couldn't cope with her agony, her guilt. I've only just found out that years ago she was pregnant and had an abortion late in the

Her Moons Denouement   Max Hardy

pregnancy. She lost her innocence, her youth, her baby and the man she loved. And I wasn't the person that she could talk to about any of that. I wasn't the person who she could talk to about how that impacted our son and our marriage. I am a coward. Too wrapped up in my own world and in my own problems to help the one person in the world that needed my help.'

My body is shaking, not at the thought of the gun to my head, but at the thought of the impact my actions have had on others. Rebecca is looking at me with open empathy as she hands me back the gun, nodding.

I put it to my forehead again and pull the trigger.

Click. Eighteen.

'Hannah was my childhood sweetheart. We had been going out since school, since Purple Rain in 1984. She was pregnant with Michael and we were having a home birth. There were complications and I decided to take her to hospital in the car. We crashed, it was my fault. She was bleeding but in the last stages of labour and it was a choice of either saving Hannah or saving the baby. I chose the baby and she died in my arms, with my wonderful baby boy screaming as we cuddled him. The same boy I fucked and killed years later. She made the ultimate sacrifice and I promised her I would look after him. I betrayed her.'

My stomach sinks. I had heard the full story on Dr Hanlon's tapes, but it made it no less wrenching, even more so as she sits crying in the shadowed moonlight. I hand her the gun, worried.

'I have to say yes, but I have to say stop. Too many people have died because of us. I don't want you to be the next.'

'Not your choice. If you think yes, I take a shot. Simple as that.' she says through tears.

'Yes.' I answer, honestly, passing the gun back to her.

Her Moons Denouement　　　　　　　　　　　　　　　　Max Hardy

'She puts it under her chin this time, caressing her jawbone with the barrel before pulling the trigger.

Click. Nineteen.

'I wanted Jacob to die. I wanted to help him die. I kidded myself that it was for him. All I saw in his eyes was the emptiness of forever and I just thought that death had to be better than the non life that he had. But it wasn't about Jacob. It was about me again. It was about me not being able to cope with a son who had a empty, endless life. It was my fears that I was trying to end, my fears of loneliness, my fears of rejection, my fears of an empty life. I didn't want that for him. But I didn't want it for me.'

She passes me the gun and strokes my hand as I take it from her and put it to my forehead.

'Thirty three and a third percent chance that I will die now.'

'So pessimistic, that's a sixty six point seven percent chance you will live.'

I pull the trigger.

Click. Twenty. Fifty/fifty chance now.

'I never knew who my parents were. I was told they abandoned me when I was born. I vaguely recall being a very sick child, spending lots of time in hospital. After that I remember lots of foster homes, lots of transient families who never really opened up and let me in, just took the money and interacted as little as possible. Even friendships were hard because I was always the new girl. Always having to start from scratch. Always having to learn to trust people again. Always fearing I would be leaving again very soon. The worst thing, the very worst thing that has ever happened in my life is never knowing who my parents were and never knowing the love and warmth of their hearts. I have always been alone.'

Her Moons Denouement　　　　　　　　　　　　　Max Hardy

Tears stream down my face in time with hers as I feel her agony, feel the anguish infused in every single painful word. I feel it because I know it. Rickety door in rickety rooms burst open and the floodgates of my fears are breached. I hand her the gun.

'I don't know why we are here, I don't know why she has involved us in her life, but if I had anything to do with your pain, I am truly sorry.' she says as she puts the gun straight to her forehead and pulls the trigger.

Click. Twenty one.

Not even a fifty/fifty chance now. Chance has run out just at the right time. I speak.

'I never knew who my parents were. I don't know what happened to them. For a long time I didn't even know what a parent was. I was a very poorly child and spent the first six years of my life in an isolation room, shut away from everyone apart from doctors and nurses. I remember every single day, every single pain, every single injection and extraction from the marrow in my bones. I remember the emptiness, the mind numbing emptiness. To this day I have no idea what was wrong with me, I just remember the agony.'

Rebecca leans over the table and puts the gun into my hand, tears freely flowing down her makeup stained face. She lifts my hand to my forehead and then leans her head right in next to mine, in line with the trajectory of the gun.

'After that I remember lots of foster homes and lots of transient families. I learnt what I thought a parent was meant to be from them, and I learnt to fear what a parent was. I learnt that even in a world of people, you are always alone. I didn't want that for Jacob. That isolation, that emptiness. The worst thing, the very worst thing about my life is not ever knowing what a parent was, and living my life trying to find out. I have always been alone, I have always been a loner. And

Her Moons Denouement Max Hardy

that has made me selfish and conceited, insular and heartless. The world will be a better place without me.'

I feel Rebecca shaking, from the emotion that is wracking us both, but also with her final affirmation.

I pull the trigger.

Chapter 19

The gun clicked for the seventh time and Saul sat bolt upright instantly, his sobbing subsumed into surprise, making his breath catch as he stared at the quivering hand holding it. Rebecca reached down and tenderly cupped the hand, steadying it as she took the gun off him. She flipped the barrel open and slipped the single bullet out, placing it in a talon of moonlight on the table between them.

'I don't understand. The bullet was in there. Why didn't it fire?' Saul asked, his eyes bewildered and questioning, staring at Rebecca's shadowed, weeping features.

'I guess in the hardest of times, when we are so absolutely alone, when we feel there is no one and nothing that can comprehend the way we feel, and we feel nothing at all can help us, that's the time we need an Angel. I don't know why he did it, but Ben Hanlon was mine. The main reason I am alive today is not because I want to find out why this is happening, it is that he asked me to look after someone.' Rebecca answered obscurely.

'He asked you to look after me?'

Rebecca cocked the trigger on the revolver and scratched the head of it with one of her cherry painted nails. 'Indirectly, yes. You were never going to blow your brains out with this revolver. I filed the trigger head down on the very first night I saw you thinking about using it.'

Her Moons Denouement   Max Hardy

Saul took the gun off her and scraped more of the back paint off the trigger, then slowly released it and watched down the barrel to see where it connected. He laughed and snorted a glob of snot from his nostril in the process which joined the tears trickling down his lips.

'So, you've been watching over me. Does that make you my guardian angel: No, a Fallen Angel? Outside of the law, outside of society, a criminal in many people's eyes with a different moral outlook. Yet still you try and help. Is that what they are doing to us Rebecca? Turning us into Fallen Angels?'

'I don't know. Until yesterday I had never even heard of the term. It was certainly not something either Madame Evangeline or Ben Hanlon mentioned to me. What I do know is that as much as she hurt me, both mentally and physically, she taught me to be strong. She taught me to challenge morality. She taught me to face my insecurities, my fears, my demons and learn to control them. He taught to me have a purpose, even if it is only to get you through the day. He taught me to open my mind to its own darkness. He taught me how to be selfless. None of those things were taught by sitting down with a book and turning to chapter three and reciting wrote. I learnt by living a different way. Perhaps it is what they are doing. Perhaps they aren't playing us. Perhaps they are preparing us.'

'Why us though. What is it about you and I that they are interested in? Are we just the next in a long line they are recruiting into their cause? Or something different. You look remarkably like Madame Evangeline. There seems to be someone out there who looks the spit of me. Are we related in some way, is that what this is all about? Or is that just another tactic they are using to draw us in. They seem to be able to look like anyone they want to, they seem to be able to construct any identity they want to and they seem to be able to disappear at will. It's hard to think why we would be special in that, two orphans with ordinary lives.'

Her Moons Denouement　　　　　　　　　　　　　　**Max Hardy**

Rebecca lifted the decanter and poured them both another whiskey, then reached over to the sideboard and took a couple of tissues from a box on top and proceeded to delicately wipe the wetness from Saul's face.

'I don't think they are questions we can answer tonight. I think the only people who can help us answer those questions are Ben and Evangeline. What we've got to figure out is how we find them. But more important than that, before I leave here tonight, I need to know that we have found a reason for you to want to live.'

Saul raised one of his hands and placed it over the one Rebecca was using to wipe his tears, directing it to his clammy cheek, where he forced it in tight, nuzzling into the flesh of her fingers.

'I have never told anyone about my childhood. I have never known anyone who I thought would understand. I have never met anyone who I thought could help me walk through that pain and face those fears because they have done it too. Until tonight. For the first time ever, at this precise moment, I don't feel a loner.'

Rebecca raised her other hand to his other cheek and stroked it tenderly, then leant over the table and pulled him in close, wrapping her arms around his back and hugged him tightly. He willingly fell into the embrace. They stayed cuddling in silence for more than a minute, just drinking in the essence of each other before Rebecca broke the embrace and sat back, still holding his hand.

'That's a start. A big start. But what about the next step?'

'The next step is taking control. At the minute, someone else is doing that and I am letting them, we are letting them. We've got trackers in our bodies that let them know every move we make. There will be people we are involved with that will definitely be feeding information back to them. They have an agenda, a purpose and they are following it through regardless of the consequence. We need to understand the bigger picture. Why are they exposing these murderers, what is their goal and are we just peripheral, or part of that plan.' Saul's voice was becoming more and more animated, full of energy and vibrancy, full of ferocity. 'I want to live so I can take my life back.'

Rebecca smiled at his fervour, adding simply, 'How do we do that?'

He jumped up from his seat, slapping the light switches on the wall as he turned, brilliant light illuminating the gloom immediately, chasing shadows from every corner of the room.

'Wow.' Rebecca whispered, in awe as she looked at the walls of the room, every single one of them covered in notes, pictures, post it's, documents, pins and strings. 'You have been busy.'

'Busy looking at the wrong thing.' he answered, darting around the room and rearranging artefacts seemingly randomly.

Rebecca stood up and moved to the middle of the room, taking in the display, watching Saul work. 'Did you bring all of this with you?'

'Yep, and added to it over the last twenty four hours. There is only one thing I have been interested in: was Jess Madame Evangeline? That's it. Everything else was unimportant. It was my guilt over the decision I made that was driving that. Primarily, I am here today because I wanted to see how she could have conceivably got out of this room without me knowing. I know that now. I also thought I would be able to talk to her and just ask why.'

'That's still a relevant question.'

'It is, but the bigger question is why us? I've not even looked at that. We have so much evidence from the Hanlon tapes, from your initial case, from what I have found out about the 'Fallen Angels' by being with the police today that we should be able to work out what they are doing. We should be able to find out who and where they are. I've got a Private Detective looking at some evidence on where Jess might have gone to on her trips to Edinburgh.'

'There is something I have too. Something which made me sure in my mind that Ben Hanlon knew Madame Evangeline, or Eve, which was another of her names.'

Saul stopped his frantic rearranging and turned to her in surprise. 'Did you say Eve?'

'Yes, Eve. I have a DVD of Michael and Eve together. Eve being Madame Evangeline. The only way he could have that is if she gave it to him.'

'At the club tonight, a woman mistook me for someone called Adam. Perhaps she didn't mistake me. At the time I thought Adam, Evangeline. Adam and Eve. Temptation, snakes and forbidden fruit. Just reinforces that thought.' he pondered, grabbing a pen and post it and writing the thought down, then slapping it onto the wall below a picture of Jess. 'Do you have the DVD here?'

'Not on me, but where I am staying, yes. When you talk about snakes, what do you mean, the one on her abdomen?' Rebecca asked quizzically.

Saul was back at the walls, moving more of the evidence around. 'Yes, it was the only concrete piece of evidence that I had at the time to say that Jess was Madame Evangeline.' He heard a zipper being opened, stopped and turned.

Rebecca was undoing her cat suit, the leather parting the reveal the swell of her breasts, the scars and scabs of her self harm, her flat, bony stomach and the top of a snake head tattoo just below her belly button.

'One like this?' she asked.

Her Moons Denouement　　　　　　　　　　　　　　　　**Max Hardy**

Shock shot across Saul's face, immediately followed by confusion and trepidation.

Rebecca saw the panic and spoke quickly. 'It doesn't mean that I am Madame Evangeline. It doesn't mean I am Jess. It doesn't mean that I am Eve. It means I have a tattoo the same as hers/theirs. What you need to know is that I have had this tattoo all my life. I don't know when it was done.'

'Sorry, just the shock of seeing it. I know you aren't Jess and I know Jess was Madame Evangeline. It is a big coincidence though. You didn't mention it at all in the Hanlon tapes.'

'No reason to really. I can't even recall mentioning that Madame Evangeline had one.'

'You did, but only in passing, you didn't make a big thing of it. It was at the foot of King Arthur's seat, when you saw Dr Ennis coming off the field. Madame Evangeline was opening her coat, showing you her naked body.'

'Yes, I remember now. God, you've got a good memory.'

'You have no idea. It remembers everything. Did you not think it strange that she had the exact same tattoo?'

'Not really. She presented her tattoo to me as a love token. She said that she liked mine so much, that she had one done exactly the same. Bear in mind she saw it the very first time we met and I hadn't seen her naked at that point. I had no reason to believe any different at the time.'

'That does add some more weight to the theory that you may in some way have connections.' Saul said, noting that down and sticking the post it on the wall under a picture of Jess, drawing an arrow on the wall pointing to Rebecca. His eyes went back to another picture, of

Her Moons Denouement   Max Hardy

the woman in Jacob's room. He picked it off the wall and turned back to Rebecca.'

'So this was you in Jacob's bedroom?' he asked, showing her the picture.

'Yes, that was me. I know you spent a lot of time in there. I went in to angle the blinds so I could see you from the tree house when you were lying on the floor.'

'Ah, thought so.' he said, nodding as he turned back to the wall and started to put the picture back, under other pictures of Rebecca this time. He paused, not turning.

'Why did you take Ian?'

'Sorry, I don't know what you mean.' She answered, confused.

'The small tan teddy, he's called Ian. I saw you pick him up and sniff in his scent. You put him in the right pocket of the coat you were wearing. Why?' he was still facing the wall, looking at the picture.

'Promise me one thing John. Promise me there is enough in your life right now not to want to kill yourself.' Rebecca asked, seriously, her voice full of crackling emotion.

Saul turned around slowly, once again surprised at her tone, his countenance confused once more. 'Right now Rebecca, I have you, and you have given me hope. Right now, I do not want to kill myself. I want to get my life back. Why?'

Rebecca approached him, taking his hand in hers and squeezed them tight. 'The person Ben Hanlon asked me to look after should never be the reason you don't want to kill yourself. That has to be about you. But they should always be the reason you want to stay alive.'

'Rebecca, what are you talking about, that doesn't make sense.'

Her Moons Denouement 　　　　　　　　　　　　　　　　　　**Max Hardy**

'It will. Your son, Jacob. He is alive John, he is alive!'

Chapter 20

Pools of light dotted the still half full car park, illuminating the vehicles as a wave of weary officers exited the police headquarters and made their way slowly back to their cars, beaming headlights of those that had jumped the crowd providing even more light to the late evening/early morning exodus.

'What a day. What a bloody four hours!' Tait exclaimed as she stepped out of the building, holding the door for Bentley.

'Aye, it's been a hectic one. You've done well lass, considering.' Bentley praised grudgingly.

'What, considering I am a girl.' she teased.

He didn't bite. 'Considering how big this fucker already was and how much it's grown in the last four hours. Eighty odd people questioned, a number charged with sexual offences, half of them prominent public figures. This is going to be one huge fucking circus come tomorrow and not one of them has come up with anything even remotely related to the 'Fallen Angels'.'

'Not yet. Its early days on that front. Let them stew in the cells overnight and they will be a bit more willing to talk in the morning.'

They crossed the car park, Bentley heading off to his clapped out Volvo, Tait towards a squad car.'

Her Moons Denouement   Max Hardy

'Look Bentley, I know it can't be easy taking orders off a lower ranking officer, especially a girl, but thanks for not being a dick about it and thanks for your help today. Get a good night's kip and let's regroup in the morning, get some focus on these fucking angels.'

'Those thanks should be the other way around. You've pulled me out of the clarts more times than you should have today and I thank you by jumping straight back into them. You're a good lass, with an incisive mind. Go on, fuck off and give your twat of a boyfriend the same kind of grief you've given me today.'

'Will do. See you in the morning.'

Tait headed off to her car, waving backhanded as she went. Bentley climbed into his, throwing a biscuit from his pocket over the back seats toward Jackson, who caught it in mid-flight. 'Come on lad, let's get home and see what grief is in store for us.' He turned the ignition key but the engine made no sound.

'Fucking great.' He pumped the clutch and then tried again with the same result, absolute silence. 'Bastard car!' he shouted and thumped the steering wheel, knocking the horn which blared across the car park. He popped the bonnet and climbed out, walking around the front of the car.

Tait drove by in the squad car and stopped alongside, opening her window. 'Problems?' she asked.

'If I was a betting man, which I'm not, I'd say flat fucking battery.' He stuck his head under the open bonnet and fiddled with the connectors to the battery, in the end whacking them with his hand. 'Aye, dead as a fucking dodo. Great.'

'Look, jump in here and I'll give you a lift home. I can pick you up in the morning as well.'

'Nah, don't worry, it's miles out your way. I'll just call a taxi.'

Her Moons Denouement   Max Hardy

'Don't be daft, you gave me a lift this morning, time to return the favour. Don't be a stubborn old fart. Girls can drive too you know.'

'Aye, go on then.' he grudgingly answered as he slammed the bonnet shut in frustration. He shouted on Jackson, who jumped over the seats and out of the open front door. Bentley slammed the Volvo door shut as hard and aggressively as the bonnet and then kicked it, shouting 'Pile of crap car.' as he did.

He opened the back door of the squad car and Jackson jumped in, then he climbed into the passenger seat, fastening his seatbelt as Tait pulled away.

'Does he come to work with you every day?' Tait asked conversationally as they pulled out onto the main road.

'Aye, he comes and keeps me company out and about.'

'No one at home to keep an eye on him: and by the way where is home, so I know where I'm going.'

'North Queensferry, off Battery Road. My sister's generally at home, but she's not that fond of him. Father's usually out.'

'No Mrs Bentley?'

'You're a nosy little fucker aren't you!' he exclaimed, frustration in his tone.

'Sorry, I wasn't prying, just making conversation. I am a woman you know, it's our prerogative to instigate idle chit chat. I could just sit quiet for the next ten minutes if you prefer.'

'No, it's me should be sorry lass. Old and cantankerous, that's me. Probably the reason there's no Mrs Bentley. I live in the same house I was born in, with my dad and sister. Sad I know, but that's my life.'

'What do they do?'

Her Moons Denouement — Max Hardy

'Dad's a Presbyterian Minister. Dessi thinks she is Fraulein fucking Maria from the Sound Of Music. She's not a nun, but she likes to think she is. She looks after the house and Father now he is getting older.'

'Must feel strange having all this religious stuff going on with a Priest in the house.'

'Aye it is. St Giles is a Presbyterian Cathedral and dad has held services there in the past. Close to home. What about you, more family than just that twat of a boyfriend?'

The car was heading through South Queensferry and Tait pulled onto the slip road leading to the Forth Road Bridge, the huge suspension span lit up in the early morning darkness.

'There's my brother and my dad. Dad's a copper too, in the force down in Sussex, that's where I'm from originally. Brother's a banker. Don't see either of them much nowadays. I occasionally get an e-mail at work off dad and we get together once a year at Christmas.'

'No mum?'

Tait went quiet for a moment, her expression hardening as she left the bridge and headed off down into North Queensferry. 'Somewhere, don't know where, don't really care. She left us when I was about five. Where do I go now?'

'Just follow the signs for Deep Sea World.'

'Is that the place built on the old quarry?'

'It is. Full of water now, like a big lake. It's where they got the stone to build the bases of the rail bridge.' he said, pointing to the large iron structure that they were approaching. 'Down right now, onto Battery Road.'

Her Moons Denouement   Max Hardy

'I've never been this close to it before, it's huge. What's it like living in the shadow of that monstrosity?'

It was Bentley's turn to pause, looking at the bridge pensively. 'You know, living around it all the time, you don't see it as a monstrosity, you just see it as part of the fabric of your life.' he eventually answered, sagely. 'Pull up that gravel track to the left and drop me off in front of that house.'

Tait parked the car up where he had instructed and looked out of the window at the derelict garden, then up to the dark, foreboding house, noticing one light on in a bedroom window, the shadow of a large torso standing looking out.

'Looks like someone is up waiting for you.'

Bentley looked up to and sighed. 'Aye, you're not the only one who has to explain why they are late. Thanks for the lift. See you in the morning.'

'No problem, I'll pick you up about eight.' Tait answered as Bentley climbed out of the car, letting Jackson out of the back.

Bentley watched her reverse out and then drive away, Jackson heading off into the overgrowth of the garden for a sniff. He turned and looked up at the bedroom as the shadow moved from the window, the light going off.

'It's not the bridge that's the monstrosity I live in the shadow of, it's that bastard.' He mumbled to himself as he headed off up the unkempt garden path and opened the front door.

Pastor Bentley was standing there, his face full of fury, a walking stick raised in his angry hands. He lashed out with it, hitting Bentley across the top of the arm, grabbing his coat and dragging him into the house as he did, using the full force of his large frame. Bentley cowered, and

Her Moons Denouement   **Max Hardy**

hunched his way into the hall as Pastor Bentley slammed the front door closed, locking Jackson outside.

'It's one o'clock in the morning Fenny. No call again Fenny. Your sister made supper especially for you and now it's cold Fenny. It's not good enough boy, not good enough at all. Where have you been? Fucking that tart in the car? Or is that what you would like to do? Are you going to masturbate about her later? You sick, twisted animal. Into that kitchen now.' he fumed as he whacked Bentley across the back while he staggered into the kitchen.

'It's not like that Father, it's not like that at all. You know what my job is like, you used to do it. I don't know when I am going to get home. I told you last night, there is a big case on and we really do need to be worried about it.'

'That doesn't stop you picking up the phone and telling us where you are. That's even more important if you think there is something to worry about. When I was on the job I would always ring one of you and let you know I was going to be late. Now sit down there and eat the tea that Desiderata so lovingly made you. We have a lot to talk about. You have a lot to get done tonight.'

The anger dissipated from Pastor Bentley almost instantaneously as he sat down in the kitchen booth in front of Bentley's tea plate and a notepad, the top page of which was full of notes.

Bentley slid in the other side, still wincing under the pain of the walking stick blows. His head was bowed, not able to look Pastor Bentley directly in the eyes. He took the silver foil off the top of his tea plate, then closed his eyes and said grace automatically.

'I'm sorry Father. I should have called. There is no excuse. I will stay under the stairs tonight as punishment. It is what I deserve.' he grovelled as he started to eat the cold meal in front of him, his face perking up slightly as he took the first mouthful.

Her Moons Denouement

'Delicious, as always. Is Dessie in bed?'

'No, she is dropping off. She left this afternoon and won't be back until tomorrow.'

Bentley's face sank again as he dropped his cutlery, rummaging around in his pocket for his phone. 'Oh shit. We have to call her, we have to bring her back and abort this now Father. Someone knows.'

'It's too late for that Fenny. What do you think someone knows?'

'Because I received an anonymous text message from someone saying just that. Take a look!' Bentley said animatedly as he opened the message and showed it to Pastor Bentley.

'We Know.' Pastor Bentley read out loud. 'That still doesn't answer my question: what do they know?'

'That's not the only thing Father. There was another murderer exposed today. He has killed five women, allegedly, although I know he can't possibly have killed one of them. Sunni Bhalla was on that list.'

Pastor Bentley's expression turned thoughtful, ruminating on the name. 'Sunni Bhalla. Two thousand and four, if I recall correctly.'

'Yes Father. They know we have done something and they know that something involves Sunni Bhalla and Heather Scott. It is far too dangerous for us to do anything else at the moment.'

'I disagree. I think it is far too dangerous for us to stop. She is in another country now. If we don't follow through on this, her boyfriend is going to start asking where she is and if we haven't finished the job, it is more likely that it will come back on us. Have you learnt anything more today about the woman you think might be doing this?'

Her Moons Denouement   Max Hardy

Bentley shook his head dejectedly, looking up beseechingly into his father's eyes, seeing that there was no way his mind was going to be changed.

'We saw Rebecca Angus on a raid we did tonight. She escaped into the Leith area. I don't know how she would know these things but I still think she has a score to settle with me.'

'You leave whoever that is to me. I will watch your back. What I need you to do tonight is finish the job. I have her boyfriend's movements for the last twenty four hours.' Pastor Bentley said, pushing the pad into the middle of the table, so Bentley could see it.

'Between 20:08 and 22:15 tonight he was in Leuchold Woods. It's a well known dogging area. If beating women up wasn't enough of a depravity, he also seems to be a voyeur. He was watching a group of people have sex from a discreet distance, masturbating.' He emphasised the last word, shooting Bentley a disgusted look. 'A few people where passing when his van entered the park and a few more when it left. I am almost positive no one saw him while he was in there. That's where you need to plant the evidence.'

Chapter 21

The man was struggling ineffectually as the two women, one dressed as a Pierrot clown, the other a Choupoao, and old Chinese Hag Clown, dragged him over the varnished oak floorboards into a room furnished as a normal study. He had a coarse grain sack over his head and tied around the neck. His orange Kashaya robe was starting to unravel, exposing the body underneath, which was naked and barefoot. His hands were tied behind his back with barbed wire, the prongs on the wire penetrating the soft flesh of the wrists, drawing droplets of blood.

The Clowns pulled him into the middle of the room and dropped him onto a Persian rug. His legs started to kick out, trying to get leverage and balance as he squirmed, muted groaning and stifled shouts coming from within the sack over his head. The Choupoao leant over and with an animalistic growl, threw a powerful sideswipe with her left fist, connecting with the side of his head, which jarred sharply. He stopped moving.

Pierrot quickly walked to a writing desk at the side of the study and grabbed a role of barbed wire from the top of it. She turned back to the rug, where Choupoao was forcing the Monks legs into a lotus position. Pierrot then started to roll the barbed wire around the legs, pulling it tight to hold them in position. Choupoao then lifted his torso up from the floor, undoing the barbed wire tying his hands, and then tore the robe away from his body, leaving him naked. She then positioned his arms on his restrained knees. Pierrot secured the wrists

Her Moons Denouement   Max Hardy

around the knees then swirled the remainder of the wire around his torso, right up to his neck. She pulled the sack cloth off, revealing a bald, young man, his mouth wide open and filled with an orange rag. His eyes were fluttering, consciousness starting to return. She finished by looping the last of the barb wire around his neck and pulled it as tight as she could, the whole length of it digging further into his naked body, causing obvious pain, enough for him to awake and scream almost silently into the orange rag.

They both pushed him into a sitting lotus position. Pierrot returned to the desk and retrieved a folder from it, passing it to Choupoao and then sat down in a leather bound chair, spinning it to face the back of the Monk. Choupoao walked around in front of him, then sat down cross legged, placing the closed folder on the rug between them.

She placed the palms of her hands together then raised them slightly in time with her head tilting forward until they touched her eyebrows and the tip of her nose.

'Namaste Chodak. Your Karma Mudra would like to speak to you tonight. Although Namaste probably isn't the right greeting at all because that was the last time I will ever bow to you. It is the last time I will ever call you Master Yogi.' she said with vitriol and disdain coursing through the words as she leant over and removed the rag from his mouth.

His face was contorted with agonising confusion. Every time he tried to move, the barbed wire dug deeper into his skin, ripping the flesh. 'Chinnamunda, what is this, why have you done this to me?' he asked, pleading.

She laughed, a wicked laugh, throwing her head back with venom as she answered. 'I now know why you gave me that name. The same name you gave the others. She is the goddess who decapitated herself. Do not plead, do not beg. There will be no forgiveness, only revelation.'

'Chinnamunda, you are confusing me with this aggression, this anger is not like you.'

'How old am I Chodak?' she questioned abruptly, ignoring his statement.

'Another strange behaviour, what is the relevance of your age to this?' he asked her, looking down at his bindings.

'Of the most important relevance. What is my age?' she reiterated firmly.

Pierrot rose from the seat behind him and grabbed the barbed wire around his neck, pulling it tight, causing him to scream. She leant right up to his ear and whispered into it calmly. 'This isn't a debate. This isn't a discussion. Answer the ladies questions, or you will suffer a millennia of hellish torments.'

Chodak froze on hearing those words, the confusion falling from his features, to be replaced quickly by a steely realisation. 'You are forty three.'

'Tell me the age when women display the unlimited manifestation of demons Chodak, tell me which demon is forty three.' Choupoao demanded.

'Thirty nine to forty six years old. You are Garuda Mug.' he answered dispassionately.

'Human beast, you are to be crushed today.' she hissed, gnashing her teeth as him wildly. 'Today I must devour your flesh.' and with her tongue trembling she finished: 'From your body I will make the drink of blood!'

Her Moons Denouement Max Hardy

'You have read the sacred texts I see. Remember your vow of absolute silence to your tantric master. Remember the penalty. If you break your vow, it will be you who will dance with insanity, it will be you who will live a millennia of torments.' he threatened with cold, harsh words.

'The same millennia of torments you have exacted on demons thirty nine to forty two.' she retorted, raising her voice as she picked up the folder in front of her, opening it and taking out the top picture.

'Dawn Evans, aged thirty nine: Dog Snout.' she spat, placing the picture on the floor in front of him.

The picture was of the room they were in, the writing desk and leather chair clearly visible in the background. In the foreground, a transparent plastic sheet covered the Persian rug. Glistening blood, congealing in pools gathering in the folds of the plastic was visible where the head should have been. Where the head should have been was a gaping, open, bleeding stump of a neck, riven strips of skin flopping from where the head had been sawn off. Blood was spattered down the naked body, all the way down to two more gaping holes where her breasts should have been. The white of ribs was visible through the hacked breast tissue that remained. Her two arms spread out slightly from the body, the hands palm up. In each hand was placed, nipple up, the severed breasts. Blood flowed down her chest to her stomach, pooling in her belly button. Past her belly button, her legs had been raised, the feet pushed nearly all the way to her buttocks, the knees forced wide, as near to the floor as was possible without touching it. Her groin was forced in the air, and sticking out from her vagina, which had been ripped by hand to accommodate it, was her bloody, severed head, staring lifelessly out of the photograph.

He said nothing, just looked from the picture up to her, eyes ablaze with tempered fury.

Her Moons Denouement   Max Hardy

'Laura Mason, aged forty: Sucking Gob.' She placed another photograph of a different woman, in exactly the same state beside the first.

'Stephanie Andrews, aged forty one: Jackal Face.' Another photographic atrocity was placed in front of him.

'Gemma Cole, aged forty two: Tiger Gullet.' She placed the last photograph down next to the others, all of the severed heads pointing towards him, their dull lifeless eyes watching him as he looked down upon them.

'All they ever wanted to do was understand Tantra. All they ever wanted to do was explore the divine energies with a yogi who could transform that erotic love into divine power. They all believed in you. They believed in the sacred oath, believed in the power of your gods and look how you rewarded them. They were your mudra and you betrayed each and every one of them, you ruled them with a fear of a millennia of hellish torment if they even whispered a single word about the sacred rites. Sacred rights that are a hypocrisy to the celibacy of monks, a hypocrisy to Buddhism.'

'You are demons, old haggard, menacing and cursing demons that would lead the uninitiated astray. Tantra is not for your kind, yet you would look to sully it with your wickedness, your selfishness. Chinnamunda would rejoice in ridding the world of such grotesques. She would dance on your rotting corpses.' He spat defiantly, flexing his muscles against the barbed wire, gritting his teeth under the pain.

Pierrot tightened the wire once more, leaning close into his ear again. 'Well let's see what the rest of your faith make of that, let's see if they agree with you because later on today, we will be showing each and every one of them the atrocities you have enacted in the name of their religion. The world will see your barbarity.'

Chapter 22

Bentley stared intently at the dust devils riding on the sliver of light shining through the crack of the under stair cupboard door. The sliver came as the morning sun shone through the dirty Fanlight above the front door, affording his dark prison a first glimpse of the new day.

He didn't move, just continued to follow the dancing dust. He listened to the heating pipes of the old house groaning, the main pipes running down the wall behind him on their way back into the cellar. They carried tales from the rooms in the house, tales of people moving, tales of people chatting, tales of people living. This morning they were lifeless apart from the natural creaking of the house as it stretched in the dawn light.

His father thought that locking him under the stairs was a punishment. Bentley had accustomed his mind early in his childhood that it wasn't. The dark confined space with its slat of a bed covered in a worn candlewick blanket was a world of possibility, his imagination using the blackness as a blank canvas to paint out the life tunes that the pipes played to him. He would hear his sister playing with her dolls, his Father reciting sermons, his mother...forgetting that he was in here when 'Uncles' called around.

Still no sound. He knew that Dessie was still away but thought that his father would be around. Then he heard a low growl from just outside the door. It was Jackson in his kennel. The growl turned into a series

Her Moons Denouement   Max Hardy

of broken, timid barks and Bentley raised his head off the blanketed slat, listening for a knock on the front door. Jacksons bark turned menacing just as a loud bang echoed down the hallway, followed by the front door slamming off the wall and urgent voices shouting instructions.

'First two, rooms to the left, second two, the right, third two upper left, fourth two upper right. GO, GO, GO!'

Bentley sat upright and put his ear to the door, listening intently, his face a mask of sheer panic.

'It's his sister we are after, but when you find Bentley, bring the waste of space directly to me. Tait, take that yapping mutt and put it in the back of the car for the moment.' Cruickshank ordered as she walked into the hallway after the main body of police officers.

'This is a throwback to the seventies. My granny's house used to be decorated like this.' Cruickshank continued as she walked down the hallway towards the kitchen, looking into each room as she passed them, watching the officers searching. She turned as she reached the kitchen entrance and paced back towards the front door. 'Too quiet gentlemen, I can't hear you sounding off!' she shouted up the stairs as she passed.

Tait came running back from the car and joined her in the hall.

'Upper left clear!', 'Upper right clear!' came the blaring retorts from upstairs, followed by the same from downstairs, the officers done with searching returning to the hallway.

'No one at all, not even Bentley?' Cruickshank asked, surprised.

'No one Ma'am.' reiterated Sergeant Calvey.

'Take the guys and search the outhouses. Check any basements and double check any cupboards. They shouldn't have been expecting us,

Her Moons Denouement   Max Hardy

but you never can tell. Tait, let forensics know they can come in and begin processing. Get them to start in her bedroom.' she ordered, walking towards the under stairs cupboard as everyone dispersed. She pulled the door open and took a step back in surprise as she saw the cowering, terrified form of Bentley staring back at her from the corner of the cupboard.

'Jesus Bentley, what are you doing in there! Get yourself out now. Were you hiding?' she shouted, her voice raised, more in shock than anger. She took in the small bench and the blanket as Bentley unfurled to his full height and girth as he stepped out of the cupboard, his generally brusque demeanour trying hard to tame the terror in his eyes as he stood and faced Cruickshank.

'I was just changing my boots Ma'am, had Jackson out for a walk and I was getting ready for work when I heard the commotion and didn't know what it was. Thought someone might be breaking in, so I pulled the door shut.'

He didn't look her in the eyes, just stared straight ahead at the wall, pulling his creased, filthy coat into some semblance of straightness on his body.

Tait entered the hallway, followed by Laurent, the Forensic Examiner. He shot Bentley a dismissive snarl and shoulder pushed him as he walked by. Tait looked at Bentley in surprise. 'Where did you come from?'

'I was just putting my boots on.' he answered, almost apologetically as he leant and grabbed Laurent by the scruff of his jacket neck just as he was nearly past, a shot of fire flashing through his otherwise still terrified eyes.

'Sorry Ma'am, I can't let any of you do anything else in this house until I've seen a warrant. I don't even know what you are doing here so I'll

Her Moons Denouement   Max Hardy

be buggered if I'm letting this French twat anywhere near my sister's bedroom.'

'That's a fair point Bentley, but let Laurent go. Laurent, you just stay there for a minute and bite your tongue.' She reached inside her long black raincoat, pulled out a tri folded piece of paper and handed it over to Bentley.

He opened it and read the text, his face falling into obvious worry once more. He handed Cruickshank the letter back. 'Did he examine the evidence?' Bentley asked, nodding towards Laurent.

'No, one of his colleagues did, and I was there watching, just to ensure that no mistakes were made this time. It is conclusive.'

'Go on, go and process the room, but don't make a fucking mess!' he snarled at Laurent.

'Come on Bentley, let's sit down and talk, I'll make us a cup of coffee.' Tait said, taking his shaking arm and leading him off towards the kitchen.

Cruickshank stood back aghast, a look of fury on her face. 'What the hell do you think you are doing Tait! He is a suspect, he doesn't get bloody tea and sympathy!'

Tait was equally as forthright as she stood up to her superior. 'Yes Ma'am he is, but just a suspect. We have no evidence linking him to what we have found and he is still a colleague, albeit one you do not have the time of day for. We have just raided his house and if I were him, I would be shocked and wanting to know what the hell is going on. In the circumstances, I don't think a cup of coffee and an explanation is beyond the realms of decency and it is certainly not something that will jeopardise the investigation.' she finished, staring out Cruickshank, who cracked first.

Her Moons Denouement Max Hardy

'Go on then, make him a bloody cup of coffee. Mine's tea, milk with two sugars while you are at it.' she replied, exasperated, flinging her arms in the air as she followed them into the kitchen.

'Where's the tea and coffee Bentley?' Tait asked as she guided him into the booth.

'First wall cupboard to the left of the sink.' he answered, shuffling up the bench.

Cruickshank sat down opposite him, using her hands to navigate her body along the cushioned bench as her feet didn't quite reach the floor.

'So what did you find?' Bentley asked, playing with his fingers on the table nervously.

'Imam Mann had keepsakes of all his murders. Little pouches made of the clitoral foreskin that he ripped from his victims. Inside the pouches he kept the severed, dried up clitoris. They were in a floor safe we found in the location Perdip directed us to. There wasn't a little pouch for Sunni Bhalla. Instead there was just a small plastic bag with her name on it. Strange, I grant you and certainly something that was planted there. But there were two sets of DNA inside the bag, one Sunni Bhalla's, the other....' She paused as Tait returned to the table and handed out the drinks, sitting down deliberately beside Bentley as she passed him a chipped and stained Celtic Mug.

'See you have one of those at home too.' she said, smiling at him encouragingly.

Cruickshank shook her head disconsolately at the overt support Tait was showing and carried on. 'The other was a fifty percent match to your DNA Bentley. Which tells us it's not your DNA, but one of your siblings. As far as I am aware, you only have one sister, Desiderata Bentley. So that's why we are here, early in the morning, to question her about the disappearance of Sunni Bhalla in 2004. If it were just that, we wouldn't be this heavy handed, but there is also the matter of Heather Scott and your dog's DNA being found as part of that investigation. Where is she Bentley?'

'She's away on a trip. She went over to Ireland for a few days with a friend. She will be back later on today.'

'Dates and times Bentley, we will check it out. Make a note Tait.'

'I don't know exactly, it was an afternoon flight yesterday, about 14:00 from Edinburgh, I think she gets back on the return flight today. It should get in at around 16:00.'

'And the friend?'

'Buggered if I know, someone called Carly I think.'

'What about your Dad, where is he?'

'I'm not sure; he went out before I got up. He could have an early service at the church.'

'Which church would that be?'

'It's over on Pennywell Road, other side of the Forth. Okay, so the evidence might not have been contaminated, but it was most definitely planted. Has it not crossed your mind that someone is out to get me and they are using my family to do that? I am telling you, this has Rebecca Angus stamped all over it. She is a nut job, she is loose, and she is after me.'

'That might very well be true Bentley, and I hope for your sake it is, because the other alternative is that in some way shape or form your family are implicated in the murder of one woman, Heather Scott and the disappearance of another, Sunni Bhalla. Given the other crimes

Her Moons Denouement   **Max Hardy**

these women are being connected to, I have to wonder, in what macabre way could your family be implicated.'

The back door from the garage opened and Sergeant Calvey came into the kitchen, approaching the table.

'The house is clear Ma'am, definitely no one here but Bentley and the dog. One thing you do need to be aware of though Ma'am.'

'What's that?'

'In the garage Ma'am, at the back there is a hidden door that leads down a ladder to a stone room. There is a made up bed and a single chair in there. It was only the disturbed dust on the floor that alerted us to the fact the door was there, it's not easy to see otherwise.'

Cruickshank looked back towards Bentley's haggard features, watching them grimace even more as she took in the news, her face full of questions and disappointment. 'I think you've got some explaining to do my lad, don't you?'

Chapter 23

'He was never in the crate John, never in danger. Hanlon had him at an apartment on the Quayside in Newcastle the whole time. When Featherstone Hall blew up, he was sixty miles away, blissfully sleeping.'

How do you describe a feeling that is at the same time euphoria and desolation? If it were a colour, it would have to be red, vivacious and vibrant, but with hidden menace. If it were a sound, the squeal of a baby pig, loud, raucous and full of excited anticipation, but painful, grating and bone curdling. Euphoria that Jacob is alive, desolation that Sarah died needlessly. All the time knowing it was my choice that killed her. But the euphoria is not just because he is alive. His eyes are no longer the emptiness of forever. They are the eternity of hope as I watch them dilate. As I watch my beautiful son make them dilate.

We are in an apartment on the Royal Mile, in one of the older tall sandstone buildings overlooking Waverley Station and across to Princess Street, to the hotel where I am staying. The second Rebecca told me he was alive last night, I had wanted to come and see him. But she dissuaded me. We had a lot to talk through other than Jacob and we needed to get a plan of action worked out. I think what she really wanted to know was: do I want to live. The Russian roulette had been intense and had opened up old rooms and deep emotions. I was hyper, my mind buzzing with a million thoughts spurred on by the revelations of the day. She was quite right to keep me away for a while longer. Surprisingly I fell asleep at around five in the morning

Her Moons Denouement   Max Hardy

and woke up at around nine with Rebecca cuddled in, her head resting on my chest It's the most sleep I have had in two weeks.

She has changed out of the black leather cat suit and is now wearing pale blue jeans and a white long sleeved vest with a round neck. She has toned down the makeup and is wearing a short blonde wig. Every time I look at her, I see a glimpse of Jess.

'It is incredible, absolutely incredible.' I say to her as I watch his eyes dilate again.

'I think he is excited to see you. Jacob, are you pleased to see Daddy?' Rebecca asks.

His eyes move just once and I smile the broadest smile ever, the corners of my mouth wanting to rip.

'More importantly, were you pleased to see Ian?' I ask, lifting the small tan bear up in front of his eyes. They move just once and I snuggle Ian into the crick of his neck. Then they flick three times quickly.

'There were three flicks there. What does that mean?'

'That means up. I think he wants to sit up a little more. He likes looking out of the window, watching the world. Four flicks means down. That is as far as we have gone: Yes, No, Up and Down. But that is amazing for someone who two weeks ago had never voluntarily moved a single muscle in his body.'

'Sarah would just be so ecstatic, knowing he can do this.' I turn away from Jacob as the words fill me with emotion. I don't want him to see my tears and my anguish as guilt once again overwhelms me.

'John, you need to be stronger than that, not just for Jacob but for yourself. Caving in under a single thought, letting the guilt overwhelm you like that is not going to get anyone anywhere. I know you had a

Her Moons Denouement   Max Hardy

nail rammed through them, but you do still have a pair of bollocks, don't you?'

I haven't known her that long and most of what I do know about her is from the Hanlon tapes, but Rebecca is real and straight to the point. Always. Is that something Madame Evangeline taught her?

'Point taken. Practically, how the hell has a mental patient on the run from the law managed to get a disabled young child up here in a day?'

'Easier than you think when we both have brand new identities and a shit load of money. No one is looking for a middle aged woman trying to get help with her disabled child. It's not out of the ordinary and practically, the ordinary is easy to achieve. However, if anyone sees you here with a disabled child, then that's a different matter. Your face has been all over the news. So practically, we meet at your hotel room and occasionally, when Anka is having time off, you can come and see him. Agreed?'

I answer, grudgingly, knowing she is right. 'Agreed.'

I turn back and watch Jacob as he looks out of the window. 'Why do you think Hanlon left him with you?'

'He kept saying, 'We have let you down.' and I couldn't quite understand why at the time. Looking back, I think he was referring to Gordon Ennis and what he did to Michael. I don't think that was part of their plan. I don't think they expected me to end up in a mental asylum being abused. Don't get me wrong, I don't think he felt guilty, I think he just wanted to give me something back that I had lost: my baby boy.'

'That reminds me, can we have a look at the DVD you have of Michael with Eve?'

She nods and walks towards the TV at the other end of the open plan apartment, switching it on. A still image blurs into life from the black

Her Moons Denouement   Max Hardy

of the screen, an image of Eve, of Jess, of Madame Evangeline: one in the same, another unholy trinity.

'You had it ready?'

'I put it on when you went to the loo. I knew you would want to see it, just to make sure.'

She's right again. I walk up to the screen and stand beside Rebecca, taking in the image.

'It's not that I don't believe you, I just don't trust my own judgement.'

'Bollocks, you were never going to believe it until you saw her with your own eyes. Now, I know you will want to play the video too. I am going to pop to the loo for a minute while you do. Not because I need a piss but because seeing Michael is still raw and quite frankly, I am struggling to grow a pair where he is concerned.'

She squeezes my hand as she slips the remote control into it and then leaves the room.

I press play and watch as the image starts to move and the woman I know as Jessica Seymour starts to speak.

'Hi Mrs Angus, pleased to meet you. I'm Eve. I would like to have met you in the flesh but Michael is a little shy about introducing me, so here I am in the pixels instead. I hope we can meet personally really soon.'

The clip ends. No doubt. The way she slinked up that bed. The way her voice sounded, deep and resonant, going deeper on the 'p's. The features, exactly the same. Not nearly the same, like Rebecca's, but exactly the same. Eve is Jessica. Now we just have to work out how to find them: Adam and Eve.

Her Moons Denouement　　　　　　　　　　　Max Hardy

Rebecca comes back into the room and walks up to me and, taking the remote control, she switches the TV off.

'Well?'

'Not a single doubt in my mind.'

'Good, now what are we going to do?'

'We need to find out where they are. I know you never knew where Madame Evangeline lived, but could you mark up on a map of Edinburgh every place the two of you ever met? We might be able to cross reference those locations and narrow down an area to search in.'

'Yep, I can start that now. Anka won't be back for a few hours yet. What are you going to do?'

'I'm going to chase up Harry Massah and visit the two Fallen Angel suicide crime scenes. I want to visualise what happened there, try and see if I can get any inkling as to where they are going reveal their next killer.'

'You think there will be a next?'

'I'm expecting four. She wiped the paint off a quarter of her face. I'm expecting the police will get another video today and I don't think they are going to be able to stop the TV's and press running with it for much longer so keep the news channels on. Expect to see a lot about the arrests last night too.'

I walk over to the window and kneel in front of Jacob, looking him directly in the eyes. 'Daddy is going for a while but I will be back. Do you understand?' One flick. 'I love you little man.' One flick. I kiss him on the forehead as I stand, walking back towards Rebecca, who I cuddle tightly.

Her Moons Denouement   **Max Hardy**

'Keep in touch anyway, but if you think of anything or find anything when you are jotting down your rendezvous, just call.'

'I will.' she answers and with that, I leave the apartment.

Before the events at Featherstone Hall, if anyone had told me that I would be colluding with an escaped murderer, withholding evidence from the police and to be blunt about it, perverting the course of justice, I would have requested they be sectioned. It's interesting how experience changes your perspective. It's amazing how the smallest thing, the simple dilation of a pupil, can change it all again. Last night, Rebecca made me want to live for myself, to gain back control. Today, that little man has made my heart feel again. I have a purpose now and that is to find out what all of this is about, not just what Jess did to me. I seem to be just a piece in their overall game. Not sure if I'm a pawn, a knight or a king. But I'm going to find out.

I turn out of a narrow cobbled alley onto The Royal Mile, a little restaurant called 'Angels with Bagpipes' directly to my right. Ironic that it is named after a statue of an Angel in the Thistle Chapel over the road. A chapel that is part of St Giles Cathedral. I turn left and look down towards the crown like dome of St Giles Cathedral that rises in the skyline about five hundred metres further down the road. It's only ten o'clock but the Mile is bustling already with tourists of every conceivable nationality heading either past me towards the Castle, or in my direction towards the main Fringe area. I overhear lots of conversations, many people talking about the suicides of the past few days, many people speculating on who the Fallen Angels are. Many more thrust flyers into my hands. A comedian cracking banal one liners, a Shakespeare look-alike spouting sonnets, a Hare Krishna singing 'My Sweet Lord', a Goth just looking mean and moody. I thrust the flyers into my jeans pocket, my mobile ringing at the same time. I pull the phone out and look at the screen. Number withheld. Not Rebecca then.

Her Moons Denouement   Max Hardy

'Hello, John Saul.'

'DI Saul, it's Harry Massah. Is it convenient to talk?'

'Harry, yes. Have you got some good news for me?'

'Getting to be good, most definitely. I have very good CCTV images of Jessica and the other man getting off a train at Waverley and some not so good footage of them leaving the station.'

'That's excellent. Were they picked up, did they catch a taxi, a bus?'

'That's why it's just good and not excellent. From what I can see they walked. I have them on one of the street camera's going onto Princess Street, but then lose them going into a shop.'

'What shop was it? They will probably have cameras. I can go and find out.'

'Already on it, I'll be seeing them in half an hour. How about we catch up for a coffee after that, say about half twelve and I'll show you what I have.'

'You're in Edinburgh!'

'Well, they weren't going to give the CCTV footage to me just because I asked nicely. Sometimes it's only the personal touch that gets you what you need. Twelve thirty? There's a café on the ground floor in Jenners.'

'I'm impressed. Twelve thirty it is.' I answer, hanging up.

I am impressed. It's not often that I've come across a Private Detective who has made me feel like that. The crowd gets thicker approaching St Giles, street performers out in force, encouraging crowd participation. Most of the noise I hear is jovial banter, rising about the general hubbub of conversation and the occasional blast of bagpipes. But in amongst that I hear some more urgent, aggressive shouting.

Her Moons Denouement   **Max Hardy**

My feet and groin are tender from yesterday's exertions, but I gently jump up in the air, trying to see over the dense crowds in front of me. Just outside St Giles I can see a melee of police officers. I see arms being raised, truncheons being wielded, bottles being thrown, vulgarities being screamed. I push through the crowd, apologising as I do, trying to get closer. Words reach me before I arrive, startling my mind.

'Not all like him! What about the bloody paedophiles, what about the fucking Magdalene Nuns. It's one atrocity after the next with you catholic scum and all the Pope and his cronies ever do is cover it up!'

I reach the edge of a line being pushed back by police officers and see through their cordon, to a crowd of Catholics outside the entrance to St Giles holding banners proclaiming 'Jesus Forgives', 'In God we Trust', 'Faith Is Not Fear', 'Suicide is for Sinners' amongst many others. A further line of police officers is attempting to hold back a smaller crowd of....they just look like tourists, yes, they are tourists. They hurl Starbucks Coffee cups, plastic Coke bottles, in fact anything they have to hand over the barrier they are trying to breach, the officers wrestling them to the ground as they rush their line.

'How insensitive can you get? So bloody inappropriate. In the light of what's happened, they are just wrong! It's those Catholics you should be arresting.' a man next to me shouts, barging in to the police officer in front of him.

I quickly look down the police line. He isn't the only one trying to break through. I start to reverse out of the crowd as people behind me push forward, feeling anxious in the crush. I duck between them as they do, seeing the feet of the police line, seeing it being forced backwards. I manage to reach the kerb behind me, the crowd thinning, and push my back against the wall beside a small whiskey shop.

Her Moons Denouement   Max Hardy

It is pandemonium on the Mile. For every tourist trying to get away from the small riot growing strength in the shadow of St Giles, another two are pushing towards it. In the distance I hear sirens blaring. The small contingent of officers start to get overwhelmed and over the frenetic heads of the crowd, I see the catholic banners being ripped to shreds, the poles that hoisted them being used as weapons as I see them thrashing up and down, as I hear the screams of those being beaten.

It's interesting how experience changes your perspective on the world. The world has just changed again.

Chapter 24

Blue lights start to flash and a siren screeches into life as another police van loaded with officers in riot gear heads out of the Headquarters car park, passing an incoming van laden with people arrested at the fracas in front of St Giles Cathedral. Another van is unloading people in front of the Headquarters entrance, Officers leading them into the reception to be processed.

The Duty Sergeant was screaming orders out over the incessant din of the ever growing line of people to be booked in, three other officers helping him with the processing. As well as the new arrivals, there was also a steady stream of those arrested the previous evening at Sodom & Gomorrah leaving. In amongst those arrested, many more police officers were mobilising and getting ready to head out to the centre of Edinburgh.

As most officers were heading towards the exit, a few were heading up the corridor towards the interview rooms, DI's Purves and Gregory following them, deep in conversation. Ahead of them, the door to the Superintendent's office opened and Cruickshank backed out of it, looking flustered.

'Certainly Sir, we'll get on to it right away.' she said, closing the door as she turned into the corridor, seeing the Detectives.

'Right boys and girls, how are the interviews with last night's crowd coming along? We need to finish processing them as quickly as possible. There is a lot of pressure coming down on us to get any relevant information out of them quickly and get them bailed.'

Purves consulted the clipboard in her hand, taking a moment to gather the facts before answering. 'We have ten left to finish interviewing Ma'am. All the rest have been either released without charge or bailed on sexual offences charges. At this point, no one is admitting to knowing Elvis Aarons or Tej Mann, our second suicide, not even with the sweetener of dropping all charges. To a man and woman, they all looked blank when we tried to get anything on the 'Fallen Angels'.'

Cruickshank started striding down the corridor a few feet in front of them, spouting off orders to uniformed officers as she passed them.

'Gilberts, clear the main incident room, Command and Control is going to be initiated very soon and Super wants it ready for Silver Command. Hodgson, have you cascaded the call in's for standby yet?'

'Yes Ma'am, half an hour ago. We have had responses from twenty who are on their way in.'

'Good work. Purves, did forensics find anything at Tej Mann's house?'

'Nothing Ma'am. It was very similar to Elvis Aarons, very sparsely furnished, only a painting on the kitchen wall and a photograph of Imam Mann on the table in Military fatigues, having a drink with the same person who was on the O'Driscoll picture. They are LISF fatigues, the Libyan Islamic fighting Group. We have had nothing back from forensics about the identity of the other man in these two pictures.'

Cruickshank threw her arms into the air in exasperation not turning to the Inspectors or breaking her stride as she spoke. 'Bloody great. I'm sure you have impressed the urgency of this to them?'

'Yes Ma'am.'

'Gregory, have you passed all of your notes from the Scott and Bhalla investigations on to Tait? I need you focusing on finding out who the hell these 'Fallen Angels' are now.'

'Yes Ma'am. She has all the notes and is prepping her interview questions for Bentley.'

'Good. Did you find any religious link between the two of them?'

'No link whatsoever. Bhalla is a Muslim and Scott was christened a Methodist although she wasn't practising and hadn't attended church since the day she was christened. Tait also has a list of women who loosely fit the profile of being physically abused and going missing. It's a long list.'

'I bet it is. Where is she?'

'Interview room six.'

'Thanks. Right, get to it and spread the word that briefing has been pulled forward half an hour to eleven.'

Cruickshank headed off down a narrow corridor at the rear of the interview rooms and tapped a code into a control pad next to a nondescript door. She strode into the interview control room, pulling the door closed behind her. There were two officers in the room sat in front of a bank of monitors on a bench running the length of the wall. The bench was in front of a number of one way mirrors set into the wall, each framing an image of the interviews taking place inside the rooms beyond. She looked to a mirror on the far right, where Bentley was sitting alone at the same table Liam O'Driscoll had been interviewed at. He was staring down at his fingers with a vacant expression, not even seeing that he was picking the nails from his grubby fat fingers and flicking them onto the table.

Her Moons Denouement   Max Hardy

'Have you got your questions prepped?' Cruickshank asked Tait as she stood beside her, looking over her arm at the manila file she was holding.

'Yes Ma'am, just going over them one more time.' Tait answered nervously.

Cruickshank noticed the nerves. 'You are alright about doing this? I know you have a soft spot for Bentley, but this isn't a time for misplaced loyalty. You need to ask the tough questions.'

'Totally Ma'am. It doesn't mean I don't feel a little sorry for him, but I won't let that sway my judgement.' Tait answered with a little more authority in her tone.

'Good, now get in there and give him hell. We know we have no concrete evidence against him or his family at the moment, it is all just circumstantial. But something is going on and you need to press the right buttons to find out what.'

Tait nodded and grabbed a hot coffee in a Celtic mug from a table at the back of the room as she left. A few seconds later Cruickshank saw her opening the door to the interview room and watched as she sat down opposite Bentley and passed him over the coffee. She watched her smile at him as she put the manila folder down and then mimic his hand gestures, scraping fingers down her own nails.

'Good body language Tait, show a little empathy to get a rapport going. Don't go overboard though.' Cruickshank mumbled to herself as she stood watching.

Bentley picked up the mug of coffee and took a long lingering gulp of the heady brown liquid, a modicum of life entering his eyes as he looked at Tait, then over to the mirror on the wall.

'You poor, poor bastard. Shankers has really done for you. I can think of a thousand and one things on this case that would speed up your career other than interviewing a waste of space tosser like me. I think I did warn you against raiding the club. No one is ever going to talk. And here's your reward. Demoted to harangue me. Poor, poor bastard.'

'DC Annie Tait interviewing DI Fenny Bentley. Time is 11:10 am.' Tait announced, ignoring Bentley's comments as she opened the file in front of her and calmly picked the top sheet of paper from within, laying it down in front of Bentley.

'Heather Scott. A known victim of domestic abuse. One of your very first cases as a DC. Her body was never found although the large quantities of blood and part of her ear at the marital home were enough to convict her husband. Your dogs DNA was found in a sealed bag which had the name of Heather Scott on it.'

'Aye, facts we found out two fucking days ago.' Bentley sounded off, agitatedly, rubbing his chest uncomfortably as he did.

Tait carried on, unperturbed, taking another sheet of paper and laying it on the table.

'Sunni Bhalla, aged twenty six. Went missing in two thousand and four. We have a history of domestic violence recorded on file allegedly perpetrated by her boyfriend. While he was questioned about her disappearance, there was no evidence to suggest that anything untoward had happened. Your sisters DNA was found in a sealed bag along with that of Sunni Bhalla.'

'You are storming this lass. Another friggin blinder we all know!' Bentley shouted in frustration, grabbing the Celtic mug and taking another swig of coffee. 'It's not helping anyone this! Did anyone see your fucking interview strategy before you came in here?' he finished, grimacing.

Her Moons Denouement   Max Hardy

'Are you all right Bentley, you look a little flustered. Is your chest alright?' Tait enquired, concern in her tone.

'Just fucking annoyed at the stupid bloody questions?' Bentley blasted, flapping his hand at her, dismissing the concern.

Tait looked straight into his eyes, her gaze calm and measured, not flustered at all by his outbursts. She took a third sheet of paper from the file and placed it in front of Bentley, watching him intently as he looked down at the page. Watching the agitation ebb from his body. Watching his ruddy complexion turn pallid. Watching his large broad frame sag. Watching a shaking hand reach out to the paper. Watching a quavering stubby forefinger trace a line over the name on the page.

'Abigail Bentley. Known victim of domestic abuse. Went missing in nineteen seventy three. You were thirteen at the time. Her husband, your father, Edward Bentley was questioned at the time about her disappearance. It was discovered that she had been having an affair and that the abuse by your father was as a result of that affair. At the time, it was assumed that your mother had run away with her lover. No trace of her has ever been found. Your father was dismissed from the force after admitting to beating your mother.'

Bentley stared at the page, not looking up, not acknowledging the facts Tait was relaying.

'Three women DI Bentley. Three woman who were victims of domestic violence and linked to your family. Someone may be trying to set you up DI Bentley, it is very possible. But the other possibility is that someone is trying to tell us something.' Tait paused for a second as Bentley stared at the picture of his mother on the sheet, watching his bottom lip quivering. Just for a second: before she lifted another piece of paper from the file and slapped it down on top of the sheet he was staring at, startling him.

Her Moons Denouement   **Max Hardy**

'This is a list of another twenty three women from the surrounding areas who have gone missing in the past forty years. All of them were victims of domestic abuse. In eight of the cases a conviction was made in lieu of a body due to overwhelming forensic evidence. Blood and body parts. You were involved in seven of those cases. Look at that list DI Bentley, look long and hard at that list of women who have disappeared from the face of the earth. And then please try and explain to me why on earth you have a hidden room carved out of rock under your garage that has recently been hosed down with bleach.'

Bentley looked emotionally drained, his eyes staring through the names on the sheet before slowly rising to look at Tait, reflecting inner conflagration. His lips moved slightly, almost speaking, but then stopped as he picked up the Celtic mug and took another gulp of coffee, holding the liquid in his mouth and swirling it around, his gaze still firmly on Tait, trying to read her eyes, trying to read her intent.

'I think I told you last night that Dessie loves the Sound of Fucking Music and thinks she's a nun. She likes stories. She likes to play. She likes dolls and she likes secret places. It's her place, her hidey hole. She goes there to be alone, to get away from us old cantankerous blokes. She also uses it as a home for any waif and stray animal she finds. Father won't let her have them in the house. Last one was a fucking mental rabbit with myxomatosis. I tried telling her it was diseased but would she listen, no bloody way. She was heartbroken when it died. We bleached the place to get rid of the virus.'

A strength started to return to Bentley's words as he spoke, his body imperceptibly straightening from its slouch as he leaned over slightly towards Tait.

'I know how this looks, and trust me, I know it looks bad. I'd be asking the same questions if the shoe was on the other foot. But I have absolutely no idea why someone would be trying to show a link

Her Moons Denouement   Max Hardy

between these different cases. And being involved in seven missing person's cases over a thirty year career really isn't that many.' he said, the words soft and considered.

Tait held his gaze with a steely resolve, not letting Bentley's cajoling demeanour distract her.

'Earlier you told us that your sister was on a trip over to Ireland, is that correct?' she asked.

Frustration flashed over Bentley features once again and he sat back in his seat, flabbergasted.

'For fuck sake! Are we back on Noddy Time now, bloody PC Plod questioning.'

'Could you answer the question please DI Bentley.'

'Jesus, yes she is over in Ireland.'

'And was that leaving from Edinburgh airport yesterday afternoon?'

'Yes it was leaving from Edinburgh airport yesterday afternoon.' Bentley parroted sarcastically.

'And just to confirm, your sister is called Desiderata Bentley, no other names?'

'Yes she is called Desiderata Bentley, no other names.' he replied, mimicking her voice.

'That's a problem then DI Bentley.' Tait said calmly, paying no attention to his parroting.

Bentley's countenance turned pensive again as he leaned over the table once more and spoke at Tait.

'And why would my sister going to Ireland be a problem.'

Her Moons Denouement   Max Hardy

'I'm sure that wouldn't be a problem Di Bentley. This problem is this. We have checked with every airline running flights from Edinburgh to Ireland. Just to be safe, we checked with Newcastle and Glasgow airports too, on their manifests to Ireland, in case you had mistaken the airport. And just to make absolutely sure, we asked every airline in the country who had flights to Ireland yesterday afternoon to check their manifests for us. The problem is DI Bentley, your sister did not take a flight to Ireland yesterday afternoon. So I have one simple question: Where is she?'

Chapter 25

Life goes on. Less than an hour ago there was a mini riot in the middle of one of the busiest streets in the City and now...

Now I am sitting in the corner of a little café on the ground floor of the biggest department store in town and everyone is going about their business with a normality which astounds me. The only token gesture to even recognising the significance of what is happening in the city is the sound turned up slightly on the TV showing the Sky News Channel in the opposite corner of the room.

They have a ten minute loop going. First minute is on Archbishop O'Driscoll, focusing on the scandal that it is causing in the Roman Catholic Church. Half a minute given up to his victims. Another minute is spent on Imam Mann with the usual slant towards Islamic fundamentalism. Half a minute on victims. One minute replaying what they call 'Highlights' of the two suicides and then three minutes of speculation as to who the 'Fallen Angels' are. No fact. Lots of religious references from the Bible and from the Koran, but all wild speculation. No mention at all of the video I saw yesterday from Madame Evangeline. The last three minutes are given over to the mini riot that happened earlier, with amateur footage of the skirmish. In between the loop they are talking to so called 'experts' in the studio, even more speculation with no substance.

Her Moons Denouement Max Hardy

Harry is late. It's almost quarter to one now. I look out of the window for the umpteenth time and see a procession of buses passing. One breaks suddenly, the others following suit. People on the pavement outside stop and look into the road. I lean over and look as well. Coming down the middle of the road, oblivious to the mayhem they are causing are a large group of Hare Krishna, the ones on the outside of the procession holding placards advertising a show. I can hear them singing 'My Sweet Lord' through the window.

I see Harry approaching from the main shop, looking out of the window, watching them too, his expression as bemused as the other onlookers. He shakes his head as he spots me in the corner and approaches.

'There's never a policeman when you want one, is there DI Saul. They are causing havoc out there!' he says playfully, emphasising the 'DI'.

'I've been told in no uncertain terms not to get involved in any kind of police work in the City. On pain of arrest. I think the main focus of the police at the minute is over on the Royal Mile. Did you hear about that?'

'Yes, I saw it on the news. Bloody stupid Catholics. I mean, there's a time and a place, come on. And that time isn't the day after one of your key leaders is exposed as a murderous loon and the place isn't in front of where he was outed! They say that faith is blind. That is definitely the case with those idiots. Totally blind to the public mood. I have no time for buffoons.'

'Would you like a coffee?' I ask, tickled by his overtly pompous heirs.

'Good god no, a tea please. My mind frazzles if I have coffee after twelve. My most profound apologies for being late. It took longer than I expected to look through the footage.'

Her Moons Denouement   Max Hardy

I order him a tea as he speaks, at ease and entranced by his larger than life boisterous personality.

'Not good news so far i'm afraid. We definitely have images of them coming into the shop, but so far no images of them leaving.'

'Which shop was it?'

'This one, Jenners. They came in the front entrance together and we have footage of them coming off the escalator on the first floor. After that they split up. He goes up another floor then we lose him. She stays on the first floor and browses for about five minutes then goes back down to the ground floor and we lose her.'

'Okay. Now I recall that you pictured Jessica coming to Edinburgh on two separate occasions, only the first with the other me. Did she walk on both occasions?'

'Perceptive of you DI Saul. Yes, on both occasions she walked from the station. On both occasions, she came into Jenners. I haven't progressed the second date yet with the security team. I will do that once we have finished on the first date.'

'Is that going to get us anywhere though? What is the best we could hope for? We see them coming out of the shop and know which direction they headed. What then, where do we go from there?'

'Small steps DI Saul. In my profession, patience is the watchword. It might get me to the next store and then I will go and talk to the security team there. And then the next, and the next and so on and so forth. Where it might get us to is the end of Princess Street. What you might find out is what stores they visit, what things they buy, who they might converse with. And if they talk to people, shop people, I can talk to those shop people too and they might remember something.'

As a Detective, sometimes there's a reason you ask a question and it's not necessarily because you don't know the answer. It's because you want to find out if the person you are asking knows the answer. It's because you want to understand how they think and what makes them tick. Harry is definitely a detail person. That one statement tells me that if there is anything on those CCTV images to help us, he will find it.

'Small steps Harry. Is there anything I can do to help at the moment?'

'No, I have as much info as I need to progress this line of enquiry. It is just time unfortunately.'

Out of the corner of my eye, I see a banner flash across the Sky News feed. 'Breaking News – Video from the Fallen Angels'. How the hell has that happened? The police wouldn't have sanctioned its release? Or are they struggling to find out who the Angels are and this is an appeal? It's not an appeal. It's not being pre-empted by anyone from the force.

'In the past half hour, Sky News has received this exclusive footage from the group known as the 'Fallen Angels'. The images you are about to see are extremely graphic and may cause some viewers distress.'

Everyone in the café without exception turns and looks at the TV.

The newsreader finishes and photographs of O'Driscoll's victims flash up on the screen, the same as the ones yesterday. Imam Mann's victims follow straight afterwards. Madame Evangeline's voice again, reciting the same message as the video I watched yesterday. The screen stops on Imam Mann's face and then fades to black, apart from his eyes, which turn green, the darkness then replaced by Peirrott's face. One of the her cheeks has no make up on it and she takes a handkerchief from the table in front of her and cleans the make up from her second cheek. She makes the speech about masks again, about us all wearing masks, then the dialogue about the 'Fallen

Her Moons Denouement   Max Hardy

Angels' being human. Much the same as the message in the previous video.

'Don't just think of that question in isolation. Look at these images of the beautiful women Archbishop Liam O'Driscoll and Imam Mann murdered and as you look into their eyes, ask yourself one question: Why do I fear my faith?'

Pictures of the women again, smiling faces, dead bodies, flicking through them at pace. They are powerful images backing up a powerful question.

The images stop and there is a picture of a different woman. It is a bizarre pixelated photo of another woman. It is hard to make out, but her head looks like it is between her legs, not on her shoulders. Her hands are out at an angle, palms up, holding something in them. Her legs are in a very unnatural position. She looks grotesque.

'Just in case you think the atrocities carried out by Archbishop Liam O'Driscoll and Imam Mann are the end of these atrocities. Just in case you think using fear and faith as weapons is confined to Christianity and Islam. Just in case you think we are extreme in our actions, look at this poor woman's face. This poor woman who has been beheaded, her head thrust up into her genitals. At one o'clock today, somewhere in the city, we will tell you all about the religious leader who exacted this brutality upon her: her and many other women. A leader from a religion that extolls peace and love as their mantra. It gives me no pleasure at all to say even that won't be the end of our revelations.'

Mantra, peace and love. Upturned palms and splayed legs. Bhuddism? What possible part of Bhuddism could exact that kind of atrocity? There is a Buddhist Goddess who beheads herself and dances over the corpses of her lovers. What is she called? One o'clock.? That's only five minutes away.

Her Moons Denouement   Max Hardy

'Think on one thing: Even Fallen Angels Have Wings. I am Madame Evangeline and we are the Fallen Angels.'

The video stops and the TV cuts back to the studio. The café is silent, everyone staring at the screen, the visceral intensity of the images, of the message from Madame Evangeline still resonating on the shocked faces of the café's customers. Harry turns back to me with the same expression.

'Who on earth is she and how do they know these things?' he asks me directly, but his question is really a bemused statement as he shakes his head.

'Who and how aren't at the top of my list right now. Where, in the next five minutes, they are going to unveil the murderer, is. It is something to do with Buddhism, I am sure. The body position, the words peace, love and Mantra. The body position. There is a god with that body position, what the hell is her name. Are there any Buddhist Temples in Edinburgh?'

I grab my phone and hit the search button, typing in 'Buddhist Temples Edinburgh'. Come on, come on. No bloody Wifi. Two results. One just off Princess Street, one in Leith. I click on the first one. The Kagu Samye Dzong Centre. It's a terraced house. Are they really going to make a statement to the world in front of a terraced house? Who is going to be there to see? I click on the second. Another house. Not going to happen. The other two have been dramatic city centre locations with lots of people. This one has to be the same, but there is no big temple. Where else could it be? 'My sweet Lord' pops into my mind, along with singing Hare Krishna.

I yank the collection of flyers I have gathered out of my pocket and throw them onto the table.

'What is it John' Massah asks me, using my first name. Why did he use my first name?

Her Moons Denouement   **Max Hardy**

'There are no big Buddhist temples in Edinburgh, but there is a show in the Festival.' I answer, finding the salient flyer. 'There, 'The Music Of Mantra'. It's in the Princess Street Gardens and there is a one o'clock matinee. I saw the Hare Krishna not long ago, probably heading off to the show. It is just on the other side of the street.

Chapter 26

I jump up from my seat and head for the exit, throwing the door open as I sprint into the street. I look back and see Harry rising, slow on the uptake, still in shock. It is one o'clock. Distant screams filter through the hubbub of traffic and pedestrians on the side street as I jostle between the heavy early afternoon crowds down onto Princess Street. The Gardens are across the road. I see people running towards them and people running away as I dart between the traffic and run up the railings separating the gardens from the main road, right next to the gothic Scott Monument. I run through a small gate into the gardens and up to a low stone wall, and look down over an open expanse of grass. There is a stage on the grass, an orange awning over the top of it. Chairs are thrown over haphazardly, decimated by the audience, most of whom are trying to get out of the vicinity of the stage, some trying to get closer.

Some trying to get a closer look at a large woman with some kind of Chinese dress on, her face made up to look ferocious. She has a Samurai sword in her hands and has it hovering against the neck of a naked man sitting bound by barbed wire in the lotus position. The loud speakers crackle and above the running feet, above the surprised and frightened shouting, above the panicked screams, a mantra blares out.

'Fear and Faith, Faith and Fear. In whose faith is your fear founded.'

Her Moons Denouement Max Hardy

This is a good vantage point. I can see the drama unfolding with an uncompromised view. Not just of the stage or the people who are gravitating in either direction to and from it, but the watchers as well. It is important to watch the watchers. Somewhere in amongst them, there is always the possibility that there will be someone who is orchestrating things. They will be close enough to have a good view of everything, but far enough away to make a quick escape. They will look unusually casual and that is how you usually spot them. In this case a Madame Evangeline, or a Ben Hanlon could be watching.

My gaze darts over heads, examining faces, watching expressions, always being drawn back to events on the stage. A large screen fires up behind the Chinese Hag, happy smiling faces of middle aged women appearing on it, slightly overlaid, names appearing below the images. Her hypnotic poetry continues.

'Which Numen's dogma is decreed, to despoil innocence last breath, forced to embrace your litany, on the sanctity of life's death. This man, this monk, this monster, deflowered and decapitated these inquisitive women. Women who's only wish was to learn the ways of Tantric.'

Young slim woman standing about twenty feet away. No shock or surprise on her face, only curiosity. My Jess radar kicks in, seeing her in the contours of the woman's face. A man of a similar age with a small child approaches her from the exit of the Scott Monument and directs her away from the show below, shielding the small girls eyes. It is not Jess.

'This monster not only deflowered and decapitated them, but then deflowered them with their own decapitation.'

More screams, more people backing away from the stage at the uncensored sight of the type of image that was on Sky News. I stop searching the crowd and just stare with my mouth agape at the abominable creation in front of my eyes. Four decapitated torsos with

Her Moons Denouement   Max Hardy

the heads rammed into the vaginas. Hard to tell who is who but why only four? There were five smiling faces.

'All because of their age. All because his faith told him that women of their age are demons. He led them into Tanra, led them into a secret sexual sect. A sect kept secret because his faith preaches celibacy. His faith uses fear to keep the women who enter Tantra quiet. His faith threatens them to suffer a millennia of hellish torments, insanity and death if they utter a word to anyone about what they know. His faith did that to them. His faith would have done that to me too. I am forty three. He was going to kill me.'

Is that why four bodies. Is she the fifth smiling face? I can't let her be the fifth one to die, I can't let her commit suicide. I jump the small wall, wincing in agony as I do and stumble down the slight embankment towards the stage. People are running up the hill and I swerve and dart to avoid them, running through the discarded, upturned chairs until I stand right in front of the Chinese Hag. Close up, she is far from a hag. She is a middle aged Asian woman with beautiful brown eyes and a round, warm profile, but with her face painted white, black makeup accentuating the eyes and lips, making them look hideous.

'You don't have to do this.' I shout towards her.

'I'm not going to kill him. Far from it.' She replies to my question, looking down at me. 'I am here today to show the world the atrocities he has enacted upon these poor women, all in the fear of his faith.'

'I know you aren't going to kill him. I meant you don't have to kill yourself. Do you really want to give him the satisfaction of knowing that his actions had such an impact on you, that they have caused you to commit suicide?'

Her Moons Denouement   Max Hardy

She laughs, throwing her head back, letting out a haggish cackle, playing the part deliberately before she looks back down at me, studying my features.

'What is most people's greatest fear John Saul?'

She knows my name. How the hell does she know my name? How you know my name is the fear at the top of my list at the moment. What do people fear most? Spiders, religion, being mugged, being killed. Death.

'Death.' she answers before I have time to reply. 'We fear death above all else. We fear it because we don't know what happens afterwards. It is instinct. But if you train your mind not to fear death, not to fear what may or may not happen afterwards, and open yourself up to the endless possibilities that lie at the other side of that closed door, you will realise that there is no reason why you wouldn't embrace death and open it's door.'

I stare at her incredulously, her focused, lucid words sending a chill through my bones, making me fear the intensity of her belief. She wants to die. She is ready to die because she wants to see what is on the other side of death, not because she doesn't want this life. I am never going to stop her. She smiles a knowing smile and continues talking.

'We will no longer stand in the shadows of their gods and let these atrocities prevail.'

Police sirens break into the din of chaos surrounding the gardens, distracting my attention back to the crowd, back to watching. I look over the far side of the gardens, to people leaning over the walls on the road up to the Royal Mile. Nothing that look ordinarily out of the ordinary.

Her Moons Denouement   **Max Hardy**

I look behind me, to Scott's Monument and the people looking down over the scene from the first level walkways of the tower. I see Jess, watching events on the stage intently, leaning nonchalantly on the barrier. Her lips move as she watches. There is no one beside her. Who is she talking to? Her gaze diverts from the stage and looks directly at me. Her lips move again. She smiles at me, a long lingering loving smile, then looks back to the stage, to the Chinese Hag taking the sword off the bound monks neck.

I turn and break into a run, heading back up the embankment, heading towards the entrance to the tower, scrabbling in my pocket for some money as I approach. I don't take my eyes off Jess as I reach the entrance and throw a twenty pound note at the man in the booth. Police sirens are getting louder and I hear cars screeching to a halt on Princess Street as I enter the Monument, heading up the narrow, dark, damp stone staircase. Sirens become muffled in the confined space. The Chinese Hag's voice does too, but I can hear the intensity of it increasing, her tone becoming more frenetic.

'Even Fallen Angels Have Wings.'

I clamber out of the gloomy stairwell, blinded briefly by the brilliant sunlight. I look through the people leaning over the balcony watching the scene below but can't see Jess. I hear an outburst of screams and hysteria. I hear the sound of heavy footed police officers laden with riot gear pounding into the gardens and look down quickly. On the stage, standing proud and tall, the Chinese Hag stretches her arms out and large feathered wings unfurl from her back as she does. The samurai sword glimmers in the sun.

'We want justice. Justice for Abigal, justice for Neeta, justice for Martha, justice for Elena. We want justice for every Angel that has died. Justice for every Angel left to bleed in the fear founded by the disease of their god's seed. We want the world to see the truth.'

Her Moons Denouement Max Hardy

Police pound down the embankment, shouting for people to get out of the way. The crowd as one move backwards as the woman raises both hands above her head and grips the sword tight between them. I push through the gawping onlookers on the balcony and reach the spot where I saw Jess. She isn't here.

'We are the Fallen Angels!'

I stop dead and stare down at the stage, see the razor sharp rapier slice through the air as the woman thrusts it into her chest, straight through her heart. She slumps down onto her knees, then flops to one side, dead, and on her way to somewhere with endless possibilities. That is not the fear of faith, that is the power of faith, of an unequivocal belief.

Pandemonium engulfs the balcony as the onlookers panic, pushing past each other to get towards the stairwells and get down onto the street. I hear some talk about getting closer to the scene, others just wanting to get as far away as possible. Regardless, their jostling is hampering me as I look frantically around for Jess. I look through to the continuing balconies on the second, third and fourth sides of the Monument, but can't see her. I look to the windows higher up the Monument, at people leaning out of them, but no Jess. I look down to street level, to the people streaming out of the exits to the Monument, but can't see her. I can see the police starting to form a cordon around the stage and disperse the crowd. I can see Harry looking around trying to see me. I can see more police cars arriving on the street, more police officers running down the hill towards the stage. But I can't see Jess. I bang both hands into the wrought iron protective rail on the balcony in frustration, immediately regretting it as pain shoots through the stigmata in my palms.

Focus John. You haven't seen her come out. Yes, but she could have gone down a different tower while I was coming up. She could have, but she might have gone up. Get down to ground level and keep an

Her Moons Denouement   **Max Hardy**

eye on the exits. The police will be clearing this area soon, they will clear the monument as well. If she is still in here, she will have to come out. I head for the nearest stairwell and quickly walk down it, out onto the pathway in front of the gardens towards Harry. The police are already taping off the entrance to the park and ushering people out.

'Harry, keep an eye on the exits to the Monument. I saw Jess up there. I don't think she has come out yet.'

'Stop exactly where you are Saul!' screams a voice I recognise. I look towards it, to DCI Cruickshank running in through the gates of the gardens, DC Tait directly behind her.

'Harry, keep an eye on those entrances, you know what Jess looks like. Follow her. Don't make out that you know me at all.' I whisper as I pass by him, looking directly ahead toward the approaching women.

'For the second time in two days Saul, I find you right in the midst of this investigation.' Cruickshank sneers in my direction as she reaches me. 'You might fool me once Saul, but never bloody twice. Either you are in this up to your neck, or you know a hell of a lot more than you are letting on. Arrest him Tait. Playtime is over.'

Chapter 27

'You have four things to hit him with Tait and not a single one of them implicates Bentley directly. But he knows something. The 'Fallen Angels' are trying to tell us something and he has to have some answers. Don't go easy on him. It's the same for you Purves. Saul is popping up in this investigation far too many times for my liking. Probe him hard on the things we discussed.' instructed Cruickshank as she settled into a hard backed wooden seat at the Interview Control Room desk.

'Yes Ma'am.' both women sounded off in tandem as they left the room, Tait last, closing the door behind her.

Cruickshank looked into the two rooms directly in front of her, Saul in the one to the right, Bentley the left. She noted Saul's calm, patient demeanour, which was at odds to Bentley's. He was agitatedly pacing up and down the room, biting his finger nails and worrying his sweaty brow with a shaking hand.

Tait entered the room with Bentley, carrying his chipped Celtic mug full of steaming coffee.

'Could you please sit down Bentley, I have some more questions to go through with you. More evidence has come to light in the past few hours.'

# Her Moons Denouement	Max Hardy

Cruickshank watched the body language between the two of them, noting Bentley's placation at Tait's stern tone.

'Before you ask any of the new questions, just see if he has anything else to add to the earlier interview. I doubt it, but you never know, a few hours stewing in the cells might have loosened his mind. He certainly looks agitated.' Cruikshank said into a thin microphone sitting on the bench in front of her. She saw an imperceptible nod as Tait sat down opposite Bentley and arranged a folder in front of herself.

'Having had time to reflect on the questions I asked you earlier Bentley, specifically, do you know anything about the disappearance of the missing girls and do you know the whereabouts of your sister, have you anything else to add?'

'Nothing to add on both questions. I have no information regarding the missing girls and I have no idea where my sister is. I am beginning to worry about where she is and I am getting a bit aggrieved at the lack of evidence you are presenting to link me personally to any of this.'

'Okay. We appreciate your co-operation and patience and I am sure you appreciate that we need to thoroughly investigate the evidence we have. Can you recall the list I showed you earlier, with the other women who had gone missing?'

Bentley huffed in frustration. 'Yes, I remember the list.'

'At one o'clock this afternoon, the 'Fallen Angels' revealed another mass murderer. One of the alleged victims was a woman called Martha Grainger.' Tait took a copy of the list she had presented to Bentley earlier out of her folder and placed it down in front of him, pink highlighter through three names on the paper. 'She is on the list. Went missing in nineteen ninety eight. He husband was charged with her murder due the overwhelming forensic and eye witness evidence.

Her Moons Denouement

Max Hardy

Several clumps of matted hair ripped from her skull were found in their bedroom as well as a large quantity of blood. Neighbours heard screaming and shouting coming from the house and immediately called the police, as there was a known history of the husband being violent towards her. Police arrived within forty minutes to find the husband almost delirious, the blood and hair and no body. He maintains his innocence even to this day. He admits to hitting her in the past but said he was sleeping at the time witnesses heard the alleged argument. He said he woke up to find the blood and the hair on the bed and his wife missing. The courts didn't agree. You were the arresting officer. Do you have any idea why this third woman would have been highlighted by the 'Fallen Angels'?'

'I have no idea other than the same one I keep repeating. Someone is trying to set me and my family up. I believe that someone is Rebecca Angus. I believe she is doing it because I was involved in her arrest and conviction. I believe she is Madame Evangeline and is at the centre of what is happening with these 'Fallen Angels'.' Bentley answered, his manner still aggravated, but his words considered.

Cruikshank's attention was drawn to the other room, where DI Purves introduced herself to Saul, then sat down opposite him, opening a file she had with her on the table and delving straight into the questioning.

'Could you tell me how you happened to be at Princess Gardens today at the exact time another 'Fallen Angels' revelation was taking place?' Purves asked, in a monotone yet assured voice.

'I was having a coffee in Jenners and I saw the breaking news on Sky about the 'Fallen Angels' video. It was about twelve fifty five. The image of the beheaded woman and her body position reminded me of a picture I had seen years ago of the Tibetan Buddhist Goddess Chinnamunda. Madame Evangeline also used words like peace, love and mantra. All key words in Buddhism. I couldn't find any large

Her Moons Denouement

Max Hardy

Buddhist temples in Edinburgh but I had seen a group of Hare Krishna dancing down past Jenners about five minutes earlier. A Buddhist show in the middle of Edinburgh. If the 'Fallen Angels' were going to make a statement, it was going to be there. I had a flyer in my pocket advertising their show in the Gardens at one o'clock so I went to see if my suspicions were correct. They were.'

Cruickshank whistled through gritted teeth and she sat back in her seat, nodding in admiration. 'Why the hell can't my Detectives see that kind of pattern!' she mumbled to herself, looking back to Tait and Bentley.

'But it's not just the fact that the name was on the list. It is also the plastic bag that was found at the house where Chodak the Monk inflicted atrocities on innocent women. A plastic bag with your father's DNA inside of it. That is now your dogs, your sisters and your father's DNA associated with these missing women. I don't think you are being setup. I think someone is telling us that you know something about this. They may even be telling us that you are involved. That you have abused your position to concoct convictions and draw people away from what is really happening with these women. I think someone is telling us that your family have been involved in their disappearance.'

Tait stared at Bentley with a firm and commanding glare, the power of her words and the intensity of her voice echoing in the force of her eyes. Bentley tried to hold the gaze but couldn't, instead looking down to his fidgeting stumpy fingers, his eyes distant, scared and lost. He took a gulp of coffee.

'Go for it Tait, he is struggling, put the boot in right now and he will crumble.' Cruickshank whispered into the microphone, leaning forward in her seat once more.

'That's not all though Bentley. We have been looking for a connection between the women on the list. We started looking for a religious connection. After all, that's what the 'Fallen Angels' are exposing. We couldn't find any. But we did find a different connection between them. All of these women were physically abused by their partners, we know that. We now also know that at one time or another every one of them attended support groups to help them with the consequences of domestic violence. We have been in touch with every one of those support groups. And do you know what we found out?'

The door behind Cruickshank opened and Laurent entered the Control room excitedly. 'Sorry for interrupting Ma'am, but we have the results back from the DNA we found at Bentley's house. You need to see them.' he said, striding to where she was sitting and placing an open file in front of her. Cruikshank looked down at the page, her eyes widening in surprise.

'And you are 100% sure about this. No fucking cross contamination?'

'100% Ma'am. Le Fenwick double checked every sample.'

Cruikshank leant over the microphone again. 'Tait, finish your current question, don't let him answer then come and see me straight away. We've got some fresh evidence. Thanks Laurent.' she finished as the Frenchman left.

'We found out that your Father provided pastoral support to all of these groups and that your sister would often attend to assist him. I have to step out for a few minutes, but in that time I would like you to think about one thing. A name on a list, a piece of DNA in a bag not directly related to those victims is circumstantial. Two people having direct contact with every victim shortly before they went missing is not. That is more than coincidence. That is a pattern. A pattern directly linking your family to those missing women.' she said firmly, then

Her Moons Denouement Max Hardy

stood up, holding eye contact with Bentley's panicked stare all the way to the door.

Cruickshank watched Bentley lean over the table and sink his head into his hands, his bitten fingernails scratching the skin on his forehead until it broke, spots of blood mingling with the beads of sweat.

'He's breaking.' she whispered before turning back to look into the other interview room, where Purves was taking some images out of the folder in front of her.

'This is a picture taken by a CCTV camera at a set of traffic lights just before the Portobello junction on the A1 in Edinburgh at 12:30 am on the 1st January 2012. It is of a limousine. Could you tell me who is looking out of the side window?'

Saul smiled, recognising the image, his manner still calm and open. 'It's Rebecca Angus. I'm sure you have another picture in your file from a different angle, showing the driver of the limousine and yes, the driver does look remarkably like me. These pictures came to light in my last case so I have seen them before.'

Purves looked at him agape, but still went through the motions of placing the second photograph in front of him. 'Yes, I do have another picture. Could you explain why you appear to be in a car with Rebecca Angus, the woman who was convicted of murdering her son that morning? The woman who was then committed to a mental institute for Dissociative Identity Disorder. The other identity she has being that of a woman called Madame Evangeline?'

'Look DI Purves, I can see your interview strategy. Place the pertinent pieces of evidence in front of me that loosely link me to Madame Evangeline and the 'Fallen Angels' and try and get me to think you know more than you do. Try to wrong foot me and get me to admit something more than you know. I get what you are trying to do and why you are trying to do it. The truth is I probably did know more than you a few days ago, but I have shared all of that information. I came here to give you that information. I called out the link on the Imam revelation. I tried to stop the woman today from killing herself. By all means waste your time trying to find out how I am connected to this. You might do me a favour and help me find out too. But just realise, all the time you are doing that, the real Madame Evangeline and whoever these 'Fallen Angels' are will still be running rings around you.'

Cruickshank slammed her palms into the desk in front of her and shouted in frustration, 'Shit, busted.' She leant over and spoke into the microphone. 'Purves, just get out of there, he has seen us coming all day. We don't have a thing and he knows it but take him down to the cells and let him stew for half an hour until I'm finished here.'

Tait entered the room and approached Cruikshank who handed her the piece of paper Laurent dropped off. 'Right, next question is the same. Hammer it home that we know there is another woman out there that fits this pattern. Then finish on this. Just tell him it straight and then ask 'Did he know?' If that doesn't break him, nothing will. What a messed up bloody family.'

Tait looked at the evidence, her expression initially shocked, then thoughtful. 'It still doesn't implicate Bentley. It still doesn't directly implicate his sister or father.'

'No, but something is not right and this adds even more grist to that mill. It's what we have and we use it.'

Tait nodded and left the room, appearing a few seconds later back in the interview room. Bentley raised his head from his hands as she sat down, his face streaked with tears, running pink with the blood flowing from the scratches in his forehead. He was breathing heavily and he took one of his hands and rubbed his chest hard.

Her Moons Denouement　　　　　　　　　　　　　　　　**Max Hardy**

'Well.' asked Tait, sternly. 'Do you have anything to say to the previous question?'

'It is his self-imposed punishment, and his redemption. He knows that hitting mother was wrong. That is why he turned to religion. To help him come to terms with what he had done. To help him find a way to help others. He goes to those places and tells them about what he did. He tells them about the things to look out for in an abusive partner. He tries to explain what drives a man to do it and what he thinks women can do to gain the strength to challenge them. He may be old fashioned in his beliefs and he may still have his faults, but he goes there to help women who suffer from domestic abuse. You might find that he has talked to twenty odd women who have gone missing, but if you ask further, you might also find that he has talked to hundreds of other woman who haven't gone missing and whose lives have changed for the better because of the insights he was able to share.' Bentley said quietly, breathing heavily, his manner conciliatory even if his words were challenging Tait's aspersions.

'The man sounds like a saint. So giving.' Tait answered sarcastically. 'Do you think he is currently helping Coleen Naismith in the same way? She was last seen running screaming from the house that she shares with her boyfriend by neighbours. That was two days ago. Today someone reported finding blood and a severed toe in Leuchold Woods. Forensics have confirmed that they are Coleen Naismith's. Three weeks ago she attended a victim support session where your father was giving a talk. Today both your sister and your father have mysteriously gone AWOL. Your family know something about her disappearance. You know something about her disappearance. What are you hiding? What are you afraid of? Is it your father? Are you afraid he may banish you to the cupboard under the stairs if you tell?'

Bentley's body stiffened, a shot of anger coursing through it, visible in eyes that went from dull to glistening, lips that went from pliant to snarling, fists that went from shaking to taught as he spoke. 'I have

Her Moons Denouement   Max Hardy

never heard of Coleen Naismith. As for my father, he is not a Saint, but neither is he a monster and what we do, how we live behind our front door is nobody's business but ours.'

'Is that right. Nobody's business but yours. Do you even know what is going on behind your front door?' Tait responded with measured aggression. 'We found signs of sexual activity in your father's bed. Recent sexual activity.'

The slight bit of fight that had coursed through Bentley's body left him again and he slumped back into his seat, his face anguished.

'DNA is conclusive. The sexual act was between your Father and your sister. Did you know that was happening behind your front door?'

Chapter 28

On the face of it three very distinct and different murderers. Yes, all religious leaders with a warped sense of their own beliefs but when you come down to it, when you come down to the animal in us all, are they really different, or is this really just about sex. Is that what the 'Fallen Angels' are trying to show?

I shuffle pictures on my hotel wall, bringing images of the three religious leaders closer together and pin a list of the women each has murdered beneath them. That's another anomaly in all three cases. Heather Scott and Sunni Bhalla have not been called out on the videos the Fallen Angels have released so far. I know that there was one more picture shown in the Chodak case as well. Who are they? Are the Angels trying to tell the police something and if so, what? Are they a bigger part of what the Angels are going to reveal? By my reckoning, there is only one reveal left to go. Patterns. It will be religious, it will be in Edinburgh, there will be an anomaly, and a 'Fallen Angel' will commit suicide. What else? Well, Madame Evangeline, Eve, Jessica will make a video of it. She will ask people to question the fear in their faith.

There is a sound of a soft footfall on the carpet behind me and the waft of a subtle encompassing scent, Coco Chanel. I don't turn, but feel Rebecca come up alongside me and mirror my gaze at the evidence wall.

Her Moons Denouement Max Hardy

'You can use the door you know. I did give you a key.' I say.

'What, and have the plain clothes police officer who is following you know you are aiding and abetting a fugitive?'

'You've seen him?'

'He's not hard to miss. If he's not lounging around the reception area looking like a desperate punter trying to score some crack, he's watching from McDonalds over the road stuffing his face with burgers. So best I keep using the window. What are you contemplating now?'

Rebecca is constantly surprising me. 'Right at this moment I'm contemplating how the hell you have become so savvy so quickly to surveillance techniques.'

'You call it surveillance techniques, I call it people watching. It's something I have always done, but I got a lot better at it when I met Madame Evangeline. We would meet up in the night and watch people, sometimes following them back to their homes. Sometimes watching through cracks in curtains as they got naked and fucked their husbands, wives, lovers: or all three. Invariably, we would play with each other while we watched. She taught me a lot about reading body language and facial expressions. Don't change the subject, what are you contemplating?'

'Three murderers. I'm trying to understand patterns so we can figure out who the fourth might be. Just wondering if this is about sex. The first set of victims were buggered, the second set had their clitorises ripped off and the third had their heads forced up their vaginas.'

'I saw the 'Fallen Angels' video on the news and do you know what struck me. Yes, she asked people to question their faith and why they fear it. Yes, the monsters who killed those girls are probably nutters and an extremely radical representation of their faith. But what struck me was the underlying tenants of those faiths and the way they perceive and treat women. It might not be about sex, it might be about the sexes.'

I look at her in open admiration, nodding my head as I write that hypothesis down on a post it and hand it to her. 'Way to go Miss Pankhurst. I think you might just be onto something there. There is no doubt that Madame Evangeline is a force of nature. She has no problem using sex to get what she wants. You know that probably more than anyone.'

'Like I said, she taught me well. Including how you use sex as a weapon to cajole and control. I'm doing it to you now. I saw your eyes light up when I talked about being a voyeur. Do you want to hear more?' she teases as she pops the post it onto the wall and then unrolls a map she is holding and pins that to the wall too.

'I heard quite a bit on the Hanlon tapes. All about your encounters with Madame Evangeline.' I answer as I approach the map, noting the clusters of dots marked on it. Three distinct areas, but the most surprising thing was the sheer number of dots.

'I don't think you've heard about them all. I counted them today as I marked up the map and it even surprised me. In the space of a year we met seventy three times. Statistically, once every five days although practically it wasn't like that. What you heard on the tapes was only an abridged version of events. I could tell you in intimate detail about every single one of those encounters if you want me to?' she teases, deliberately running the stump of her tongue as close to her lips as possible. Her eyes, full of playful wickedness make the grotesqueness of the action alluring, distracting me again.

'Trust me, my tackle is in no fit state to react to even the most lurid or erotic of descriptions and it will waste precious time finding out what we need too. Is there any significance in your mind to the clustering of the encounters?' I ask, hopefully distracting her attention from the fact that I am ever so slightly embarrassed and flustered as her candidness. It didn't work.

'The first set, around Leith are when I would meet her at clubs like Sodom and Gomorrah, where she regularly performed cunnilingus on my aching hot clitoris. Most of the legal and illegal sex scene on a club basis is centred around that area. The second set are centred on the Holyrood area. Now that was a lot of outdoor activity, a lot of alfresco sex, a lot of teasing and tantalising, flashing bare flesh and erect nipples, masturbating and fingering each other in bushes knowing we were being watched. Knowing we were being watched by politicians, or civil servants. Basically people of power. Lastly, the mews, the crescents, the courts and the squares around the far end of Princess Street, an area with a lot of wealth in a small footprint. It is true what they say, wealth does lead to excess. Your eyes would water at some of the excess we witnessed. That's where we would watch through cracks in curtains, knowing that the people in the houses knew they were being watched. We would live in shadows, mere metres away from people passing in the night. The thrill of being so close to the city centre, so close to normal life and having your lover caress and squeeze your naked breasts, having her fervently forcing her fingers in and out of your yearning cunt as you spy on others doing the same thing is just so intoxicating. The whole experience was liberating.'

She is looking at my profile, I can feel her emerald eyes burning into my ruddy cheek. I turn and see her mouth closed, her lips pouting at me, those eyes simmering. She places a hand tenderly on my groin and strokes the erection growing in my jeans, making me gasp.

'There's nothing at all wrong with your tackle.' she smirks, removing her hand and punching me playfully in the forearm, her eyes changing from simmering to soulful. 'Making someone feel like you do right now is what she taught me. I have just disarmed every single one of your defence mechanisms with a few chosen words, a single touch and

Her Moons Denouement   Max Hardy

an intensity of personality. She gave me the belief to do that. She had me challenge morality. She made me fearless of sex. Why did she teach me to do that?'

My pulse is racing, I can feel my heart battering my eardrums with the rhythm of my coursing blood. She is absolutely right. She has disarmed me. If she told me right now to lay on the bed and do any bloody sexual act under the sun to her, I would. I would have no qualms about it. Jess had the same impact on me sexually. Which isn't a surprise as she is Madame Evangeline.

I jump as my pocket begins to vibrate, sending another jolt down my erection. Rebecca giggles as I reach in there and pull out my phone awkwardly, trying hard not to touch myself.

'Harry, where the hell have you been? I've been trying to get you for hours. Did you see her come down from the monument?' I ask overtly down the phone, still trying to distract my mind from images of Rebecca naked.

'Sorry John. I had a domestic issue with one of the girls, her pony has gone lame and I needed to make some urgent calls to vets. Bloody phone ran out of battery then. I've only just managed to steal a charger.'

'No problem, these things happen. Did you see her come down?' I reiterate probably a little too impatiently.

'Sorry John, I didn't. I hung around just on the main street for about twenty minutes, well after they had cleared the area. I can only guess that she got away before you came down.'

'Shit! Okay. How about the CCTV footage in Jenners, did you get any further with that?'

'Not from Jenners. I couldn't get any further there. For whatever reason I can't see them coming out of the shop. So I moved on to the

Her Moons Denouement

Max Hardy

second date when Jessica came up on her own. That has been a little more promising and a little odd.'

'In what way?'

'Well, I have her going in and out of four shops along Princess Street, the last one being House of Fraser.'

'Where about is that on a map Harry? Is that toward the Holyrood end of Princess Street or the Lothian Road end?' I look at the clusters of dots on Rebecca's map as I wait for an answer.

'It's down towards Lothian Road. Why do you ask?'

'Just a hunch is all.' I put the phone on mute and talk to Rebecca. 'Harry has CCTV of Jessica down this end of the street.' I say, pointing at the map, 'That's not far from the Lothian cluster. I think we should put your surveillance techniques to the test around there tonight.' I suggest.

'Hello John, are you there?'

'Sorry Harry, I was just looking that up on a map here. Did you see her leave the store in any particular direction?'

'No, I didn't unfortunately, and that's where it gets a little bit odd.'

'Odd how?'

'Well, odd in that the CCTV in that store is pretty damn good. I have her moving around the floors, I can even see what she is buying. Then she just disappears. I have no footage at all of her leaving the store and I have checked it all for the rest of the day.'

'It's not that odd. You couldn't find her leaving Jenners either.'

'No, sorry John, that's not the odd thing.'

Her Moons Denouement   Max Hardy

'Oh, alright. What is the odd thing then?'

'Do you recall this afternoon when the detectives took you away. The younger one, not the stern battle axe.'

'DI Tait? What about her?' I ask, perplexed, shrugging my shoulders toward an inquisitive Rebecca who was listening in on the call.

'Well, I saw her on the CCTV coming out of the store about half an hour after Jessica went in.'

'Okay, that could just mean that they both went shopping in the same store on the same day. Or it could mean that they were meeting each other?' I pondered aloud.

'Either are possibilities, but I have no footage of the two of them conversing or even passing close to each other. But even that isn't the odd thing.'

'That's odd enough! So come on, what is the odd thing?'

'The odd thing, and believe me I have checked and double checked, is that I can't find any CCTV footage of DI Tait entering the store.'

Chapter 29

'Sorry boys and girls, I know this is another late one but as you are no doubt aware from all of the press coverage on this today, our friends the 'Fallen Angels' don't appear to be sleeping. So if they don't sleep, we don't sleep. It's another day when we have been made to look like a bunch of amateurs. A day when the Superintendent has had to step in and invoke a Major Incident. A day when we have moved from enticement to incitement. And, I have to be brutal with all of us here, another day when we don't have the first fucking clue. A Detective from out of the area who is signed off on the sick is having more success figuring this case out than we are!'

Cruickshank paced up and down in front of the evidence boards in the incident room, glaring out into the audience of tired, browbeaten Detectives with a look of simmering fury. She stabbed a finger vehemently into the latest set of pictures on the boards, those of Chodak, his victims and the 'Fallen Angel' who committed suicide.

'Another mass murderer, another set of victims, another person dead and still no clues to point us in the direction of the 'Fallen Angels'. McCalvey, have we had anything back from forensics on the search of Aira Lee's apartment?'

DI McCalvey shuffled nervously in his chair and shook his head disconsolately. 'Nothing at all Ma'am. It is spotless. There aren't even any of her fingerprints. The only things in the place apart from a few bits of furniture were a painting in the kitchen and the photograph of Chodak in military fatigues along with the same man who was in the other two photographs of the killers. We still don't have any ID on him.'

'What about the fatigues? What army was Chodak fighting for?'

'Another extremist group, the Democratic Karen Buddhist Army. They are a breakaway group who support Burmese government offensives against the predominantly Christian led Karen National Liberation Army.'

'And GCHQ are certain they have never seen this man?'

'Absolutely certain Ma'am.'

'Okay. Well, keep searching. Tait, I want you to take a different tack with Bentley. Just confronting him with the evidence hasn't worked, and by the way, you are probably the only one of us today that seems to have gathered some real leads, so well done. Is everyone else taking note?' Cruickshank highlighted, looking disparagingly around the rest of the Detectives. 'I want you to play the superior friend card now. Get in there and tell him what a bastard I am and how you realise there is no concrete evidence against him. Go all out with the empathy. Try to get him to confide in you. Not in an interview room. Keep it all off the record. Take him a cuppa in his cell. Can you do that?'

'Yes Ma'am.' Tait answered crisply, her eyes buoyed by the compliment Cruickshank paid, but her expression acutely embarrassed under the withering glances from her colleagues.

'Good, now everyone, back to it. I have to prep with the Super now for tomorrow morning press conference and have to try and present a silk purse out of this pig's ear of a case.'

Her Moons Denouement   **Max Hardy**

Tait waited for everyone to leave, then slowly and thoughtfully followed them all out. She headed down the corridor to the tea room and picked up Bentley's chipped Celtic mug, pouring coffee from the warming percolator into it. She looked around the empty room furtively, before slipped something into the coffee. She wandered down to the booking desk and smiled at the Duty Sergeant.

'Evening Fred. Shankers wants me to have a chat with Bentley. I'm taking him a coffee. Is that okay?'

'Just sign your name in blood and remember to yodel if he attacks you.' Sergeant Calvey replied with a deadpan face.

Tait smiled as he led her down the row of locked cells and opened the door to Bentley's. She walked in, Calvey locking the door behind her.

'Behave yourself Bentley and remember Tait, yodel if he doesn't.' Calvey shouted through the observation hatch before slamming it shut.

Bentley was sitting against the wall on the floor, his legs stretched out in front of him and his hands pushed deep into the pockets of the dirty raincoat he had pulled tight around him. His face was streaked with sweat and caked on blood, hair matted to his forehead. He was looking down at his lace-less, scuffed Doc Martins and didn't look up to acknowledge Tait. She sat down on the floor next to him, putting her legs out straight as well and proffered him the coffee.

'Peace offering.' she said, simply.

Bentley took a hand out of his pocket and let it circle his mug, then raised it to his lips and took a long, lingering slurp of the dark, dense liquid, not once looking away from his boots nor offering any kind of gratitude.

'Shankers asked me to come in and play the superior friend card on you. She wanted me to tell you that it was her making me ask the

Her Moons Denouement   **Max Hardy**

questions earlier. Told me to talk to you off the record, gain your confidence and see if I can wheedle out of you whatever it is you know.' Tait said, speaking softly, with a hint of trepidation in her voice.

Bentley didn't answer. He took another sip of coffee, then turned his head and looked into her wide, naïve blue eyes.

'What the fuck's going on Bentley. Did you really know what was happening between your dad and sister?' Tait asked in a hushed voice brimming with incredulity.

His gaze dropped in embarrassment, looking back to the scuffs on his boots. The only sound in the cell was the slight wheeze of his breath and the crinkling of his raincoat as his chest rose and fell. They were augmented by a loud slurp as he took another gulp of coffee.

'Yes, I really knew. Just as I really know that your boyfriend hits you. Just because you know something, it doesn't automatically give you the right to have an opinion. It certainly doesn't give you the right to interfere.' he answered quietly, not looking from his boots once.

Tait's jaw dropped in surprised panic, her bottom lip trembling as she tried to compose herself to speak. 'He...' she started but was immediately interrupted.

'I don't want you to defend him. That's not why I said it. My point was, we all have lives behind closed doors. I can see you find the life behind my closed door disturbing. I could say the same about yours, but I don't. I know it's not something anyone would level at me, but I would like to think that I have a little empathy for the things people want to keep private. It's only if you laud your life in front of me that I'll rip you to shreds.'

'Sorry, I didn't mean to judge, it's just, well to be honest my gut reaction was shock. Shock that you knew.'

Her Moons Denouement   Max Hardy

'I understand that. Thanks for the coffee, you didn't have to make a peace offering. You did a good job in the interviews earlier. If I had those facts, I would have done the same, but probably with a bit more fucking swearing.'

'It didn't break you though, so either there is nothing there to break, or you are one hard heartless bastard.'

'Which one do you think it is?' he said, a glimmer of a smile crossing his anguished lips.

'I think it's the far end of both. Something there to break, but with a big soft heart.' she replied with candour.

'Is that why you aren't playing superior friend?'

Tait paused, her bottom lip trembling again as she gathered her composure. 'You know, over the past few days working with you, you have been nothing but supportive. Challenging, bloody minded, belligerent and boorish, yes: but my overriding feeling is of being supported. I don't want to be a boss. I don't want to be superior. Right now I don't even want to be a police officer. I just want to be a friend. Not because I think you haven't done anything wrong. But because I think you have.' she finished, fidgeting with her fingers as she looked openly at him.

Bentley stared at her for the longest of moments, taking in every aspect of her gaze. He looked back down at this boots and took another slurp of coffee.

'I was thirteen when mum left. Dessie was just coming up to her sixteenth birthday. Father took it hard. In the space of a few days he lost his wife and his career. He knew it was his fault. He knew there was no one else to blame. But it didn't stop him trying to blame someone else. I guess I was the one that got the brunt of that. Dessie is bipolar. When she is up, she is really up and when she is down: well.

Her Moons Denouement   **Max Hardy**

But she is good at controlling it, she know what helps to keep her up. What helped to keep her up back then was becoming Mum. She looked after us both, stepping in to do the cooking, the cleaning and the washing. Organising the two men of the house. She thrived and because he didn't have to worry about anything other than himself, Father did too. He found religion then as well, taking the Presbyterian stance that everyone is born a sinner, and as such is subject to God's wrath and the punishment of death. By God, did he use that wrath on me, literally.'

'Were they intimate, even back then?'

'No. Please don't think that Father was a paedophile. That isn't the case at all. Dessie became more than a Mum over time. Dessie wanted to be more than a Mum and Dessie can be very persuasive when she wants to be. She wanted to be a wife. She wanted to do everything a wife would do for her husband. She wanted to have a sexual relationship with Father. For a long time he refused, but she wore him down. She was twenty. It was then they started helping out at support groups for domestic violence. Father felt it was something he could give back, to help atone for his sins. I think it also helped him reconcile the relationship he has with Dessie. I am worried for them. I think they may be scared and hiding.'

'Hiding from what?' Tait queried.

'I told them someone was trying to set me up by involving people they had helped in the past. I think they are scared that if people start looking into our family, society will judge their relationship, just as you did.' Bentley responded, eyes filled with sadness.

'Where do you think they are?'

'I have no idea at all.' he began, still looking at his boots. Then his eyes shot up and he stared at Tait. 'Where's Jackson, is someone taking care of Jackson?'

Her Moons Denouement

'I think he's still at your house. There's an officer stationed there at the moment.'

'Could you find out for me?' he asked imploringly, fear furrowing his forehead.

'Don't worry, as a friend, I'll find out. I'll take him home if needs be.'

'Thanks.' Bentley said, relief washing over him. He took a last swig of coffee and passed the cup back to Tait. 'Thanks for listening and not questioning. Best of luck explaining that to Shankers!' he finished, the briefest flash of his fiery temperament enlivening the words.

Tait stood up and approached the door, banging on it loudly. 'Just leave her to me.' she said, smiling down at him sadly.

Sergeant Calvey opened the door and Tait left the cell, walking back to the Sergeant's desk. Cruickshank was sitting perched on the end of it, her arms crossed sternly, her expression just as severe.

'Well, did the superior friend garner any compelling evidence?'

'No Ma'am. He was tight lipped, hardly said a word.'

Chapter 30

It is disappointing not to find any sign of Madame Evangeline but I enjoyed my time with Rebecca. To watch her reminisce about the things they did at the places we visited was uplifting. The sheer love that oozed from every word she extolled, no matter how lewd they were, was just so heart warming. My empathy was in overdrive because the way she talks about Madame Evangeline is exactly the way I feel about Jess. My emotions are still so mixed up about her. I know Rebecca is finding it hard too. We love her, but we both know that she has played us. We both know she was involved in the deaths of other people we loved. That doesn't seem to stop our hearts yearning for her again. Why is that?

I pop the keycard into the lock of my hotel door and open it into near darkness. I enter the room and close it. I don't put the light on, but walk over to the window and open it, looking out over the city, seeing the nearly full moon peeking out from a layer of cloud low in the late evening sky. I turn to the left as I hear a window being raised and watch as Rebecca swings her legs out of it, her knee length pencil skirt rucked up around her hips to give the legs freedom. She smiles over to me with that same playful look she has had on her face all night as she prowls the narrow ledge with feline elegance and arrives in front of the window, not once using a hand to steady herself.

'Would you help a lady in kind Sir?' she mocks, managing a small curtsy on the ledge. My heart jumps as I briefly think she is falling.

Her Moons Denouement

Max Hardy

'More a whore than a lady tonight I think.' as I hold her hand and feign helping her through the window. Not that she needs any help at all as she demurely steps onto the carpet in her black stilettos and adjusts her skirt.

Suddenly, her hand grips mine tight and I feel her whole body tense.

'There's someone in the room John.' she whispers sibilantly, looking at the degrees of darkness over by the wall where most of the evidence is pinned. I look over as well, towards the outline of a chair which I know is over there. There is a subtle movement of shadows on the chair and the sound of ice clinking in a glass as it is placed on a table.

'I am so pleased the two of you have met at long last. I am even happier that you are getting on so well.'

Rebecca grips me even tighter and I reciprocate, the voice causing my throat to constrict, my heart to race and my whole body to start quivering. I know the voice. I know the woman.

The shadow stretches as she stands and slinks into a sliver of illumination sculpted by the moon, her long slender legs visible all the way to toned, bare thighs hugged by a short red leather skirt. A black sleeveless camisole top floats over her slim torso, swishing in the breeze of her strides as her long black hair framing a delicate, beautiful face enters the shaft of moonlight.

'Not even a 'Hello' from either of you for your old lover?' she says, her tone low and sultry, simmering and provocative.

I can't even speak. I am mesmerised. She is alive. There is no doubt. She is right in front of me. She is walking right towards me in the flesh. In the most beautiful, sensual, curvaceous flesh I have ever known.

Jessica takes one last stride and is right in front of us. She raises a hand and my gaze follows it hypnotically as she cups Rebecca's chin

Her Moons Denouement Max Hardy

and pulls it towards her face, to her parting lips, to her protruding tongue that sinks itself eagerly into Rebecca's opening, reciprocating mouth. Rebecca yelps as the urgency of the kiss overwhelms her, her knees sagging slightly. Jessica breaks the kiss suddenly, staring straight into my eyes and tilting her head towards me, mine moving closer to hers of its own volition until her tongue eagerly explores the inside of my willing mouth. My body aches under her touch. She breaks and takes a step back.

'You will have questions. Tonight, I will answer three, so think carefully on what they will be. But I will only answer them if you agree to do whatever I want in return. Whatever I want. There are no safe words. I will do exactly as I please. You both have to agree. If you don't, I leave.'

I start to speak, my countenance expressing concern, my mind screaming a million things at me, a million things I want to say. She puts a finger quickly onto my opening lips.

'Shush. There is no debate in this. You have a choice, but those choices are 'Yes' or 'No'. They are the only words I want to hear. Anything other than two 'Yeses' and I leave.'

I cannot take my eyes off her commanding emerald eyes. Her voice is intoxicating. I can't let her go. But can I agree to anything in return? Will Rebecca agree to anything in return? I feel her hand squeeze mine: just once.

'Yes.' we both say simultaneously, uncontrollable yearning dripping from the word.

'Rebecca, you have a few minutes to think of your first question while I do one of the things I want to do. Just stand there and watch while you think.' Jessica orders, taking a step closer to me.

Her Moons Denouement

Max Hardy

Her hands reach out to the buckle on my belt and I instinctively step back. She grabs it and pulls me forward, right into to her chest, into the heady fragrance of her perfume. She kisses me forcefully, undoing my belt and my trousers deftly, yanking them down and taking my underpants as well. I grimace as she kisses, as her hand catches my still scabbed and slightly weeping penis. My now fully erect scabbed and slightly weeping penis. She pulls her short skirt the small distance up over her pantie-less buttocks and then raises a long leg and circles it around my back, pushing her groin into my cock, roughly jiggling her hips until my tip finds her wet, gaping lips.

She grabs my hands as she lowers herself onto me, standing on one leg, pulling her other leg tight into my backside. She presses her thumbs into the stigmata in my palms and bites my tongue as she kisses me furiously, her hips moving up and down along my length, the muscles of her cunt constricting tightly around my aching cock. She pulls my hands around from my sides and forces them onto her bare behind, breaking the kiss for a frantic breath. She sneers at me, forcing my hands hard into her arse.

'Fuck me hard and don't stop until you come!' she orders aggressively, pushing herself down onto me quicker and quicker. My heart is racing, blood coursing through my veins all the way down to my groin as the mixture of pleasure and pain overwhelms my mind. My balls start to tighten in the glow of orgasm as she pumps harder and harder, my cock swelling uncontrollably inside her as the rush starts and I grunt with every earthy thrust. I throw my head back, clasping her bum so tight I lift her off the ground as the first spurt of ejaculate shoots up inside her and I scream, inflicting half a dozen more forceful thrusts upon her, before I am spent, my face ruddy, my whole body dripping in sweat. I pull her torso tightly into me, still deep inside, feeling her whole body against mine, bathing in the afterglow.

She reaches up and kisses me, taking a lip between her teeth and biting it, drawing blood as she breaks.

Her Moons Denouement   Max Hardy

'I have missed that John. I have missed you.' she says through tear filled, sweating eyes, her smile soft and radiant. Still sitting on my length, she turns to Rebecca.

Rebecca who has her skirt around her waist, who has a hand in her panties pleasuring herself.

'I've taught you well.' Jessica says, still squeezing me inside her.

'But you might want to stop while you ask me your question.'

Rebecca didn't stop, just looked deep into Jessica's eyes with a fiery unrequited passion.

'Who are you, really? John knows you as Jess, I know you as Madame Evangeline, Michael knew you as Eve.'

'I am all of them, depending on who I want to be. But it's not the name that is important, it is the person that I am. The person you all fell in love with. I was born Jessica Seymour. My father was Henry Seymour, although you will know him as my late husband. I have had many names in my life, but the one I go by most of the time nowadays is Eve. I would like you to call me Eve. That is all. Now John, your turn to think of a question. I think Rebecca may need a hand.'

Eve lifts herself off my still erect penis and walks the single step to Rebecca, slinking a hand inside her panties to join the one already in there. Eve grabs Rebecca's free hand and thrusts it between her cum dripping thighs, forcing three of Rebecca's fingers deep inside herself. My penis is still rock hard and I stroke it as I watch them, kicking my trousers from my ankles as I do. Eve pulls Rebecca tight into her, so that their groins are almost touching, so that the frantically moving hands are banging off each other. They both lean heads in forcefully and start to kiss frantically, the agitated excitement building, their hands moving more rapidly. Both start to moan amongst the kisses, hips bucking under the intensity of the fingering. My throat is dry, my

Her Moons Denouement   Max Hardy

own pulse racing watching two women frig the life out of themselves. They break mouths simultaneously, both breathing heavily, both staring intently into their glistening emerald eyes. Deep frantic panting, forceful finger thrusts, faster and faster, until they both throw their heads back and scream in the throes of orgasm.

Eve looks longingly at Rebecca, takes a hand from between her legs and licks the glistening juices off her fingers. 'It has been far too long my beautiful lover.' she says wistfully, running one of those fingers down the outline of the scars on a cheek. 'We let you down. You should never have been in that hospital. Your question John.'

Oh god, my mind isn't even thinking about questions, it is thinking about the two of them pleasuring each other, it is thinking about fucking Eve. They let Rebecca down. Why?

'Why did you do this to us? Why did you put Rebecca in a position where she fucked her son? Why did you put me in a position where I killed my wife and thought I had killed my son?'

'Life is about choice. Life is about experience. Experience dictates the choices you make. Experience defines your life. We all have filters. Fears, ideals, morals, beliefs. Things that can influence the choices we make and the experiences we expose ourselves to. Why? We wanted to see how you would react with the filters taken away. My last desire now before your last question, so think carefully.'

Eve backs away from Rebecca, running her hands down between her own legs pleasurably as she does, then running them up her body, over her breasts as she reaches the edge of the bed. She sits down and pushes her body backward onto the bed, onto her back, head resting on the pillows, knees in the air, legs wide apart. Her shaven, glistening, gaping lips stare out at me and make my thick length throb. I want her again.

Her Moons Denouement   Max Hardy

'Rebecca I want you between my legs, licking my lips, sucking my clit, hands playing with my breasts, bringing me off. Take your panties off. John, I want you behind Rebecca, watching her cunt as she pleasures me. I want you to do what your body tells you to do. Every single thing your body tells you to.'

Rebecca looks at me and reaches out a hand, squeezing it once as she leads me over to the bed. She slips her panties off and then crawls onto the bed, between Eve's thighs, her stunted tongue going straight in to drink the mix of love juices. I watch as her behind rises into the air, as her shaven, naked cunt and pulsing anus stare right up at me. Eve is watching me, her face contorted in pleasure, her hands pushing Rebecca's head into her groin, her lips whispering encouragement. Rebecca starts to gyrate her hips, the rhythmic motion hypnotising me, drawing me in. I step closer and take my penis in my hand. I let the tip touch her moving bum cheeks, let the feeling of the wisps of her flesh against it wash over me. My mind is telling me that I shouldn't be doing this. I don't really know Rebecca. But every other sinew of me being is willing me to enter her. I move my cock closer, letting it linger in the cleavage of her cheeks, letting it ride with her rhythm. I slide it down the crease, letting it rest on the slightly open anus. I push gently, the minutest part of my tip entering her and hear a timorous shriek. I pull back, scared that I have hurt her. But that is what I want to do, with every single fibre of my being.

'Do it John. Do what your body tells you to do.' Eve says as she sees me pull back, her eyes rolling ecstatically as she speaks.

I move back in, letting my end ride her crease again, letting it naturally dance with her cheeks, letting it find a natural place against her anus. And I push. And Rebecca screams, forcing her backside against me. I put my hands on her bum cheeks, grabbing them and pulling as she forces back onto me, sinking my whole length inside her, then using my hips to pull it back, then in, then back. I slide my hands down her back, watching Eve loll her head in the bliss of cunnilingus, hearing her

Her Moons Denouement

Max Hardy

moaning grow in intensity. I slip my hands under Rebecca's blouse, and around her front, cupping her braless breasts, circling the nipples between my thumb and forefinger. I squeeze them tight, moving my hips faster and faster, sliding in and out of her, feeling another orgasm growing, feeling Rebecca pushing herself hard against me, feeling Eve's eyes burning into me passionately. I start moaning, start growing, start throbbing, and jerk, forcing the orgasm hard into Rebecca's arse, forcing Rebecca's head right into Eve's cunt, forcing both Eve and Rebecca to scream.

Rebecca slumps to the bed, taking me with her, my penis sliding out as we both land next to Eve in a heap. Eve pushes herself up on the cushion and slings her legs over the side of the bed.

'One last question Rebecca, what do you want to know?' Eve says, standing up and pulling down her short skirt, it barely covering her false modesty.

Rebecca raises her head from the bed, my body rising slightly as she does. 'Who are the Fallen Angels?'

'A group of people who have a belief. A belief that fear is what stops us from becoming everything we can be. A belief that the faiths we have all been fed are founded in fear. We have walked the earth for a long time and there have been many of us, many that you would know by name. We have been living, experiencing, watching and waiting. Waiting for our time. Our time is now.'

Eve turns and slinks to the open window, her silhouette framed in the light of the moon as she turns back to us. 'I checked your wall earlier. I am impressed. You know more than I thought, but there were a couple of things in the wrong place and a few things missing. I did a bit of rearranging. You might want to check it out.'

Her Moons Denouement   Max Hardy

Eve slings her legs over the window sill and looks back one last time. 'Everything we do, we do because we love you. Always remember that.' She smiles a melancholic smile and then is gone.

I back off the bed, half naked, not bothered about it in the slightest and bang the switch on the bedside lamp, illuminating the room, illuminating the evidence wall. Rebecca rises too, equally as unconcerned about her state of undress. We both approach the wall, looking at the things that had been moved. The main things that had been moved were clearly visible. Four groups of three pictures.

Archbishop Liam O'Driscoll, Elvis Aarons and a man I don't recognise.

Imam Mann, Tej Mann and the same unknown man.

Chodak, Aira Lee and the same man again.

Then that man, in a picture with Edward Bentley, Fenny Bentley's image pinned just below it. The next murderer is Edward Bentley.

Chapter 31

The police car drove slowly down the incline towards the peninsula below the Forth Rail Bridge, Tait staring into the illumination of the headlights, looking for the side road up to Bentley's house. She put her foot down and speeded up slightly when she saw it, powering the vehicle up the small gravel track to the edge of the garden where she parked up behind another police car.

Tait got out of the car and looked up to the foreboding, dark lifeless façade of the house, her expression perplexed when she saw no rooms illuminated. She looked into the drivers window of the other car, shaking her head when she saw it empty.

'Strange, I wonder where Cummings is?' she said to herself, walking up the weed infested path towards the front door, carefully watching her footfalls in the soft light from the moon shining down from above the bridge.

The door was slightly ajar. Tait took a pen light from her pocket and shone it into the small gap, before pushing the door wider. She heard a low whimpering and dropped the light downwards to the source. Jackson sat in his small kennel shaking, his innocent, doe eyed Labrador face staring back up at her.

'Hello son.' she said, leaning down to stroke the top of his head. He took a few steps out of the kennel, wagging his tail and sinking his muzzle into her crotch. 'Whoa boy, less of that now. Is there anyone

Her Moons Denouement   Max Hardy

here son, have you seen Cummings?' she finished, ruffling his ear before standing back up.

She reached to the left and flicked a light switch on the wall, expecting illumination. The hall stayed dark. She flicked it a few times with no change in outcome. 'Okay, not strange at all then.'

She shone the pen light into the oppressive blackness of the hallway, letting the focused beam dance over the floor and the walls. There was no movement. 'Cummings, are you there?' she shouted, standing up and flashing the light up the stairwell, resting the beam upon each step. The house was silent, apart from the soft panting of Jackson beside her and the breathing of the breeze behind her. She walked down the hallway, angling the light into the open doors to the rooms on the right, not catching any movement as she did, the dog following along behind.

'Where are you Cummings.' she whispered under her breath, scanning the kitchen in front of her, casting the pen beam over the table and the worktops, all the way to the back door out into the garage. The back door that was open.

'He doesn't seem to be here.' Tait said, apropos of nothing, talking into the air as she walked through the kitchen quietly, with Jackson in tow, to the back door. She angled the beam into the garage, picking out the bits of car dotting the floor and the hidden door that was propped open on the back wall. She stepped into the garage, flashing the light down the front end, seeing nothing moving in the consuming darkness obscuring the dust encrusted remnants of vehicles.

Jackson was about to step into the garage after her, but she put out a hand and with a firm voice said 'No Jackson, stay.' The dog sat, head tilted to one side, tongue lolling out of his panting snout. 'Good boy.' she praised, then turned and approached the opening in the back wall,

Her Moons Denouement

shining her light down the step ladder, letting it play on the hewn granite.

'Cummings, are you down there?' she shouted, listening intently to the silence emanating from the hole. No answer. She pulled the cord for the light and smiled to herself when nothing illuminated, and then started to descend the step ladder, looking down and flashing the pen light into the base. She reached the bottom and stepped into the small room, letting the beam move over the wooden floor, up to the empty bed and then around the bare stone walls. Nothing. She approached the nearest wall and started to run her hand over it methodically, starting at the top and going from left to right.

'No sign of Cummings. Mark my location.' she said, again into the air, to no prompt. She moved down the wall, crouching as she got lower, focusing the pen light under the bed, seeing a piece of cloth poking out from between one of the floor boards. She sunk to her knees and reached under the bed, pulling the material out.

'Looks like a ripped piece of a police uniform. My guess would be Cummings. He may have caught them coming out.' she said, putting her hand to the floor as a confused expression crossed her face. Her hand started to vibrate, in time with the floorboards that started to shake.

'Somethings happening. The floor...' she screamed just as the boards beneath her feet fell away from behind her, into the ground, knocking her off her feet and causing her to slide down the opening floor. She scrabbled for purchase, trying to grab the leg of the bed that wasn't falling. She missed it and tumbled down into a dark, consuming pit that swallowed her whole.

Chapter 32

'More skirmishes broke out yesterday at churches over Edinburgh with a total of twenty five arrests being made. The heightened police presence in the city and the zero tolerance approach we are taking ensured that they were all short lived. In all cases, the incitement was instigated by groups protesting in defence of their particular religion. Police Scotland are running the protection of the City and the containment of the skirmishes as a Major Incident and will keep a focus on it until the troubles die down.' Cruickshank started, speaking into a bank of microphones in front of her, looking out into a sea of vulturous faces feeding on the intonation and inference of every word she uttered, rolling them around in their mind into lurid headlines. The press room was packed, every seat taken and every alleyway and gap in the room filled with TV crews, reporters and photographers.

Cruickshank continued indomitably, her features stoic, her voice trembling with authority. 'We are still pursuing criminal investigations into the three mass murderers, the three suicides and the identity and whereabouts of the group calling themselves 'The Fallen Angels.' If any member of the public has any information that may help us with any of those criminal enquiries, especially if they know any of the people identified as being involved in them, then please ring Police Scotland immediately. A number of prominent politicians and business people were arrested as part of our investigation, but I can confirm that they have all been released and no charges relating to this investigation were made. We did however make a number of charges relating to other offences. That is all I am able to say at this point.'

Camera's started flashing followed quickly by and a crescendo of questions blurted out from the crowd of journalists, all vying for immediate attention. Cruikshank stood and addressed the audience again. 'I am sorry ladies and gentlemen, that really is all I am able to say at this point. There will be another press briefing at eighteen hundred hours and we hope to have some more information for you then.' She turned from the briefing bench and walked stiffly, head held high, out through a door to the left, questions still being hurled at her receding back.

She shut the door and leant against it, closing her eyes and taking a deep breath, before opening them again, three of her Senior Detectives waiting in the foyer for her.

'I couldn't even say we have a number of people helping us with our ongoing enquiries. We are exposed and the press are gunning for us. Riots in the city, murders and suicides: it is chaos out there. We need to focus today and show that we are making progress. Where the hell is Tait, she's ten minutes late!' Cruickshank admonished, as she strode past the three Detectives.

DI Purves spoke up bravely. 'I haven't seen her this morning Ma'am. I left a message on her mobile about fifteen minutes ago.' she finished, falling in line behind her.

'Not what I expect from a senior on this team. Has anyone been to check on Bentley this morning with her not being around?'

'Yes Ma'am. Le Fenwick was down earlier. Bentley had pains in his chest. Le Fenwick thinks he's suffering from stress. He's advised us to wait a while before we start questioning again.' Purves answered.

Her Moons Denouement   Max Hardy

'For fucks sake, he's the only unofficial suspect we've got and we can't question him because he's feeling a bit stressed! Gregory, go and find Le Fenwick and tell him to come and see me.'

'Will do Ma'am.' Gregory answered as he peeled off the back of Cruickshanks entourage and headed back down the corridor. Cruikshank entered her office, Purves and Trentor following her in.

'Now, we have a briefing at ten and I want a plan of attack from each of you on every single lead we have outstanding. I want a dust down of everything we have already checked and a peer review done on our assumptions. We need to break something today and that has to be before another person ends up dead. Any questions?'

Purves and Trentor shook their heads simultaneously, speaking in tandem as well, 'No Ma'am.'

'Well, what are you waiting for, get to it!' she shouted as she dropped her eyes back to the open folder on the desk in front of her, just as the phone beside it rang, the two Detectives turning to leave.

'Yes!' she barked down the line, her expression turning from frustrated to serious as she listened.

'Purves, Trentor, back her now!' she shouted towards the receding Detectives, who turned on their heels and walked back into the office.

'Yes Ma'am.' Trentor asked, entering first, noting her agitatedly pointing digit instructing them to sit.

'And the press have it already? What time is it going out? Shit, that's in fifteen bloody minutes. Have I got it?' Cruikshank asked, urgency in her voice and actions as she quickly turned the computer monitor next to her on and started wiggling the mouse beside it agitatedly. She looked at her e-mail. 'Right, got it.' she finished, hanging the phone up without a goodbye.

Her Moons Denouement   Max Hardy

'We have a video already this morning from the 'Fallen Angels'. The press have it too and the major news channels will be airing it in fifteen minutes. Let's see what they have in store for us today.' Cruickshank said sarcastically, clicking on the MP4 file attached to the e-mail.

Windows Media Player started up and the screen went black. Four tiny letters popped up in red in the middle of the screen, then started to grow, filling the screen with the word 'FEAR'.

'What do you fear?' the words burst out of the computer speakers loudly, the voice filling the room, the screen changing to show images of Liam O'Driscoll, Imam Mann and Chodak's victims quickly flicking by.

'Do you fear someone you ask for help?' An image of Liam O'Driscoll appears, lingering for a moment to be replaced by Imam Manns, then after the same interval Chodak's, pausing on his face.

'Do you fear the faith that is meant to comfort, that is meant to love, that is meant to forgive, that is all about peace? That is his faith.'

The screen turns black. Two green circles appear, slowly growing to reveal two eyes, the eyes blinking as the blackness fades out, to be replaced by the half white painted face of Madame Evangeline in her Pierrott outfit, sitting behind the same nondescript desk, with the same Cezanne picture behind her.

'This man, Chodak, a Buddhist Monk, let his victims believe in the spirituality of love and of sex. He was meant to be celibate but he lured women into a secret, forbidden world of Tantric sex. They participated willingly, becoming his Mudra, believing that they were entering into a spiritual relationship, but in reality becoming victims of the tantric female sacrifice. His intent was always to kill them because they were older women, because the way of tantra identified them as demons.'

Her Moons Denouement

Max Hardy

Madame Evangeline's face is replaced by another picture, of an Asian woman, with a short brown bob, slight wrinkles on her brow and crows feet in the corner of her eyes, but with unblemished smooth skin otherwise, her dark brown eyes intense and her smile effervescent.

'Aira Lee was one of his Mudra. He made her swear to keep their tantric relationship secret. He made her swear, using the fear of his faith, of a millennia of hellish torments if she told anyone, as a threat. But she was stronger than the fear of his faith, strong enough to discover what he was really doing, strong enough to expose him and his faith.'

Aira's image faded, replaced once again with Madame Evangeline, who raised a tissue to her face and wiped away the white paint from around her left eye.

'We have exposed three murderers and their fifteen victims. We have one more to go. One more vicious, evil murderer to expose. One more man who has killed more women than the other three monsters combined. One more man who, somewhere in Edinburgh right now, has recently trapped their latest victim.'

Cruickshank's phone starts ringing and she looks at it in frustration, picking it up and turning back to the screen. 'Yes!' she shouts.

'His faith tells him that everyone is born a sinner, and as such is subject to God's wrath and the punishment of death, which means eternal separation from God in Hell. Do you fear his faith?'

Cruickshank turned from the screen, shock overwhelming her face as she looked at her colleagues. 'What time did they find the body? Any indication yet how long it had been in the water? He was here at nine last night, I saw him just before he went out to the house for the evening. Is there any sign of Tait? What the hell was she doing there?'

Her Moons Denouement   Max Hardy

'Tonight at nine o'clock we will reveal his faith, we will reveal who he is and we will reveal the atrocities he has enacted upon this world in the name of his faith.'

Cruickshank replaced the receiver, still looking at her colleagues in disbelief, shaking her head. 'Campbell is dead. They found his body floating in the Forth, just down from Bentley's house. He was strangled. The car Tait has booked out is at Bentley's house as well. There is no sign of her. Do either of you know why she was there?'

'We do not ask you to believe in us. All we are doing is revealing the atrocities that these monsters enacted in the name of your faith. We only want you to ask yourself one question, as you look into the eyes of his next victim.'

All three detectives turn to the screen on hearing those words, watching the image fade to near darkness, only Madame Evangeline's eyes left. They turn from emerald to blue, then the blackness starts to fade out and a face starts to appear.

'Ask yourself, why do I fear my faith? Even Fallen Angels Have Wings. We are the 'Fallen Angels' and I am Madame Evangeline.'

The face on the screen shifts into focus and Cruickshank jumps from her seat, grabbing the phone and hitting the last call button furiously. 'How the hell can that be!' she shouted, panicking, looking incredulously at the two Detectives who were just as dumbfounded.

'McCalvey, we have to stop them broadcasting that video. This one isn't just about people who are already dead. They have one of ours. It's Annie. Whoever this person is, they have Annie Tait.'

Chapter 33

The police car pulls away from the kerb and heads off down into Randolph Crescent away from DI Tait's apartment. I watch from a little way down the street, standing behind an outcrop of trees on the roundabout at Ainslee Place, waiting to see if anyone else comes out. It was strange seeing the images of Madame Evangeline quickly followed by DI Tait on the news. In succession, the bone structure is nearly exact and the general proportions of the face are the same. Massah had me thinking yesterday that Tait was another of Eve's aliases. I find it hard to believe, considering I had sat in a room right next to her and not even got an inkling of that. That's not possible considering how intimate I have been with Eve. She was also at the foot of the Monument yesterday a few seconds after I saw Eve. She couldn't have been in two places at once. But then, neither could Jess when I knew she was in the hotel room with me on that fateful New Year's Eve. We've got to check it out, because Tait lives slap bang in the middle of where Rebecca and Eve used to meet.

I walk over the road onto the pavement by her apartment, nonchalantly strolling by, gazing up to the windows as I do, looking for any sign of life. There is none. I take my mobile from my jeans pocket and call Rebecca.

'The police have just gone. Meet me around the back in five minutes.'

Her Moons Denouement   Max Hardy

We walked down this street last night on our reconnaissance and had checked out the backs of the apartments, voyeuristically peeking through gaps in curtains. Rebecca was right. We saw some hellishly depraved sights last night. The back of the buildings are accessible via Dean Gardens, just around the corner. I walk swiftly in that direction, gazing into every window of the terraced Edwardian Townhouses as I pass them. Most are offices, or consulates on the first couple of floors, with the apartments being on the top floor generally. I turn a corner into Dean Gardens, walking through the dense verdant trees and thick luscious grass until I reach the back fence to Tait's townhouse. Rebecca steps from behind a tree and joins me at the gate leading into the long, well maintained garden. Today she is wearing a blonde wig in a short bob, with huge black mirrored sunglasses covering most of her face.

'Are you sure it's empty?' Rebecca asks, leaning over and pecking me on the cheek. She does it so naturally, with a warmth to the touch of her lips that is comforting.

'I saw the boyfriend leave shortly after the police arrived. He seemed to be upset, stomping off in the direction of the park. It doesn't mean he won't come back so we better get in and out quickly. Remember, anything that would suggest Eve. Think about make up, prosthetics, wigs. Think about the clothes you know she wears. Think about perfumes, jewellery and intimate things. It will be that type of thing that will give her away.'

'I don't see how she can be Eve. You saw the news this morning. I mean, why would the 'Fallen Angels' put out a video with Eve and Tait in it if she is the same person. What are they trying to achieve?'

'I don't know. What I do know is that this building is slap bang in the middle of your old whoring ground and there's just the slightest chance Tait is Eve. Anything is possible with these guys.' I answer as we stalk down the side of the garden, keeping close to the boundary

Her Moons Denouement   Max Hardy

fence. We arrive at the base of the outside fire escape, blooming flower pots sitting on the rusting wrought iron steps. I step a careful path through the vari-coloured flora, Rebecca close behind, and ascend all the way to the back door of Tait's apartment. I quickly look around, watching for watchers. I can only see a few people strolling through Dean Gardens, enjoying the late morning sun. I can't see anyone in the gardens of the other houses.

I slide a pick into the Yale lock on the back door and wiggle it agitatedly. It turns and I push the door open, surreptitiously slinking into a small kitchen, Rebecca directly behind me.

'I'll check the bedrooms, you check the living areas.' Rebecca instructs, surprising me with her forthright command of the situation. Her dominatrix coming out. I nod and then start searching the kitchen. What strikes me immediately is how sparsely furnished it is. Apart from two cups and a still wet spoon, there is no other crockery visible, either on worktops or in the sink. I open a few cupboards, which are also empty and pull a few drawers, not surprised to see they are empty too. I walk from the kitchen into a narrow short hallway, the main front door at the far end of it on the right, a bedroom at the far end on the left and two doors opposite me.

Two doors with a wall in between them. A wall with a picture on it. The picture is a Cezanne. 'The Abduction'. It's believed to represent the abduction of Proserpine by Pluto. Gods and Goddesses. I don't need to see any more. Eve has been here.

I hear a click to my right and the handle on the front door turns.

'Rebecca, hide!' I whisper loudly as I start to step back into the kitchen just as the door opens, catching a glimpse of a man in a tweed suit. A man I recognise instantly. I stop on my heels, staring down the hall in utter disbelief as Harry Massah enters the apartment, smiling in my direction as he sees me.

Her Moons Denouement   Max Hardy

'Good morning John, where's Rebecca?' he asks conversationally as he approaches. My mind does somersaults. He is not surprised we are here? How does he know Rebecca is with me? How does he know that I have even met up with Rebecca, I never told him? Where the hell did he get a key from? Does he know Tait?

'Harry, what are you doing here?' I ask lamely, flabbergasted by his presence in the apartment.

'All three of us need to talk and we need to talk now. Rebecca!' he says, his voice taking on an Irish lilt as he calls out the name, walking towards me, still smiling.

Why am I in Edinburgh? I am here because of pictures of Jessica and I boarding a train. Pictures that Harry showed me. Why did we search this area? Partly because of Rebecca, but also because the CCTV Harry discovered showed Jess heading in this direction. Why am I in this apartment? Because Harry told me that he saw Jessica enter a shop and Tait leave the same shop shortly afterward. He led me to believe they could be one in the same person. Why am I standing here right now, utterly surprised that Harry is in front of me: because he wanted me to be.

'Adam, or Ben, or Rob or the 'Unknown Caller' I take it.' I say as Rebecca comes running out of the bedroom, bewildered and confused.

'Doc?' she questions, looking from me to Harry, confounded when she doesn't see who she is expecting to see.

'Answers to both those questions in a moment, but follow me please. We don't have a lot of time and I have a lot to tell you.' Harry answers, walking past me and towards Rebecca who is still looking confused.

'Good to see you filling out a bit again, you were a rake a few weeks ago.' he says in his Irish accent, passing Rebecca and stroking her arm

Her Moons Denouement Max Hardy

as he walks into the bedroom. I follow behind Rebecca who slipstreams his authoritative strides.

Harry walks straight to the back of the room, which is decorated in tongue and groove panelling painted duck egg blue, and presses the palm of his hand forcefully against the end of one of the grooves. There is a click and with a slight whoosh, a door opens up into the bedroom, revealing a very short dividing walkway. Harry enters it, takes a key out of his pocket, and opens another door at the other side.

'Come on through. This adjoins the house next door. John, pull the door closed behind you please.' Harry instructs, in his Harry accent, upper-class and precise.

We are in another bedroom, very much like the one we have just left, but this one without a bed in. Harry walks toward the back wall of this room, which is also tongue and grooved in the same colour, and presses his palm firmly against a spot about halfway up a groove that looks no different to all the rest. There is a low whirr of an electrical motor and the whole wall of panelling starts to move sideways, exposing row upon row and column upon column of monitors. Eighty in total, all with different images on them. Some have images of rooms, some of people, some of maps with flashing red dots. Some are full of notes and pictures. It is like an electronic version of an incident wall.

Harry quickly glances at the screens, his gaze pausing on one with a map, a still dot and the name 'Eve' above it, before turning to face us both. Rebecca is at my side and her hand snakes into mine, squeezing it nervously.

'I have a lot to tell you and I know you will have a million questions so I want to start by saying we don't have time to answer them all right now. Either you live with that, or you leave now. It is entirely your choice. What do you say?' Harry asks.

I squeeze Rebecca's hand once, and she speaks. 'We can live with it. We just want to know why Doc. Why are we here?'

'Right at this moment, you are here because we need your help. Eve has been abducted and we do not know where she is. We need your help to try and find her.' Harry asks, openly and with sincerity.

'Hold on.' I say, just a tad sternly. 'Is it Eve who was disguised as Annie Tait?'

'Yes, Eve is Annie.'

'Well, you already know that Annie, sorry Eve is missing, you broadcast that on your latest video. I'm confused.'

'Yes, we did broadcast that. That was our plan. But the plan wasn't that Eve would really be abducted. The plan was to make it look like she had been abducted. It was meant to apply pressure on Bentley and give the police some more ammunition to use against him. It was also to allow Eve time to focus on breaking him down. But Eve genuinely went missing last night and our Plan A is currently in the balance. I am hoping you will agree to be our Plan B. Look, I am answering things out of turn here. I need to tell you what is going on so at least you have the right information to make an informed decision. Let's start with who I am.' Harry finishes, raising his hands to his face, and rubbing his fingers over his cheeks, eyes and brow, harder and harder. Skin breaks, or at least that's what it looks like, but I quickly realise it is painted latex from the mask he is wearing as he pulls it off his face.

I always question myself when I look in the mirror. Ironically, I think it makes you reflective when you are looking at your own physicality. It makes you question who you really are. You see the wrinkles starting

Her Moons Denouement   Max Hardy

to show around the eyes from too many late shifts. You see your lips frowning from not enough smiles and far too much pain. You look into eyes that wear the weight of the world.

Rebecca gasps, looking quickly back and forth between the two of us, mouth agape.

But when you see your own face, and there are no wrinkles, and the lips are smiling with no frown lines, and the eyes are alive with possibility, it really brings home how much we wear our experiences on the outside, for all to see. It shows how two people who are otherwise identical, who must be twins, can look so different. I see me, but I don't see my soul.

'Are you my brother, my twin brother?' I ask, the questions coming out broken, from a dry throat.

'Unfortunately, that's not for me to say. It is for you to discover, and right at the moment, it is not why we are here. What I can say is that I am Adam and I am the father of the 'Fallen Angels'. I was born Robert Caldwell and over the years I have had many names. You have known me as a few of them.'

He can't tell me! He is standing right in front of me, a man that is my fucking double, must be my fucking twin, must know where I fucking come from and who my fucking parents are and he can't tell me! He sees the fury in my eyes and his own fill with empathy as he approaches me and holds my arms.

'John, I am sorry for being so brutal. I know you want answers and while it is a simple question, believe me, the answer is far from simple. We don't have time and I have to be honest, and yes, brutal, you aren't ready to have that question answered, not yet. Now I need to tell you what is going on. I need to ask for your help. Can we focus on that please?'

'Better do as the Doc says John. He knows what he is doing. He saved my life and led me on the road to redemption.' Rebecca adds, squeezing my hand tighter, winking at me.

The fury is still bubbling in my stomach, but I can see that he isn't going to tell me anything. I can see that clearly in his eyes. 'Okay, so this all has to do with Fenny Bentley, does it?'

'This part does. Our bigger plan is about exposing the hypocrisy of religion, about exposing the monsters out there that use faith as a weapon and about asking people to question their fears. This last part is about the Bentley family. Eve has been living a life as Annie Tait now for just over eighteen months, shortly after you were convicted of murdering Michael.' he says, looking over to Rebecca.

'Something went wrong in our plans Rebecca. Michael was never meant to die and we certainly didn't know that Ennis was going to mutilate him in the way he did.'

'So I was part of a plan, even back then, just a pawn in your sick game?' Rebecca asks. I feel her hand tensing and shaking and I can understand why. She is feeling like me, a pawn again.

'That's not important right now. Eve is important and she is in grave danger. She may already be dead. Now, I know this is hard but we have to focus.' Adam answers, seeing the anger bubbling in Rebecca.

'We knew that Bentley had carried out an atrociously bad investigation into Michael's death and we wanted to know why. Eve became Annie and started to investigate. What she found out was that his investigation into Michael's death was non-existent. He took the professional medical advice of Ennis and the detailed forensic evidence and didn't question one single bit of it. What she did find out, when digging into case histories, was that over a number of years women who were the victims of domestic abuse have been going missing, never to be found. She discovered that Fenny Bentley was involved in a number of those investigations. She also found out that Bentley's father and sister had met every one of those missing women at victim support groups shortly before they disappeared. Eve recently found out that Bentley's mother was beaten by his father and that she went missing too.'

'So you think that Bentley is involved in these disappearances. Do you think he has been murdering them, similar to the other religious leaders that you are exposing?' I ask, the information stirring my interest.

'He is definitely involved, and we do think the women are all dead. But it's his father that is the killer. We are sure of that. What we don't know, is if Bentley knows that, and we definitely don't know how they are killing them. We think Bentley may genuinely believe that he is helping victims of domestic abuse escape their abusers, and is helping them escape to a life in another country. Eve found that Bentley has been getting false passports made for a number of years, all for women. All provided shortly after a victim went missing. Today she was going to confront Bentley with that theory and show him that not a single one of those women ever made it out of the country. She was going to show him a photograph of his father with this man.' Adam points to a picture on a screen, the same one Eve put up on my Evidence wall last night.

'You have pictures of him with every one of the religious leaders that you have exposed, who is he?'

'That's another conversation for later. The conversation for now is that she can't do that anymore because while she was searching for more evidence at Bentley's house last night, we believe his father abducted her.' Adam says, pointing to a still red dot on the screen with Eve's name above it, the map showing the North Queensferry peninsula.

Her Moons Denouement   Max Hardy

I look at the screen above it, a screen with my name on, a map of Edinburgh and a red beating dot over this house. There is a screen for Rebecca and one for Adam and another dozen or so with different names above them. I look down at my arm. Have they always known exactly where I am?

'So what's your Plan B Doc? Can we stop pussyfooting around and can you tell us exactly what is it you want us to do? If Eve is in danger, we should get cracking.' Rebecca interrupts, stepping forward and looking at the images on the screens. Eve has taught her well. She is a leader.

'We want you to interview Bentley. We want you to find out where his father is keeping Eve. We want you to find out if he is involved.'

'Okay, only one problem there as I see it, he is currently sitting in a police cell. I don't think Police Scotland are going to let an escaped murderer and a Detective who has already been warned off the case three times anywhere near him.' Her voice is loaded with sarcasm as she stops in front of an image of a police cell, Fenny Bentley sitting on the floor of it.

'How the hell have you got a CCTV stream from his cell?' I ask as I scan the other moving images, seeing a few that look familiar. There is one of the kitchen in the apartment next door. There is one of the hotel room next to mine. There is one of my hotel room. They have cameras in the pictures! That's why there are so many Cezanne's, they are using the pictures as cameras. Why Cezanne though?

'We have walked this earth a long time John and there are a great number of us, in every walk of life. It is not hard to open a locked door when you either have the key, or know the person who does. We were never going to carry out Bentley's final interrogation at the station. We were always going to do that here.'

Chapter 34

'Ma'am, you need to come down to the cells, quickly.' Calvey said over the phone, Cruickshank rising from her seat the second she heard the frantic tone in the Sergeant's voice.

'What is it Fred?' she questioned as she rounded the table, still holding the phone to her ear.

'It's Bentley Ma'am, Le Fenwick thinks he is having a heart attack.'

'Shit.' Cruickshank cursed, throwing the receiver onto the table, not even trying to hit the phone cradle as she turned and headed for the door at pace, striding down the corridor. She barged past people in her way unceremoniously, her whole manner brusque, not offering any apologies and then sprinted through the Duty reception towards the holding cells, towards a small crowd of people listening intently to the sound of a commotion.

'Come on people, let me through!' she barked, pushing the milling officers out of the way, the sound of Le Fenwick's voice rising above the general chatter.

'Come on Fenny, stay with me, breathe slowly, in and out.'

Cruikshank arrived at the open cell door and stepped through to see Bentley splayed out on the cell floor, his whole body tense and jerking. Coffee was pooling around him, coming from a broken Celtic mug next to his quivering head. Le Fenwick was leaning over his torso, still undoing Bentley's top shirt buttons and trying unsuccessfully to remove his Mac.

'What's happened Dick?' Cruickshank questioned, crouching down next to Le Fenwick.

'He keeled over Ma'am. I'd just given him a coffee and was about to assess him to see if he was fit for questioning. Can you help me get his Mac off? We need to make the clothing around his chest as loose as possible.'

Cruickshank leant over and pulled the Mac off one of Bentley's twitching arms, watching as his eyes rolled in his head, spittle dribbling from his shaking lips. 'He's losing consciousness Le Fenwick. Have we called an ambulance?'

'I can see that Ma'am. Yes, I called one about five minutes ago.' Le Fenwick answered, pulling Bentley's other arm out of the Mac and yanking the dirty stinking garment from underneath his body. He threw it onto the bed and grabbed a pillow at the same time, raising Bentley's head slightly and putting it underneath.

Calvey came running into the cell. 'Here you go Dick, two aspirins and some water.' he said, leaning down and passing the tablets and drink to Le Fenwick.

'Come on Fenny, we need to get these inside you.' Le Fenwick anxiously said, popping a pill into Bentley's mouth and dribbling a stream of water after it, before holding it closed, feeling the swallow, then repeating. 'That might help. Fred, go outside and when the ambulance arrives, tell them to get their defibrillator ready, he could go under at any point.'

Her Moons Denouement
Max Hardy

Calvey nodded and backed out of the cell. Le Fenwick started rubbing Bentley's chest lightly with one hand, holding Bentley's shaking arm with the other.

'I think the stress of everything has gotten to him Ma'am. He's not in the best shape as it is and layering the stress on top of that has sent him over the edge.'

'Let's just try and keep him alive for now and worry about the whys and wherefores afterwards.' Cruickshank answered with concern.

'Through here guys.' called the voice of Calvey from the corridor as he led two paramedics carrying a stretcher into the cell.

'Gents, I'm Dr Le Fenwick. I was with the patient when he started to convulse. Symptoms are difficulty breathing, abnormal chest pains, dizziness and shaking, anxiety, palpitations and cold sweats. He is flowing in and out of consciousness. He is having a heart attack. His pulse rate is very low so I suggest we get him straight onto a stretcher and off to hospital.' Le Fenwick instructed.

'No problem Doc. I'm Ernie and this is Val. Have you administered any drugs?' one of the paramedics responded as they both laid the stretcher down beside Bentley and carefully lifted his heavy frame onto it. They strapped his legs and waist, keeping the chest free.

'I've just given him aspirin Ernie.' Le Fenwick answered.

'Le Fenwick, you go with them to the hospital and take Calvey with you. He is still a suspect and needs to be under police guard.' Cruickshank ordered as she and Le Fenwick followed the paramedics and stretcher out of the cell and into a crowded corridor. 'Will you vulture's piss off back to your jobs right now!' Cruickshank shouted, the onlookers dispersing immediately.

The paramedics loaded the stretcher into the ambulance, Le Fenwick and Calvey jumping in the back alongside the still shaking Bentley. Val slammed the back doors shut and ran around to the drivers cabin, jumped in and pulled out of the headquarters car park, lights flashing and sirens blaring.

'Has his heart stopped at all Doc.' Ernie asked as he unpacked the defibrillator just above Bentley's stretcher.

'No Ernie, but his pulse is very weak. Have you got adrenaline shots ready just in case?' asked Le Fenwick.

'To the left in the fridge Doc. I don't mind you prepping one while I get the defrib charged.' Ernie answered.

'Is he going to be alright Dick?' Calvey asked, his voice worried, his features drawn.

'Well, his heart hasn't stopped, which is promising, but he is in a bad way. Can you hold his arm, just keep feeling for a pulse while I prep this syringe?' Le Fenwick asked, standing and moving to one side, allowing Calvey to move up closer to Bentley.

Ernie knelt back down next to Calvey, loosening a few more buttons on Bentley's shirt before he looked up to Le Fenwick. 'Is the syringe prepped Doc?'

Le Fenwick was standing above Calvey, drawing liquid from a small phial into the syringe in his hand. He looked down towards Ernie with a focused, determined expression.

'I'm ready Ernie. Are you?' Le Fenwick asked.

Ernie nodded imperceptibly. Le Fenwick lowered the syringe and quickly thrust it into Calvey's neck, injecting the contents into his body. Calvey sat up in surprise and tried to turn to see what Le Fenwick was doing. Ernie grabbed his arms as he was turning and pushed him backwards off the small seat, onto the floor of the ambulance. Ernie jumped over his torso as Calvey tried to wriggle free of his hands.

Her Moons Denouement   Max Hardy

'Don't fight Fred. We don't want to hurt you. In a minute the GHB will kick in and you will go to sleep, so don't struggle, you will only hurt yourself unnecessarily.'

Calvey's stopped struggling, his eyes rolling, the pupils dilating. His body went limp and his head lolled back, eyes closing. Ernie let go of his arms and climbed off his chest.

'That' him out for at least four hours.' Ernie said, turning back to the stretcher, where he checked Bentley's pulse. 'Bentley is alright as well, the pulse is getting stronger.'

'The potassium chloride should wear off soon. Val, how far are we away from the house?' Le Fenwick shouted through the small observation hatch into the cabin.

'Only a couple of minutes away now Doc.'

'Good.' Le Fenwick responded, leaning over Bentley's slightly shaking, unconscious body. 'It's time for us all to find out exactly what you do know about what your father is up to.'

Chapter 35

So, here's the choice this time. The woman that we love has been abducted by a killer and is almost certainly in grave danger. The clandestine organisation that she belongs to wants us to question a man who they have broken out of a police cell, to try and find her whereabouts. If we say no, she dies. If we say yes, we are drawn further into a world of questionable values, a world a long way away from legal and still no further forward finding out if we are pawns, knights or kings and queens. There was only one squeeze of the hand, one flick of the eye. There comes a time when you have to recognise the only way you can have a chance of winning any game, is to understand that you are taking part, whatever part you are playing. That answer was always going to be yes.

I sit on a white painted wooden chair in a crisp clean three piece suit, my legs crossed, hands resting clasped on top of the knees. A few feet away from me, Rebecca is sitting on a similar chair wearing a black backless trouser suit, red Jimmy Choo high heels and a long auburn wig. Her legs are crossed and her hands are clasped, similar to mine. Behind us is a wall of pictures. A picture of every single woman that we think Pastor Bentley has abducted. Above them, there are pictures of the three revealed murderers and a picture of Pastor Bentley, all of them with the same man. In the middle of the photographs is a painting. It is an original Cezanne, called 'Harlequin'.

Her Moons Denouement

Max Hardy

We are in a drawing room, with oak beamed floors and white painted walls. There is no furniture in the room apart from the chairs we are sitting in and the one in front of us, which Bentley is tied to. He is stirring, his head lolling from side to side, his eyes starting to open.

'Are you ready for this?' I whisper over to Rebecca, smiling in her direction, slightly distracted by how beautiful she is looking.

She returns the smile, then looks back at Bentley, her features becoming fierce. 'Oh yes, I am ready.'

Bentley's eyes fully open and he squints, looking around the room, his eyes focusing, trying to get his bearings. He stares at me for a few seconds, his gaze then drifting towards Rebecca, looking her up and down, staring into her eyes before he starts laughing uncontrollably.

'Fucking hell.' he squeaks out after a few moments, through the laughter, 'You had me, good and proper. Both of you have been fucking me over.'

'Bentley, look at the wall behind us, do you see the pictures of those women. Do you know what happened to them?' I ask, not moving in my seat, keeping my tone calm and conciliatory.

'What the fuck has that got to do with you? Either of you? You are a loon on the run from the law and you are a washed up DI helping her, why the fuck should I answer any of your questions?' he spits in our direction.

'You think that every one of those women is living a new life in another country. You think that your father, your sister and you have saved them from a life of domestic abuse. That's what you think.' Rebecca says as calmly and conciliatory as I did.

Bentley pauses, a look of concern entering the anger, a guarded expression rolling over his features.

Her Moons Denouement   Max Hardy

'Look at them again Bentley. Look at them closely. Look into their eyes, notice the smiles on their faces, their unblemished skin. It's easy to see how you might think they are living a good life now, when you don't know the consequences of what you have done.' Rebecca uncrosses her legs demurely and stands up as she speaks, taking a handkerchief out of a pocket in her trouser suit. She stands directly in front of Bentley, staring directly into his eyes, and takes her wig off, exposing her near hairless head, with the flesh riven and scarred from where she ripped her hair out.

She leans over slightly, letting Bentley see the full extent of the damage, opening her mouth at the same time and flashing the stump of her chewed tongue. 'Did you have any idea that this would happen to me when you left me in the hands of the monster Dr Ennis?' Rebecca asks as she starts wiping the makeup off her face, revealing the scratches, cuts and burns all over it.

'Is that what all of this is about? You getting revenge for what Ennis did to you? Fucking up my life because he gave you a hard time. You fucked your son, you killed him, you deserve every fucking thing he did to you.' Bentley antagonised, snarling at Rebecca as he spoke.

Come on Rebecca, keep it calm, don't let him intimidate you. She raises her head and pushes her shoulders back, standing tall and proud. 'And your father fucks your sister. Do you think either of them would deserve this?' she replies with an impeccable level of calmness.

Bentley just stares at her, gobsmacked.

'I am not showing you what happened to me as any kind of revenge. I am trying to show you that we all have things we keep behind closed doors. I am showing you what is behind my closed door because the three of us in this room need to find out the truth before the two women at the bottom of those photographs end up dead, if they

Her Moons Denouement　　　　　　　　　　　　　　　　Max Hardy

aren't already.' Rebecca adds, walking over to the wall and pointing to the pictures of Coleen Naismith and Eve.

'I have lied to the police about what I know of this case. I have been tracking down Madame Evangeline for the past few weeks and I found her. I withheld evidence from my last investigation, using it to track her down. If my superiors were to find out, I would be arrested straight away and would undoubtedly serve a long prison sentence. But no one else was going to help me find out the things I needed to. This isn't about the law Bentley and this certainly isn't about what any of us would traditionally think of as right or wrong. Right now, this is about two women who are in danger: two women who are in danger of your Father.'

Bentley stares at me, thinking, his eyes then darting to the pictures of the women on the walls, settling on the two at the bottom.

'What exactly is it you think my Father has done?' he asks quietly.

I stand up and join Rebecca at the wall, pointing at the pictures of the killers. 'You see this man with O'Driscoll, Mann, Chodak and your Father. Do you know him?' I ask.

'No, never seen him in my life.'

'Not many people have, yet here he is with three mass murderers and your father, a man who had contact with each and every one of the women on that wall before they disappeared. When it comes to evidence, that is a lot more than circumstantial, that is bordering on compelling. At the least it should make you want to ask questions. Questions like, where did my sister take Coleen if she didn't leave the country.' I finish, walking back to my seat and sitting down, crossing my legs.

'I know you think I am Madame Evangeline Bentley, but you are wrong. Annie Tait is Madame Evangeline. Annie Tait has been trying to find out what happened to those women for quite a while now. Annie Tait found out that your sister has never flown out of Scotland. Annie Tait is risking her life to try and find out the truth. We have to help her. We need to know what is going on so that we can help her.' Rebecca says as she returns to her seat and sits down, crossing her legs.

'We think your father has abducted and killed these women Bentley. We believe that you genuinely think these women have been saved and spirited off to another country. We believe that your intent in this was to make sure they were safe from their abusive partners. Fenny, none of us are perfect. All of us make mistakes. I just want you to think about the things we have shown you, just think: what if I have made a mistake. There might still be time for Coleen and Annie. It's your choice.'

Bentley sits quietly, looking between me, Rebecca and the pictures on the wall, the cogs whirring as he flits between us. His lips start to move, but say nothing for a moment. I can tell his mind is trying to think of the right words.

'Father would always find them. Women who couldn't escape from their abusive partners, women who wanted help. We would take them in, giving them a place to stay out of the way and help them think about a life without abuse. So we helped. I would organise alternate identities and Dessie would arrange onward arrangements, a new life in a different country with a new identity. Some of their partners were monsters and the women wanted to see them punished. Sometimes, when they wanted me to, I would plant evidence incriminating the abusive partners. I would like to say that I did that just for the women, but I wanted to get those scum off the streets as well. I don't believe that my father has killed anyone, I don't believe that Dessie didn't take them to their new identities. But I can see that there are inconsistencies and I can see that there is a wealth of evidence to suggest otherwise. What do you want me to do?' Bentley asks as his body sags in his bindings, his spirit broken.

Her Moons Denouement   Max Hardy

'We need you to take us to where they are hiding.' Rebecca asks.

Bentley sneers as he looks towards her, then at me. 'Alright, but you might want to get changed out of your gladrags first, it's a bit dark and dingy where we are going.'

Chapter 36

The first thing to assail her awakening senses was the smell. The smell of freshly lain motorways, the tarmac still warm and bubbling, mingled with the odour of burning flesh, acrid and sickeningly pungent. Her eyes started to open, blurred darkness the only thing visible in the periphery of her vision. The floor felt cold and wet, some kind of stone, and she was leaning against something ridged, which was digging into her back. The only sound she heard was a low, quiet whimpering a short distance to her right.

'Hello, is anybody there?' Eve asked, her voice groggy and hoarse.

The whimpering stopped, silence filling the darkness with trepidation. Eve tried to sit upright, but knocked her head on something metallic about a foot above her head. She raised a hand and felt the air, connecting with a bar. She felt along its length to an edge, then followed this as another bar descended to the floor. She shuffled around, stretching her legs and arms, feeling for the extremities of her confines, then ran her hands up and down her body.

'I'm in a metal cage, about four foot long by four foot wide, only two foot in height. It is complete darkness. I mean complete. No ambient light at all. A few cuts and bruises but no broken bones. I am naked. Someone else is nearby.' Eve whispers as she lies still and listens intently to the silence.

Her Moons Denouement   Max Hardy

'Hello, is that Coleen?' Eve asks, hearing a muted intake of breath on the sounding of the name.

'Coleen, if it is you, I am not here to hurt you, I promise.'

A sad, desolate, terrified, tear filled giggle broke out in the air, followed by a low murmuring whimper. 'Just like they promised?'

'What did they promise Coleen?'

'They promised to help me. And they did, to start with. They helped me get away from Richard, my boyfriend. They promised me that he would be out of my life forever. They promised me I would never be afraid again. I am more afraid now than I have ever been. You should be afraid too, very afraid.' Coleen replied, her tone timorous.

Eve shuffled over to the end of the cage where the voice was coming from and stretched out a hand through the bars. 'Perhaps you can help me understand what I need to be afraid of. I am reaching out my hand towards your voice. Could you do the same, so we can hold hands, so we can help each other through this?' Eve asked, moving her arm from side to side through the air, waiting for a reciprocal response.

Instead there was another painfully anguished laugh, followed by shuffling married to agonising whimpers. 'She is the worst. She laughs, smiles and is so, so jolly with you. She will play with you like you are a doll, being nice, being friendly. And then she will break you, as though you were no more than a doll. He just watches and does things to himself. Apart from when she breaks you, then she does things to him.' she finished, her voice falling low and sinister.

'Is that Dessie and Fenny, or Pastor Bentley?' Eve asks, still reaching out her hand and feeling for Coleen's.

'Dessie and Pastor Bentley. I haven't seen Fenny down here. How do you know who they are? Did they promise to help you as well?'

Her Moons Denouement

Max Hardy

'No, but I know who they are and believe me, I am not afraid of them. I am here to help you. I am here to find out what they are doing and to stop it. I can help you Coleen, reach out your hand and hold mine and we will get through this together.' Eve said with conviction, the words filled with strength and optimism.

Another soulless laugh, filled with anguish. 'You can't help me. You won't be able to help yourself. We won't get through this together. Together we will slowly be ripped apart, piece by piece, until we die. And they will smile while they do it. Can't you smell the burning flesh? I can't reach out my hands to you because they have chopped them off, all the way up to the elbow.'

Silence, utter silence, then: 'I know that there is nothing I can say that will give you any hope Coleen. But I can promise you this, before the day is out, you will fear them no more.'

At the far end of the room, a sliver of orange light seared a line into the absolute darkness, startling Eve's eyes temporarily.

'You need to be afraid, because they are coming. You are fresh meat. Just listen. You will hear her singing.'

Eve listened as the light started to rise up the walls, framing the outline of a door into the darkness, throwing shadow into the room, shadow that revealed shapes. Eve looked at the shape of the bars coalescing in front of her, then at a large oblong object forming beyond the cage before her eyes moved to the right, where a shadow moved in the cage next to her. Then she heard the singing.

'Doe, a deer, a female deer, Ray, a drop of golden sun. Me, a name I call myself. Far, a long long way to run.'

The door burst open, a bright orange glow from a handheld lamp illuminating the room, dispersing the shadows instantaneously, revealing a large cavern hewn out of granite, fully ten metres wide by

Her Moons Denouement   **Max Hardy**

about the same across, the top of a domed ceiling so far up, it was still lost in shadows. The large object in the centre of the room reflected the lamp light from its shiny, clean stainless steel surface. It was an autopsy bench, with a tray of accompanying autopsy equipment set out at one end of it. Steel bindings were soldered onto the bench at intervals where legs, arms, waist, neck and torso would be. There were steel hooks around the walls, filled with further saws and knives of every size. At the far end of the room, opposite the entrance, was another long stainless steel bench with a sink in the middle and steel fronted cupboards underneath. There were three metal cages bolted to the floor, two occupied by Coleen and Eve. On the opposite wall to them, there was a single wooden chair, facing towards the autopsy table.

Eve looked over to Coleen. To her naked, bruised and battered bloody body, her face swollen and almost unrecognisable as human. To her arms. To the two amputated stumps of her arms, black and still bleeding, that had been sealed with tar.

Eve looked back up towards the door where Dessie Bentley waltzed in, pirouetting, letting the lamp swing around her in an arc as she did. 'Oh today is such a fun day. Look Coleen, we have a new friend to play with, won't that be fun.

Coleen didn't say a word, just stared in horror through the tiniest of puffy slits which were her eyes. Dessie span right up in front of Coleens cage, her voice changing, becoming infuriated. 'I said, won't that be fun Coleen!' She grabbed a knife from the wall above the cage and quickly rammed it into Coleen's shoulder viciously, withdrawing it just as fast. Coleen screamed, shuffling herself as far back as she could into the corner of the cage, away from Dessie.

'Oh you wuss, it's only a little nick, stop the hysterics. You are such a girlie girl.' Dessie sang, the infuriation all gone, replaced by joviality once more. She approached Eve's cage, crouching down on her haunches, deliberately pulling her long blue dress up to her knees, exposing her naked genitals beneath.

'I hope you aren't as much a wuss as Coleen. It's not as much fun when they cry all the time. Do you like what you see down there Annie?'

'Now Dessie, stop getting the girls excited, there's plenty of time for play.' Pastor Bentley admonished as he slowly walked into the room, pulling a small trolley with a smouldering bowl of tar on top of it. 'And we don't know that she is even called Annie. Get her out and strap her to the bench.'

Eve was watching her every move silently, not even blinking, her features calm. Dessie reached above the cage again, Eve's eyes following where her arm went, and grabbed a cattle prod. She stuck it through the bars and directly into Eve's exposed chest. Eve didn't flinch as the prod came down, and relaxed her body just as it touched, moving in time with the electrical shock that paralysed her.

Dessie leant over, unlocked the side of the cage and dragged Eve out, scraping her naked body over the rough stone floor, grazing it. With remarkable strength, she lifted Eve up in one movement, dropping her unceremoniously onto the autopsy bench. She proceeded to strap her into the bindings.

'I forgot to say, I really love your tattoo, it is so erotic. So naughty. Father thinks it is evil and that you have been sent to tempt us.' she said out loud, then leaned into Eve's ear and whispered 'But I just couldn't resist licking it, all the way inside your lovely juicy cunt while you were sleeping.'

'Father has a few questions for you before we start playing. If you don't give him the answers he wants, he just might let me play with you early, which will be so much fun!' Dessie exclaimed as Pastor Bentley walked up to the side of the autopsy trolley.

Her Moons Denouement

Max Hardy

'You might not have noticed, but one of your contact lenses came out when you fell down into our pit. Your false teeth dropped out too and for some reason, you appear to have some latex prosthetics on your face. So Annie Tait, would you like to tell me who you are?'

'I think you know the answer to that Pastor Bentley.' Eve slurred, movement coming back into her body as she stretched against her restraints.

'Oh father, she is feisty. Can I play? Please, please can I play?' Dessie pleaded, bouncing up and down on the opposite side of the bench.

'Alright, but just a little, you know how excited you get.'

'I am already dripping Father, already ready for you.' Dessie's voice went deep and sensual as she picked up a small bone saw from the instrument table. 'You might want to answer Father's question directly, rather than with another question. I will stop sawing when you do.' Dessie finished, looking manically and smiling wildly down at Eve, who just looked back calmly and said nothing.

Dessie's face filled with fury. 'Alright Miss Smartypants, see how you like this!' She thrust the saw into the flesh of Eve's arm, just above the binding securing her wrist and started to cut fervidly, watching Eve's face as she did. Eve's features didn't flinch, not even when the rough serrated saw tore through the tendons and started gnawing into the bone, shattered splinters bursting into the muscle. All she did was perspire and purse her lips. Dessie became even more furious at the lack of screaming and at the lack of an answer and at the new sensation of not being in control. She forced the saw through the bone even more vehemently, breaking all the way through, blood spurting all over Eve's naked body, all over Dessie's dress, pools of it collecting in the indents around the bench. The saw screeched on the stainless steel bench, the whole hand flopping away from the arm, amputated.

Her Moons Denouement   **Max Hardy**

Pastor Bentley wheeled the bowl of tar around to where Dessie stood and picked up the severed hand as Dessie grabbed Eve's arm and thrust it into the liquid tar. Eve groaned, biting her lip until a single drop of blood oozed out. But she didn't scream, and after a second, as Dessie placed her tarred stump back on the bench, her face once again wore serene.

Dessie was furious, her features incandescent with rage. Pastor Bentley passed her the severed hand and spoke to her calmly. 'Settle down Dessiderata. This one is special. She is something different. Taste her, feast on her, let her body become yours and you will know her.' he said, looking directly into Eve's eyes.

Dessie took the hand off her father and lifted it to her lips, sucking the blood off the severed stump, then pulled the raw sinewed flesh off the bone and chewed it heartily as she too looked down upon Eve.

'Thank you Pastor Bentley for showing me who you are.' Eve said, her voice measured with a slight edge of intimidation. 'You know who I am. I am Eve. He will have told you all about me. And if he has told you who I am, then you will know there is nothing you can do to me that I will ever fear. But you should fear me. You should fear me because you have shown me who you are: and now that I know who you are, I know what you fear. Before my moon's denouement tonight Pastor Bentley, the world will know what you fear.'

Chapter 37

A gentle breeze wafts the salty sea air into my nostrils as we walk along the stony shoreline just around the corner from the North Quensferry Peninsula, underneath the Forth Road Bridge. Battery Road, where Bentley's house sits perched on top of the peninsula is visible across the small harbour. There are still police cars sitting outside, their quietly flashing blue lights still signifying activity in the descending gloom of the evening. The full moon shines through the ruddy steel of the Forth Rail Bridge, its three huge spans impressively brooding over the calm, lolling waters of the Forth.

Bentley stands beside me, taking in the view, his countenance reflective, his demeanour a little lost. 'I've lived in this bay all my life. Mrs Perkins at the White House over there, at the end of the harbour, brought me into the world. She in her eighties now. She told us about the tunnels when we were kids. Before they built the rail bridge there was a rail tunnel that ran from here to Rosyth. It's long gone now, and unless you know where to look, you'll never find the entrance. It's linked to more tunnels that were hewn when they were taking stone for the bridge. There's some natural caverns underground as well. It's where Dessie always goes when she is in a mood. I haven't been down there for years. She left me alone once when I was a kid, in the darkness, in the damp, in the silence, all alone. Didn't go back in after that.'

Her Moons Denouement   Max Hardy

Rebecca is standing at the other side of Bentley, dressed in blue jeans, walking boots and a North Face jacket, watching his features, reading his emotions. She looks over at me and shakes her head gently, looking perturbed. I know what she is thinking. Bentley seems so genuine, it is hard to think that he knows anything about what his father and sister might be doing. But we have to be realistic. He could know everything about what they are doing and this could very well be a trap. I know Adam isn't too far away from us and just hope that he can keep up with us when we go underground, because he won't be able to track us.

'Come on, let's get going before we lose all of the light.' I suggest.

Bentley sighs heavily, then turns and heads towards a large copse of trees at the edge of the Forth as Rebecca and I follow a pace behind, letting him have space, letting him reflect.

'Just through here.' Bentley instructs, ducking under the rotting trunk of a dead oak and falling onto his stomach at the foot of an outcrop of rock covered in foliage. I look down and see the narrowest of gaps hidden by the overgrowth.

'Don't worry, it's only this narrow for a few feet, then it opens up to head height.' he says as he shuffles into the gap, disappearing from view.

I look at Rebecca and see concern in her eyes. 'Just be careful. Remember this guy could be a killer. We have to trust what Eve thinks about him. We have to be strong for Eve.'

'It's not that. I feel for him. I feel his world is about to be blown apart. I know how that feels. We are pawns again John. I'm still uncomfortable.'

Her Moons Denouement   **Max Hardy**

'I know, and I am too, but we are in this now. We are in it to find out who we are and why we are here. Come on, we will either find out, or die trying.

Rebecca drops down onto her stomach and slithers into the gap. I follow suit, feeling the damp cold rock wrap itself around me, the shadows rushing to my body, consuming it in darkness as I slide though the narrow space, light visible at the far side, from the torches held by Bentley and Rebecca. I stand up once through and dust my jacket and jeans down, noting Rebecca doing the same. Bentley stands and watches us belligerently, leaving the dirt on his already filthy clothes.

'There is a large cavern about half a mile to the east. The tunnels veer around the harbour. Your footing should be fine, but watch out for slippery stones and rats.' he says, heading off down the narrow, enclosed, roughly hewn tunnel, his torchlight dancing on the walls up ahead, making puppets playing in the shadows, being controlled by the erratic beam.

We walk in silence, the only sound the crunch of feet over stone, intently listening for any noise, Bentley in front, Rebecca in the middle, me at the rear. Rebecca reaches a hand backward, searching for me as I offer mine, hands clasping and squeezing tightly. She is shaking slightly. I would guess she is worried, I know I am. We don't really have any idea about what to expect. One thing's for sure, they won't just be sitting down, having a cuppa and partaking in idle banter. I just hope that Adam is able to keep tabs on us and that there is some backup if we need it.

Bentley turns a corner up ahead and we lose sight of him for a moment, the way ahead falling dark. A brief surge of panic overcomes us both, I can feel it in Rebecca's squeeze, before we have a chance to lift our torches upwards in front of us. I see the bend and we walk around it. Bentley is standing dead still in front of us, his torch now

Her Moons Denouement   **Max Hardy**

off. I see why and motion for Rebecca to switch hers off as I do the same.

Up ahead there is a door in the wall. A stainless steel door. A door with a rim of light emanating from its edges. A door from which the sound of singing surges.

A song from The Sound Of Music.

Chapter 38

'The hills are alive, with the sound of music, with songs they have sung for a thousand years.' Dessie sang, pirouetting around the room holding Eve's severed hand, waving it as she twirled and swopped with the ululations of her voice.

Coleen was whimpering in her cage, facing the wall, not wanting to look at what was happening in the room.

Pastor Bentley was sitting on his small wooden seat to the side, his trousers around his knees. His penis was erect and one of his hands was circling it, tugging gently. He lewdly glared at Eve, who was looking straight up at the darkness in the vaulted void above. Her legs had been prised open and a metal beam with semi circular grips on each end had been wedged between her knees to stop them closing. Blood was dripping from her exposed vagina.

'The hills fill my heart with the sound of music, my heart wants to sing every song it hears.' Dessie continued as she spun all the way around the autopsy bench, arriving back at Eve's open legs. She took Eve's lifeless severed hand and stretched three fingers out on it, squeezing them together before thrusting them forcefully into Eve's parted vagina lips.

'Father likes the hands. He likes me fingering our girls with their own hands. Look at the pleasure on his face. He is enjoying it so, so much, and that makes me happy, happy happy.' Dessie purred, forcing the hand in and out of Eve, harder and harder, blood from the severed end flying everywhere. She pulled it out quickly, and danced over to Pastor Bentley, sticking the glistening fingers into his expectant open mouth as she arrived, pulling her dress up and straddling him at the same time.

The door burst open, Fenny Bentley barging through, his face determined and angry. The anger dissipated in a second, to be replaced by utter and complete terror as he saw his sister astride his father. He froze, looking on in shock.

Saul was behind him and bumped into his large frame as he tried to get into the room. He sidestepped the large man, for the first time able to see what was happening. Rebecca was following him closely and swore when she saw the vista in the room. She saw Eve on the autopsy bench, looking back over to where she stood. She strode purposefully towards her.

'Nooooo. Leave her alone!' screamed Dessie as she climbed off her father and careered towards Rebecca, ducking as she approached her and forcing the whole weight of her quite considerable frame into Rebecca's midriff. Rebecca went sprawling over the floor, Dessie's hands wrapping around her waist as they both fell.

Saul, surprised by the stealthy intensity of Dessie's attack reacted. He crossed the floor quickly to where the two women were scuffling, Dessie trying to get purchase around Rebecca's throat. Saul grabbed Dessie's wrists and tried to pull them away, but she was strong.

Behind him, he felt a whosssh of air and then a second later a fist slammed into the side of his head, knocking him off balance. Pastor Bentley hurled his ample, half naked body into Saul, not caring that his erection was scraping on the floor as he landed on top of him.

Bentley was immobile, his gaze transfixed on the scuffles happening on the floor in front of him but his body not moving at all.

Her Moons Denouement   Max Hardy

'Help them Bentley.' Eve shouted. 'I know that this had nothing to do with you. Please, help them. Look at what they have done. Look at Coleen, look at me, look at my hand. I know that is not you Fenny.'

'Don't listen to her Fenny, you will help your Father boy.' Pastor Bentley roared as he wrapped an arm around Saul's neck, pulling it tightly around his throat. Saul flailed his arms backwards, trying to make contact with Pastor Bentley's head.

Dessie had Rebecca pinned to the floor and was climbing astride her, but Rebecca managed to raise a leg and furiously kneed her in the genitals. Dessie screamed and toppled to one side, allowing Rebecca to scramble from underneath her and scrabble to the stone wall, pushing her back against it, breathing in fast noisy pants. She scanned her surroundings, looking for something to grab and use as a weapon. A glint of metal above caught her eye and she looked up to see a machete on the wall. She started to push her aching body up the wall, stretching out her hand to reach it.

Saul's legs were pumping furiously as his neck was being crushed by Pastor Bentley. He was trying to free wheel, to push himself around and slide out of the neck hold or at least to get traction to thump his assailant. One of his feet caught the edge of the autopsy table, and gained purchase. Saul pushed hard, forcing Pastor Bentley back, forcing him to lose balance, forcing him to loosen the grip around Saul's neck.

'You can help them Fenny. I know you think you have been helping all of those women over the years, but you haven't. Your father and sister have been mutilating and killing them. But you can help John and you can help Rebecca and you can help Coleen.' Eve pleaded, her face ingrained with the pain of seeing him standing there, doing nothing.

Rebecca's fingers scrambled for the edge of the blade as she forced herself upward, not quite able to reach, her legs weak and shaking, not able to raise her body any higher. Dessie rolled over and onto all fours, snarling at Rebecca as she sat hunched, sneering at her, ready to pounce.

'This is my family, they are all I have ever had.' Bentley whispered as he looked down upon his sister and father viciously fighting on the floor, his features alive with disbelief.

Pastor Bentley kicked his legs up as Saul stopped pushing, forcing the bare skin of his legs around Saul's midriff, squeezing the thighs tightly around Saul's chest. Saul started banging his fists off Pastor Bentley's legs, trying to dislodge them, trying to ease the increasing tightness in his lungs. His face started to turn red, his eyes bulging as Pastor Bentley forced the air from his lungs.

Dessie pounced, throwing herself across the short distance to where Rebecca was still scrambling for the machete. She hit her directly in the stomach, causing Rebecca to bend double and topple to the floor in agony, winded.

'You are a very naughty girl and naughty girls need to be punished!' Dessie screamed as she started to throw hard, hammering punches into Rebecca's stomach, pummelling her senseless.

'This is my family.' Bentley whispered again, looking around the room. Looking at the autopsy table, Eve lying on it, her legs akimbo, her genitals bruised and bloody, a stump whose hand lay discarded on the floor. Looking at the cages, at Coleen cowering in sheer terror, trying to wrap non-existent arms around her ears to block out the horror. Looking at the walls, at the sharp and dangerous implements of torture and dissection. Looking at the cattle prod sitting above the cages.

'This is my family.' Bentley repeated as he moved for the first time, almost in slow motion, across the room and took the cattle prod off the wall. There was a psychotic glint in his bulbous eyes, his hands

Her Moons Denouement   **Max Hardy**

shaking furiously as he walked firstly towards Dessie and Rebecca, lowering the prod to where they were fighting.

'Fenny, what are you doing?' Eve cried, not able to turn her head enough to see him.

'This is my family.' Bentley repeated again, thrusting the cattle prod down as he continued: 'I have to protect my family.'

Chapter 39

Dessie convulsed, her body going rigid, shaking agitatedly as the electric shock overwhelmed her, knocking her to the floor. Bentley stepped over her and strode directly to where Saul was gasping for air, his lips turning blue and puffy. He thrust the prod past Saul's head, straight into the chest of his father. Pastor Bentley's legs shot out straight, as did his arms, his whole body wracked with the electric shock. Saul started to cough uncontrollably as he collapsed on the floor beside Pastor Bentley's twitching torso.

'They are my family and I have to protect them from themselves.' Bentley reiterated quietly as he stood immobile once more and dropped the cattle prod to the floor.

'Fenny, you need to restrain them, the shock will wear off in a few seconds and they will attack again. Put them in the cages.' Eve instructed, staring at his immobile back. 'Fenny!' she screamed.

'I fucking heard you!' he shouted back as he bent over and grabbed his father's leg and started to drag him unceremoniously toward the cages, mumbling under his breath. 'All the fucking grief you have given me over the years for wanking, and you are up to this. You fucking hypocrite, you sick, twisted fucking hypocrite.'

Bentley hoisted his father up a few inches, then swung him into the cage Eve had occupied, slamming the door shut and locking it. He

Her Moons Denouement   Max Hardy

slouched back over the room, to where Dessie lay on the floor, the twitching of her body subsiding.

Bentley stretched down to grab Dessie's leg but before he reached it, her foot shot up and smacked him ferociously in his left kneecap, making his legs buckle, making him stumble to the floor. He screamed in agony, gripping the edge of the autopsy bench as he fell. Dessie pushed her arms down hard into the ground, forcing her torso into the air, sitting up and turning onto her haunches as she did.

Bentley was directly in front of Dessie and she snarled at him, baring her teeth as she spoke, spitting. 'You always were weak Fenny. You always were a let down. You always were a waste of space. I should have killed you when I killed mother. It would have made life so much simpler.'

Then she screamed and leapt at him, fists flying as she started to pummel his head, forcing him to the floor. 'Cleaning for you.' she punched, hitting him directly in the eye. 'Washing for you.' she punched, cracking his jaw. 'Cooking for you.' she punched, breaking his nose. 'Sharing our fresh meat.'

She pulled her arm back, ready to strike again and then stopped suddenly, anger dispersing from her face, to be replaced by surprise, then agony as she thrust her head back, howling. The screech became guttural as blood shot out of her mouth, bubbling down her chin as she jerked forward, the front of her dress ripping, the tip of a blood stained metal blade appearing through the rip. She jerked again as the blade exposed itself further, her head lolling to one side, limp as she collapsed forward, falling lifeless onto her battered brother, the blade just missing his chest. The handle of a knife was sticking out of her back. Rebecca sat on her knees just behind Dessie's dead body, hands shaking with shock and with the exertion she had put into thrusting the knife through Dessie's heart.

Her Moons Denouement   Max Hardy

Saul pulled himself slowly across the floor, still gasping for breath as he headed towards Rebecca, looking at her stunned, quaking body, watching her lips start to quiver as the realisation of what she had just done started to overwhelm her. 'Rebecca, keep calm!' he shouted.

'John, what's happened, is Rebecca alright? Is Fenny alright?' Eve asked, trying to bend her head to get a glimpse of the floor.

'Rebecca stabbed Dessie. She's in shock. Bentley looks beaten up but I can see him breathing. I'm crawling as fast as I can. Where the hell is Adam!' Saul wheezed.

'He will be on his way. Look after Rebecca, calm her down.' Eve instructed with authority.

Bentley stirred, groaning as he forced the heavy dead weight of his sister off his chest. Dessie rolled onto her back, the knife blade forcing itself further out of her chest. She say there, lifeless eyes staring vacantly at the cage her father was in. Bentley turned on his side with effort, blood pouring from every orifice in his face, pain searing into every difficult movement. He lifted his head with effort and looked through already puffing eyes to the cage where Coleen lay curled up foetal in the corner.

'I am so sorry Coleen.' he apologised, dragging himself closer to the bars of her cage. 'I had no idea that they were going to do this. I thought they were taking you away to a better life. Not this hell. You are safe now. The bitch is dead and the bastard is locked up. My bitch and my bastard. I should have known.' he said, shaking his head disconsolately, 'I should have fucking known.' She didn't look up, she didn't even move, just stayed tightly curled in her protective, quavering ball.

With one last stretch, Saul reached out and grabbed Rebecca's shaking arm and pulled her towards him. 'It's alright, you did what you had to do, just breathe.' he said reassuringly, feeling her body fall into him

Her Moons Denouement   Max Hardy

with relief, feeling the outpouring of emotion as she cuddled tightly into him, feeling a maelstrom of tears roll down her cheeks.

Bentley turned his head toward the cage his father was in. He was lying still on the bottom of it, watching his son intently, occasionally glancing over to the dead Dessie, a look of anguish apparent every time he did, a look of animosity appearing when he looked back at his son.

'What the hell have you done, you sick bastard.' Bentley scowled towards his father.

'I just finished the job their spineless partners didn't have the balls to follow through on. They weren't proper women, who looked after their men, not like Desiderata. If they were, they wouldn't have needed a beating. Same as your mother, if she were any kind of wife, rather than a whore who would drop her pants at the sniff of another man, then things might have been different.'

'What the fuck are you talking about! You are blaming her for this! So if she hadn't fucked another man, you wouldn't have killed twenty six women?' Bentley spat furiously, his body shaking with rage.

'Trust you to side with her, you dirty disgusting little urchin. I'm sure all you miss about your mother is listening to the sound of her fucking coming down the pipes under the stairs, while you lay masturbating.'

'Fuck father, can you hear yourself. You're half naked, your daughter fucks you. You kill people and you think you have the right to belittle me!'

'Dessie was right, we should have killed you. She wanted to play with you, but I would never let her. More fool me. You were a waste of space and a good waste of fresh meat.'

'Fresh meat again, what the fuck does that mean.'

Her Moons Denouement   Max Hardy

'Look at your sorry little friend over there, weak and worthless: and armless. We take a piece at a time. Dessie likes to play when we take it. And then we fry, or roast, or boil or casserole the meat and we all have it for supper. But it's wasted on you. The flesh and blood of those made in the image of our lord is lost on you.'

Bentley's face, already battered and bleeding froze in terror, taking in the words his father had said. He looked into Coleen's cage, at her amputated arms, then over the floor, to Eve's discarded hand. He wretched, his stomach convulsing in disgust.

'We eat them! You keep them alive, taking a bit at a time off them and then we eat them? I've been eating human flesh. How long have I been eating human flesh?'

'Your mother was the first. It was especially pleasing when we fed you her vagina in a stew. Coleen was your last.'

'And all because a woman wouldn't do what you wanted her too? Where the fuck does religion come into this father. Where the hell does it say anything about this being a good fucking thing in the bible?'

'Flesh of his flesh, blood of his blood. We take it every week.'

'Fucking figuratively, yes, not bloody literally.'

'You can't reason with him Fenny. He has taken his religion to its extreme and there is no way back for him.' Eve's voice came floating down from above, breaking the intensity of the conversation with its conciliatory air.

'But the world should know what he has done in the name of his faith. The world should know the atrocities he inflicted on all those poor women. You can help with that. You can expose him.'

Her Moons Denouement   Max Hardy

Bentley moved his prone body onto its side with a pained effort and then forced his torso off the ground, sitting up. He grabbed the side of the autopsy table and used it as a support to pull himself up from the floor, until he was standing over Eve. He took the metal post from between her knees and then started to undo the bindings, setting her free.

'You want me to tell the world what he has done and then kill myself, is that it? Just like your other nutters?' Bentley asked as he helped Eve sit up. He took off his blood stained, filthy Mac and wrapped it around her shoulders, covering her nakedness.

'No, I don't want you to do that at all. The other Angels left this earth because they were ready for the next experience, not because they wanted and end to this one. You might want to do it for yourself, for your own peace of mind.'

Bentley laughed hysterically, his body convulsing with the guffaws. 'You are some kind of clown, make no mistake about that. What peace of mind could I ever have knowing that my father and sister are killers? That they tortured and mutilated dozens of women. That they killed my mother and fed her to me. That I have been a party to their cannibalism. That I helped bring each and every one of those women to this table. Thank you for showing me what I was too blind to see, ut there will never be peace of mind.'

Bentley looked at Eve with sorrowful tear filled eyes, the anger of the revelations being subsumed by the guilt of the part he had played in them. He started to shake his head gently, looking around the room. Looking down to Saul comforting Rebecca on the floor. Looking over to his father staring at him without even a modicum of remorse. Looking at Coleen, naked, mutilated and terrified. Looking down at his dead sister, the bloody blade of a knife sticking ten inches out of her chest. Tears rolled down his cheeks, his mouth shivering with the intensity of his emotions. He turned to face his sister's body.

Her Moons Denouement　　　　　　　　　　　　　　　　**Max Hardy**

Eve looked into his eyes and looked at his body position, her face filling with dread as she reached out an arm quickly to grab him. 'Don't do it Fenny.' she shouted.

'Sorry Eve, I'm not ready for the next experience, I just want to end this one. Look after Jackson for me.' he tearfully whispered, letting his body fall forward, the full weight of his huge frame impaling him on the knife sticking out of Dessie's chest.

Chapter 40

Is it courage or cowardice? To have nothing left to live for, to have everything you have ever believed in and have ever loved taken away from you, to be left bereft and alone, in a world where there is no one left to love you, no matter how warped the love. Is it courage or cowardice to end your own life? I look over at Bentley's still twitching body, walking into the rickety rooms in my own mind, the ones with the Russian revolver pointing at my head, which hold everyone I have lost. The ones with the empty childhood, locked in a lonely room, nothing but the sound of my own voice for company. The ones where I have never known the love of a parent. In so many ways I have lived every single emotion that flashed across Bentley's face as he fell to his oblivion. I don't think he knew the heart of a loving parent either. Perhaps we are not as alone as we think.

Eve throws her legs over the side of the autopsy bench and hops lightly down, smarting in pain as she does. She kneels beside Bentley and feels for a pulse, sadness bubbling into her expression, telling me there isn't one. She looks up to me and smiles mournfully.

'How's Rebecca doing?' she asks me as she stands and walks towards us.

Rebecca lifts her head out of my chest as she hears the question, her face smeared with tears, her eyes puffy and red, but lucid.

Her Moons Denouement   Max Hardy

'I'm not the one who has lost a hand. How are you?' Rebecca answers as she reaches out and pulls Eve into us, wrapping her arms around her back. I join in the embrace, join in the tears and join in the relief that she is alive.

'It's just a flesh wound.' she answers dismissively, pulling back from the embrace, her features turning from empathetic to authoritative in the blink of an eye.

She looks at Rebecca sternly. 'Can you do me a favour? Coleen is still highly traumatised in that cage, can you try and get through to her and calm her down. Here, cover her with Bentley's coat.' Eve instructs, passing Rebecca the coat, leaving herself naked.

'John, I need you to search the room. Somewhere in here there will be trophies. It's what he teaches them. They all keep trophies.' she orders me, rising and walking over to the caged Pastor Bentley before I have time to answer.

She looks down, totally unconcerned about being naked in front of him. 'I was wrong. I don't think you have a fear. I thought it was Dessie. I thought you would fall to bits when she died. He taught you well. But tonight, the world will see what you have done old man.'

'So be it. Perhaps I am ready for the next experience.'

'That's just it old man. You don't get that choice. You will be kept in a prison for the rest of this life and have to suffer an existence with no experiences at all.'

Rebecca opens the cage and I see her trying to coax Coleen out, gently stroking her arm to reassure her. I look around the room to see likely places to search and walk towards the line of cupboards. I open one, which turns out to be a freezer. It's just about empty apart from a blue bag which looks like it has a forearm inside of it. Coleen's forearm? I shudder as I open the next one, the shudder turning into a wretch.

Her Moons Denouement Max Hardy

In the cupboard there are dozens of transparent Tupperware containers all filled with a cloudy liquid. In the cloudy liquid I can see fingers and palms and thumbs and severed wrists. Their trophies are severed hands.

'I think I have found them.' I call out. Eve walks over to me, her snake tattoo ululating on her stomach as she sways with each stride. She crouches down beside me, grabs a container and takes the lid off, sniffing the contents.

'Formaldehyde.' she says, picking the hand out of the liquid. 'She examines the fingers closely, noticing a few pubic hairs caught in the nails. 'Different coloured pubes. These aren't just trophies. I think they used them over and over again on their victims.' she shakes her head disconsolately.

'Who is he, this man you keep referring to. Is he the person in the pictures with the killers?' I ask her, studying her countenance as she answers.

'Every faith has its extremists. Even the extremist groups have uber extremists within them; someone who will go that one step further. He takes the things we believe in, living a life without fear, and embraces the absolute chaos of that. He is the man that makes murderers: and he was one of us. Do you have the time?' she asks, quickly changing the subject, her eyes visibly doing a spot check on where thing were in the room.

'It's eight fifteen.' I answer.

'Adam, time for you to come in.' she says, looking directly at me as she does, but not talking to me. She smiles, leans over and kisses me on the lips and then stands and walks over to where Rebecca is helping Coleen out of the cage.

Her Moons Denouement

Max Hardy

What was that? Has she got some kind of communication device on her? If she has, how long has it been working? Could she have called for help at any time? I hear footfalls coming from outside the door and a few seconds later Adam walks almost nonchalantly into the room carrying a large holdall which he drops onto the top of the autopsy bench. 'Is everything under control?' he asks Eve, smiling toward me as he sees me looking at him.

'All under control. Did you bring the spare clothes as I asked? Coleen needs them. What about the GHD? Have you mailed off the final video to the BBC?'

'Yes, got them both here.' he answers, pulling a pair of jeans and a T-Shirt out of the bag and passing them over to her, along with a small syringe. 'The video is timed to be sent at 20:45 so we are now on the clock. We will only have fifteen minutes until the police and press arrive after that.'

Eve grabs the syringe and without any warning sticks it into Pastor Bentley's arm through the bars of the cage. 'The start of your journey into oblivion old man.' she says. He scowls back, opening his mouth to reply, but then flops unconscious.

Eve turns back to Rebecca and helps her dress Coleen. I watch Adam unpack the bag. I watch him take out a black metal spring loaded box. I watch him take out a black and white Pierrot outfit. I watch him take out a bag of make up. And my mind starts adding up. At nine o'clock tonight the fourth mass murderer will be revealed. That's in forty five minutes. Where is the Angel who is going to expose him? Why did Eve ask Bentley if he wanted to expose him?

Adam walks over to me, seeing the cogs of my mind wheeling in my animated face. 'What's troubling you John. Plan B worked. Bentley showed us where he was keeping Eve and Coleen. We have rescued Eve and Coleen and Pastor Bentley has confessed to his crimes.'

Her Moons Denouement Max Hardy

'Yes, I know. What I don't know at the minute is whether it was really Plan B, or we have been part of Plan A all along. Eve has some kind of microphone. She has been talking to you. If she has been talking to you, then you must have known where she was. If you knew where she was then perhaps her kidnapping wasn't coincidental, perhaps it was planned.' I throw the thoughts of my cogs out to him, my frustrations creeping into the words.

'Perhaps John. But does it change the outcome. Does it change what you have learned from the experience?'

I don't answer his question. I don't answer it because I am distracted. Coleen is now dressed and Rebecca is leading her to the wooden seat at the other side of the room, away from Eve, but that isn't what has distracted me. What has distracted me is Eve. She is getting dressed. She is pulling on the legs of the Pierrot outfit. There are no other Angels here. There been no other Angels involved in discovering what Pastor Bentley has done, only Eve. Which can mean only one thing.

I push past Adam, who raises his hands conciliatory and steps out of my way. I slam my hands down hard onto the top of the autopsy bench, on the opposite side to Eve, facing her, my mind full of fear as I stare at her, willing her to speak.

She looks at me steadily and with an understanding patience as she continues to get ready, strapping the boxed up wings onto her back. Adam comes alongside her and helps to position the release straps on her arms.

'Aren't you going to stop her?' I implore him, my frantic gaze darting back and forward between them both. Rebecca must have heard the panic in my voice because a split second later she is alongside me.

'What is it John?' she asks as she strokes my arm affectionately.

Her Moons Denouement   Max Hardy

I look into her open, questioning face as my mind screams agony, not wanting to speak the truth that they know. 'She's putting on the wings Rebecca. Eve is the person who is going to expose Bentley tonight. Eve is the person who is going to commit suicide.'

Rebecca physically slumps and I reach out a hand to steady her as the fear in my mind starts to dance in her eyes. She looks over as Eve pulls her Pierrot outfit up over the wings and starts to fasten the buttons down the chest.

'It was always going to be me. Now is my time. I have done everything I had to do in this life and I am ready for my next experience.' Eve says with a serene calmness in her tone.

'But you can't, we've only just found you again. There must be so many experiences left to live for!' Rebecca exclaims as she pushes herself closer and hugs me tight, her fingers digging into my skin.

'Last night was our beautiful and memorable goodbye. It was my last time with you, it was your first time together. Please, and I know this will be hard, but try and be selfless. What you feel right now is only natural, it is your needs and your desires controlling your mind. You have to learn to control them and to remove them. That will come in time.'

I can't control them. I feel cheated. I have lost her once already and I do not want to lose her again. All I feel is betrayed. All I feel is played.

'Are we just pawns to you, playthings in a fucking plan? A means to an end. Dispensable. Is that what we are? Was this always about Bentley, was your reason for living to expose him and now that it's done, fuck the rest of us?' I can't keep my feelings in, I just don't understand.

'John, I only ever had one purpose in my life and I couldn't be happier that I have fulfilled it. My one purpose was to make sure the two of

Her Moons Denouement   Max Hardy

you met. My one purpose was to make sure you got to know each other. Do you want to know how important the two of you are? I have heard you ask if you are pawns, knights, kings or queens. Well, I am the queen in our family and all three of you are more important than me. I would gladly give my life a hundred times over for the two of you and your son.'

She was looking at Rebecca: when she said 'Your Son', she was looking at Rebecca. Eve can see the questions in our eyes, the confusion in our minds.

'I didn't get that wrong Rebecca, Jacob is your son too.'

Chapter 41

The small motor boat pulled out from the shoreline and headed off into the Firth of Forth, towards the looming frame of the Rail Bridge. A full moon shimmered in a cloudless sky, its reflection floating on the gently lapping waves as they smacked into the wooden panels of the boat, rocking it gently. Pastor Bentley sat at the back of the boat, naked and unconscious, his body wrapped in barbed wire. Twenty six Tupperware containers with the severed hands inside them sat in the bottom of the boat along with a manila folder containing pictures of the women Pastor Bentley had killed. Adam was at the helm, directing the boat toward one of the supporting bases of the rail bridge out in the middle of the Firth. Eve sat behind him in her Pierrot outfit. One of her eyes was covered in white makeup.

The boat butted up against a small jetty floating on the granite base of the bridge and tied the mooring rope to it. He jumped onto the jetty and grabbed Pastor Bentley's shoulders, heaving his heavy body over the side of the boat. He dragged him a short distance to the base of the main steel span of the bridge. A lift used for painting the bridge was sitting parked on the base, its safety doors open. Fastened to the metal cage of the lift was a wooden crucifix. Adam dragged Pastor Bentley up to it and hauled his body against the down beam. He grabbed a length of barbed wire that was sitting in the cage and wrapped it around Bentley's midriff, fastening him to the crucifix. He then secured his arms to the cross beams.

Her Moons Denouement   Max Hardy

Adam picked up a hammer and some nails. He positioned one of the nails in Bentley's right palm and smacked it through the flesh into the wood, unflinching. Bentley awoke and screamed, the noise lost in the open, empty expanse of water. Adam repeated the action on the other hand, Bentley screaming again. 'Time to face the music old man.' he said, Pastor Bentley scanning his surrounding in confusion.

Eve arrived beside him, carrying some of the Tupperware containers and the Manila folder and dropped them into the bottom of the lift next to a megaphone. Both of them returned to the boat and retrieved the remaining containers and brought them back to the lift.

Eve climbed into the lift and closed the safety door, stepping to the far side of Bentley, where the controls were situated. Adam followed her on the outside.

'Look after them. They have a lot to learn and not all of it is going to be pleasant. But they did well today. Our family is stronger now they know we exist. It will be stronger still when they know everything.' she said to Adam, leaning over and kissing him full on the lips, letting her tongue dance inside his willing mouth. She pressed the 'up' button, tongues still entwined as the lift started to rise, their lips touching until the last possible moment.

Across the Firth the noise of blaring sirens broke the quiet tranquillity of the lapping waves, the flashing blue lights of police speedboats visible on the horizon.

'You better get going Adam, the police and press are on their way.' she said, smiling sadly down towards him. Adam blew one last kiss and then jumped for the boat, quickly unfastening the mooring rope as he landed on board, then sped off out into the mouth of the river, away from the oncoming lights.

The lift slowly ascended the bridge, passing the main railway bearing, on which more flashing blue lights were visible in the distance,

Her Moons Denouement Max Hardy

approaching quickly down the rail track. Blaring sirens coursed around the frame of the bridge, echoing off the steelwork as the police boats arrived at its base and the police vehicles on the track. Up above, the distinctive sound of helicopters filled the glowing night sky, heading in from Edinburgh Airport a few miles away.

The lift was near the top of the main beam now, almost one hundred feet in the air. Eve looked down at the larger flotilla of vessels arriving and at the TV cameras mounted on their surfaces, pointing at the lift. Helicopters started circling around and above, less than twenty metres away, the cameramen visible as they captured the vista.

Behind her, the full moon hung low over the Firth, the bridge bathed in its glorious glow. With her one remaining hand, she picked up a megaphone from the bottom of the lift and raised it to her mouth, speaking.

'Fear and Faith. Faith and Fear.' she repeated, then recited in full the poem that the other Angels had said in part. 'In whose faith is your fear founded, which gods atonement do you seek, whose penance keeps your soul grounded, when spirits avarice is preached. What mortal flesh would you divest, to appease your saviours wrath, who's pious wrote would you impress, while seeking raptures righteous path. Which numen's dogma is decreed, to despoil innocence last breath, forced to embrace your litany, on the sanctity of life's death. Interring loved ones in the ground, in whose faith can your fear be found.'

Eve put the megaphone down and took a handkerchief out of a pocket in the Pierrot costume. She wiped the last of the face makeup away from her eye, picking up the microphone once again.

'We all wear masks. We all hide behind out fear and insecurities. Mine is now removed and you see me as I really am. I am Eve. I am the mother of the 'Fallen Angels'. Tonight I bring you the last in a line of religious leaders who use faith as fear. This man has killed twenty six

Her Moons Denouement   Max Hardy

women. He has tortured them, he has mutilated them, cutting off body parts which he then subsequently ate.' Eve announced, her voice filling with fervour.

'He lured these vulnerable women with the opportunity of freedom, with the opportunity of a future without abusive partners. Then he imprisoned them and made their remaining life a living hell. And why? Why did this man, Pastor Bentley inflict such atrocities on these women? He did it because they were women. He did it because in his world, in his religion, like every other religion, women are a considered substandard. He expected these women to be subservient, to do everything their men told them to do. He had no sympathy at all that their partners beat them, in fact, he believed their partners were weak for not taking it further. He definitely took it further. He took it to the extreme.'

Eve paused, looking out over the Firth, watching as more vessels approached the bridge with more camera's pointing towards her. Spotlights started dancing over the structure of the bridge, illuminating Special Forces Officers starting to scale the steelwork towards the lift. She took the whole scene in, her whole demeanour serene.

'We will no longer stand in the shadows of his god and let these atrocities prevail. We will no longer let the prejudices of the sexes, of women, be a weapon for fear. We will no longer allow innocent Angels to bleed in the ignominy of his seed. Even Fallen Angels have wings.'

Eve raised her arms, pulling the release cords tied around her wrists. The Velcro on the back of her Pierrot suit ripped apart and two glorious white wings unfurled along the length of her arms, shimmering in the orb of the moon behind her. She moved her arms and the wings flapped in the gentle breeze. She opened the safety door at her end of the lift and stepped up to the edge, looking down

Her Moons Denouement

to the granite base of bridge one hundred feet below. Eve raised the megaphone to her lips one last time.

'We are the Fallen Angels.' she finished, throwing the megaphone away.

Eve jumped, thrusting her arms out as she did, the wings ruffling furiously in the turbulent air as she descended. Steel flew past, her Pierrot outfit buffeting in the wind. She forced her eyes to stay open, tears streaming out of them as the cold air smacked onto the balls. She looked down at the onrushing granite base, a contented smile sailing across her face as first a wing, then a torso followed by her legs and lastly her head smacked into the uncompromising stone, killing her instantly.

Her body twitched once, then sagged lifelessly on the edge of the base, her open emerald eyes catching a mirage of the moon one last time in the slowly dilating irises. After a second a trail of blood snaked from under her crushed skull and trickled down the granite, meandering slowly through the grooves in the old stone, seeping into the water, where it pooled on the surface. It flowed further, catching the edge of the rippling white reflection of the full moon, turning it blood red: Her Moons Denouement.

To Be Continued……

The thrilling conclusion to the trilogy will be published in 2015

Visit my website at

www.maxhardy.co.uk

or Facebook at

www.facebook.com/themaxhardy

or Twitter at

www.twitter.com/themaxhardy

e-mail to

max.hardy@live.co.uk

Printed in Germany
by Amazon Distribution
GmbH, Leipzig